SIN DEEP

JODI PAYNE
BA TORTUGA

SIN DEEP

Sin Deep is set in The Cowboy and the Dom universe and features an opposites attract, May-December relationship.

Winter Love knows how to give. He gave himself his own name after all, and he's given love to many young men who later moved on with someone they wanted more. Too many. So he's stopped putting himself out there to be hurt by the young little birds he prefers, though he does still enjoy going to the gentlemen's club where he has a membership. He's older, old-fashioned, eccentric, and content to be more about people watching these days.

Harley McBride is new to New York City, having left his home in Texas for a more welcoming town. He's hard-working, friendly, and has a curious nature, which means he's having a great time meeting people. When his roommate takes him to an interesting new club, he decides to introduce himself to a man who is fascinating to him, even from across the room.

Caught off-guard, Winter takes a chance in return, and asks Harley to let him make up Harley's dark eyes. Things begin to heat up, and the two of them connect in ways that neither of them could have anticipated. But Winter knows he needs to tread carefully, and Harley is used to being independent and handling things on his own. Will they be able to find a path that suits them both, or will their relationship stay simply sin deep?

Sin Deep
Copyright © 2022 by Jodi Payne & BA Tortuga

Edited by LC Hinson

Cover illustration by AJ Corza
http://www.seeingstatic.com/
Cover content is for illustrative purposes only and any person depicted on the cover is a model.

ISBN: 978-1-951011-82-6

Published by Tygerseye Publishing, LLC, July, 2022
Printed in the USA

As always, to our wives.

1

Winter Love wasn't giving up anything for Lent; he never had and he never would, but he participated in Fat Tuesday every year as if he planned to starve himself until Easter. He'd pulled on a rich, green shirt, a gold tie, and a brand-new purple and gold masquerade mask for the occasion, and he was looking forward to a night out. Maybe Mardi Gras was a New Orleans tradition, but The Big Apple could give The Big Easy a run for its money.

Along with the New Year's Eve ball and the Halloween costume party, Mardi Gras was one of his favorite nights at Sin Deep. He'd been a member of the kinky club almost as long as he'd lived in New York. Nearly as long as he'd held his job at the public library. He'd started out as a young man, eager to experience new things, to lose himself in the scene.

Winter studied his boots as he sat in the back of a black sedan. He'd been through countless pairs of chunky, authoritative black boots over the years—boots with buckles or zippers, punk and biker and military style, even a tall pair with silver studs going up the back when that was in fashion. The pair he'd stepped into tonight was new; he'd treated himself as an early fortieth birthday present. They had a nice western heel and toe and the leather was rich and soft. They were more stylish than intimidating, but possibly the most comfortable pair of boots he'd ever owned.

They suited his almost forty-year-old image better too. He wasn't eager now. He wasn't cocky like he used to be, or forward, and he wasn't one to pursue men anymore. He didn't feast quite like he used to; he'd grown into a man who preferred to taste and savor rather than devour. He'd earned plenty of respect and was one of the establishment members now; he didn't need to impress anyone. He liked to watch, have a drink, occasionally make an overture...and he was never turned down.

Winter's car pulled up in front of Sin Deep, and he stepped out onto the sidewalk. The tall, heavy front doors stole his breath for a moment as they always did and he instantly broke out in goosebumps.

Who was he kidding? That confident, forty-year-old club elder was essentially a fantasy. He'd never hunted anything more than a drink at Sin Deep, and although he knew that man intimately in the privacy of his own mind, the persona vanished in a puff of awkward smoke every time he walked through the front doors, leaving little more than a facade behind.

He needed the place though. It was the closest thing to home he'd ever had. He was never more present, more relaxed than when he was here. Sin Deep was his drug of choice, his pleasure and his weakness, and Mardi Gras was always a good party, even for wallflowers.

2

"Lord have mercy, man." Harley plopped down with a sigh, grinning over at his roommate. "I busted my hump today."

No one had ever warned him that Yankees were just as bad about ragging the little guy as any bunch of rednecks. He'd done proved himself—he was nothing if not strong as an ox and stubborn as a mule with a burr biting his butthole—but Giorgio and Miguel knew what he could do and drove him like a prize pony.

Paid him damn well for following directions, carrying shit from one place to a truck, then from the truck to another place. All-in-all, he came home with cash, burning muscles, and the knowledge that his muscles didn't come from a gym.

Today was a harpsichord. Who the fuck used a friggin' harpsichord? Who moved a goddamn harpsichord?

This little gal with fake boobies, bright pink hair, and a tattoo of a bird on her goddamn face, that's who.

Oliver snorted. "You bust your hump every day. Jackson told me two things about you. He said we were going to get along great, and he said I would definitely not have to worry about the rent while you were subletting his room. I totally believe him. What do you do for fun?"

"Sleep." He sprawled out, as far as he could. "Uh...back home I went to a couple bars, hung out, I guess."

"Exciting." Oliver rolled his eyes and wandered into his bedroom. The apartment was small enough they could carry on their conversation without even raising their voices. "What is your drink of choice?"

"I drink Bud Light. Shiner if we're being fancy. I been known to like a margarita too." But that was something you drank with your momma or your cousins. Not with the guys, which was stupid, but true.

"Oh no, no, no, Harley. Sweetheart. That won't do. Why don't you come out with me tonight and let me buy you a real drink?"

That 'sweetheart' always made him blush.

He'd come to stay for a couple months just because Jackson swore this was a friendly place, somewhere he could just be him, and he was having a ball. Especially now that Jackson had decided to stay in Rome for another couple-three months, and he could keep on keeping on.

"Yeah? You want to?" He had a pair of pretty clean jeans.

"Yes. Be my date. It will be an adventure. Trust me. Go get dressed." Oliver came out of his bedroom in his signature skinny jeans and a shiny gold jacket. He didn't comment on the gold high-heeled booties, but they made Oliver look tall and lean, and there was glitter in Oliver's short but curly dark hair. "It's a Mardi Gras party."

"Oh. Uh. Okay." He put on his cleanest jeans and a black t-shirt with his leather jacket and his boots. He didn't wear his Stetson, because he'd learned quick that meant getting knocked around a ton. He had a cap.

"Oh, you look so handsome! No hat? Are you sure? Would you like some glitter for your hair?" Oliver held out a mask covered in purple sequins. "And here. You'll need this."

"No glitter, thanks." Lord, could anyone imagine? "I'll wear my cap."

Oliver rolled his eyes so hard he thought they might pop out. "Suit yourself. Take the mask, though. You ready? My Uber is here."

"I am." He grabbed his wallet and the mask. "Let's hasta."

He did like him an adventure.

The car ride didn't take that long, but that didn't mean he had any idea where they ended up. "My guess is you've never been to a party like this one, sweetheart. Just stick with me for a bit until you get your bearings."

They got out of the car and walked up to a set of crazy tall doors that looked heavy but seemed to open by themselves anyway.

"Is this, like, a funhouse? It seems like something in an amusement park." That would be cool. He was up for it.

"It can be. Tonight it's just a party." Oliver took his hand and pulled him inside. It took a second for his eyes to adjust to the sudden change in lighting and by the time he had, Oliver was taking off his jacket. "I'll check your coat with mine, okay?"

Harley blinked, staring at Oliver, a little agog. "Dude! You are sparkly!"

And wearing, like a...a...tube top. A sequined Harlequin tube top where his nipples showed, which made sense, since Oliver didn't have himself boobies. It was like nothing he'd ever seen, but it was so totally Oliver that he just grinned and applauded.

"Do you like it?" Oliver beamed and turned for him, showing off.

"Oliver!" A guy in a purple vest and a feathered mask gave Oliver a hug.

"Jesse! Oh, Jess—can you tighten me up?"

"Of course. Let me see." Jesse moved around behind Oliver and tugged until the top Oliver was wearing went taut across his chest."

"Ooh. Perfect. Jesse, this is Harley. He's subletting while Jackson is in Rome."

"Harley? Like the motorcycle? I'm Jesse. Like the outlaw." Jesse offered a hand like he expected Harley to kiss it.

Harley shook, careful not to squeeze, because he wasn't an asshole. He'd figured that out, and he wasn't interested in seeming mean. "Pleased to meet you, sir. How goes?"

Jesse laughed. "He called me 'Sir', Oliver. Where are you from, honey?"

"Just west of Fort Worth, and I mean no offense." He winked over. "Polite is part of my charm, I'm told."

"Oh my god I *love* him!" Jesse stepped between him and Oliver. "Welcome to the club, darling. Do you want to dance?"

"Jess—"

"You hush, Ollie. You brought me a handsome cowboy." Jesse leaned a little closer to him, big blue eyes flashing, and he got a whiff of sweet cologne.

"Now, can I trust you to keep me safe? Because Oliver's told me to stick to him..."

Jesse's eyes went wide. "This is a very classy club, Mr. Harley. But don't you worry, you're safe with me."

"He is; his virtue on the other hand..." Oliver laughed.

"I will be very, very careful with the cowboy, I promise."

Jesse took his arm. "It's just a dance. You can dance, can't you?"

"Believe it or not, I can, and I like it." He could do everything from wild flailing to waltz. He wasn't fancy, but he wasn't going to embarrass himself or his dance partner.

"Charmer." Jesse pulled him into the crowd. Oliver shouted after them that he'd be at the bar. "Is this your scene? How long have you been in town?"

"Three months, two weeks, and five days." Harley winked, laughing at himself. "And I don't know that I have a scene yet, but this is absolutely my first time here!"

And it was electric—sparkling and loud, exciting and overwhelming in the best way.

Jesse laughed as they wove through the crowd, finally finding the dance floor. The lighting was purple and green, shifting with the music. "I can tell. You're not dressed like you expected to be here tonight. I'm not complaining though, that t-shirt fits you just right." Jesse's hands slid over his chest before finding his shoulders and staying there.

"Oliver didn't need me upstaging him in his...top." His hands landed on Jesse's hips so he could find the man's rhythm. "This okay?"

Jesse nodded, stepping closer. "So okay. Go on and lead, honey. I can follow."

They started dancing, laughing as they figured out how not to murder one another's toes. Three songs in, the DJ played a slow song, and he didn't know Jesse that well, so he backed off. "Want to get a drink? I'm dry as a bone."

"That sounds—"

"Jesse."

Jesse froze for a second and gave the tall man in a mask that covered half his face a sheepish look. "Oh, hi."

The man crossed his arms, silently, and Jesse looked at

Harley. "Oops! I think I'm in trouble." Jesse winked at him. "But you were a lovely dance partner. Tell Oliver to buy you that drink for me."

"Now, Jesse."

"Yes, Sir. I'm sorry, Sir. Coming. Bye, Harley!"

The tall man caught Jesse by the nape and steered him away. He started to go after Jesse; that couldn't be right. Was Jesse okay? But only made it one step before a hand caught him in the chest.

"Let them be. It's okay. This is their thing."

"You sure? We just met. He knows my roommate." His brain insisted he needed to make a fuss, but his gut wasn't near as sure about that...

The man that stood there wasn't so tall he was staring at his bellybutton, but at his chest, and the green eyes were sparkling at him.

"I'm sure. I've known them both for years. You're here with Ollie." It wasn't a question. The guy offered a hand. "I'm Winter."

"Winter." That was a great name! "I'm Harley. Pleased to meet you, sir."

Winter. That was something else. Green-eyed Winter.

"Hello, Harley. I don't want to keep you from your friend. It was good to meet you. Enjoy your evening."

"Have a good evenin'!" He braced himself to head toward the bar, which was sure a crush of folks. There were more people in this building than in his whole hometown.

Oliver wasn't hard to find, being taller than most men and colorful too. "You're back! I thought Winter might have scooped you up." Oliver tapped the bar "Two whiskey gingers, Leighton."

"He wasn't interested." That was okay. He'd met two guys

in five songs. One that was wanting to be friends was fucking great odds.

Oliver snorted, eyes darting to the crowd and then back to him. "No? He's been watching you all night. He's watching you now."

"Stop it." He was the least sparkly guy in a universe of glitter. A damn accidental black hole. "If he wants a drink, I'll buy him one."

"He doesn't." The bartender sat two drinks down and pushed one toward each of them. "He'll nurse the one he's got for a while. And he'll watch, it's what he does. He's definitely watching you."

"Thank you, sir. What do I owe you?" Now that the guy mentioned it, he could feel eyes on his back.

"Nothing. A good time. You're off to a good start. Did you have fun with Jesse?"

"He's fun, yeah. Have y'all been friends long?" He sipped the drink, finding it smoky and spicy, but with bubbles. He approved.

"I guess. Maybe...five or six years? He's been with Theo all that time. Very taken. So naughty." Oliver sipped his drink. "He cooks too. Oh my god. Amazing. And this is a silly party night, but you should see him on a regular night. He's beautiful. He's just... I mean, you wouldn't believe it."

"He likes to dance. I didn't know he was with someone. I don't like to be rude." It wasn't in his makeup unless he was fighting.

"No worries. He liked you, but he was just playing, showing off for Theo. And even if you'd known he was taken, it was just dancing, Harley. Just fun."

"Cool. I just don't know all y'all's rules. If I can dance with him, that was good." He thought it was something—how every group of folks, every single one, had their own sets of rules, and if you figured them? Then things worked easier.

"Everyone's rules are different, but in here everyone is family. No worries. You can't get in trouble for having fun." Oliver sipped his drink. "So Jackson says he's staying in Rome for a while; are you staying in New York?"

"I intend to, yessir. I think we do okay, rooming, you and me." In fact, Oliver seemed happy as a pig in shit.

"We're good, sweetheart." Oliver sipped his drink, then looked at him with a slight frown. "You know he's not there alone, right?"

"Jackson? Did he hook up with someone out there?" How fucking cool was that. Then he'd have a reason to go to Italy sometimes. It was always good to have a buddy to visit.

"No. He went with his partner, Harley. He didn't tell you he had a boyfriend?"

"Nope. I mean, he never said one way or the other." Which was sort of weird. They'd talked a lot about Jackson's schooling, about Oliver, about the restaurant that he waited tables in, but not a lover?

"Oh. Well. I'm sure he had a reason." Oliver shrugged, and he had to wonder if Oliver knew what the reason might be. "Anyway, I don't think he'll be back for a while. Last I heard from him he was happy."

"Good. I'm all over happiness. He's my good friend, you know?" He'd worry about whether or not he needed to worry about things later.

Maybe Sunday.

"Oh yeah, for sure. He talked about you a lot."

"Hello again!" Jesse was suddenly there, grinning widely with hands full of Mardi Gras beads. "I've been tasked with handing these out. Here, cowboy, you need some bling."

Jesse hung a handful of them around his neck. "Oh, much better."

"Good lord and butter." He rolled his eyes, but he'd play along. No one'd asked to see his titties to get them, and he could use them to decorate his room.

Jesse hung a handful around Oliver's neck too. "See? I was careful with the cowboy."

"I appreciate it. He's delicate." Dude, butter wouldn't melt in Oliver's mouth.

"That's me. Like blown glass and shit."

Jesse rolled his eyes. "I want to see you dressed up. Dress him up next time, Oliver. Don't you think he'd be beautiful?"

Oliver nodded. "Go easy, Jesse. He's new-new."

"Oh." Jesse nodded. "Don't worry, cowboy. You won't be new forever." Jesse kissed his cheek and moved down the bar, hanging more necklaces on people as he went.

No. No one was new forever. He was going to enjoy all the fun of this, new or not.

3

Winter sipped his drink, eyes on the bar, watching Ollie and his guest talk and laugh. He was proud of himself; he'd promised himself he'd do something, anything other than just watch tonight, and he finally had.

He'd actually touched that boy.

And he'd only just stopped trembling from the adrenaline rush.

Harley was a wonderful name. He assumed it was after the motorcycle, not the comic book character, but who was to say anymore? People named their kids after food and medical conditions these days.

"Harley," he whispered, liking how the name felt on his tongue, which made him wonder how the boy would taste. He didn't imagine he'd ever find out, but that was okay. He could watch.

Harley ordered another drink, and he didn't judge. This was a night of excesses. It shocked him when Leighton handed him two bottles of water.

It shocked him more when Harley finished his whiskey and then headed into the crowd with the waters.

Was Harley headed his way? Surely not. He glanced quickly over his shoulder and back again, then swallowed hard against a sudden pang of anxiety in his stomach. Why on earth would this boy be coming to him? Certainly Ollie had explained he wasn't great at conversation.

Sure enough, Harley stood at his table. "Howdy, sir. It's hot as all get out in here. I thought you might could use a water."

Winter stared for a second, thinking the boy sounded genuine, but certain that someone—Jesse perhaps—put him up to this stunt. "Thank you." He didn't reach for the water. The polite thing would be to invite Harley to sit, but sitting meant talking, and he was going to have to dig deep to find something to talk about with a lovely Texan boy—or he assumed Texan, the "might could" was certainly southern, but the cadence usually gave a Texan away.

"You're more than welcome." Harley looked over the party, then he smiled at Winter. "You mind if I park my butt? I won't bother you, I swear. I worked all day, and I didn't know I was fixin' to party."

"Oh. Please. I'm sorry. I didn't mean to be rude. I was just—surprised. About the water. Very kind." He was sorry, because he was terrible at this, and he'd honestly thought Harley would just put the water down and walk away.

Maybe the boy was upset that he'd been watching. Maybe he'd made Harley uncomfortable. He should have known better; he knew this was Harley's first time here. He knew a little something about everyone at the club.

"No, no. I'm being pushy. I just want to take a load off for a minute. I promise not to be all Chatty Cathy on you." The smile he got was warm, almost sweet.

He smiled at that. "Please, sit." He opened the bottle of

water and took a sip, finding it cool and refreshing so he took another. "I'm actually quite thirsty. I didn't realize."

"It's warm in here, I tell you what." Harley drank too, throat working. He was broad shouldered, for all he was on the short side, and he had dark, short hair, dark eyes, and long black eyelashes.

He was especially fascinated by those eyelashes. "Too hot for your mask, hm?" Winter liked his mask, it put up a little barrier and he felt braver behind it.

"My..." Harley reached up and touched his face. "Oh! Right. I forgot. I got to staring at all the sparkles, and it totally slipped my mind."

He knew Harley had one, the young man had caught his eye the second he and Ollie walked in the door. It was in the boy's back right-hand pocket, a little gold sequined corner stuck out and caught the light at the bar. "It's not a requirement, and it would hide your lovely dark eyes."

A compliment wasn't too forward, was it? He wasn't sure one could be too forward at Sin Deep.

"Well, thank you, sir. That's a helluva compliment coming from you. You got pretty eyes yourself, Mr. Winter."

He'd had his share of compliments, but no one in his entire life had ever called him pretty. Or anything about him pretty. "Thank you. They're green, like my mother's were." He lifted his mask off to allow Harley to see him better. "It feels strange to be masked when you're not."

"Mine look like my momma's too. Daddy's are dark also, but more stormy."

"Mm." He nodded. "I'd say my father was stormy too." He took another sip of his water, a bigger one this time. "So what brings you to New York? I assume you're a friend of Jackson's? Are you staying with Ollie while he's away?"

"I am. I wanted to come and live up here, see something

new, and I'm having a ball. I've learned a ton in a little while."

So young. So enthusiastic. "Yes, so much to learn." Winter wasn't a teacher anymore. So much investment just to watch the pretty birds fly away. He was done with being left behind. "Ollie is sweet, isn't he? I'm sure he's been helpful."

"He's a sweetheart. I've been friends with Jackson since I was a kid, and when he offered me an out, I came."

"You felt you needed an out, hm?" Interesting.

Those dark eyes twinkled. "Yeah. The factory I was working in closed down, my mom got remarried to a preacher man, and it was time to hasta."

Goodness, Harley was fascinating to him. So easy in his skin, so sure of himself.

He nodded. "Sounds like it. Well, you'll find plenty of family in the city." He said that, knowing that he had found people when he needed them who led him here, and that was all the family he'd wanted.

"I've had a ball, I swear to God. I work my butt off, but there's so much to do. Jackson's staying gone, and Oliver likes me well enough, so I have a room for another few months."

"Work hard, play hard." A responsible young man was a rarity these days. "It's good to have a safe home."

Well, well, Winter. You're having a real conversation.

And something about Harley put him at ease instead of making him anxious.

"Yeah. I'm into having things like hot water and a bed. I mailed a big old box of my important stuff, even, so I have my favorite pillow." Harley winked at him. "I was fixin' to bring my truck, but Jackson said it would cost a fortune and that part of the experience was learning how to use the subway and all. I've met some neat folks."

He had to smile. It was possible that conversation with Harley wasn't difficult for him because Harley could carry on most of it all on his own.

As Harley spoke, Winter imagined the boy cinched into in a stylish, hourglass corset. He wondered if Harley's skin had that permanently tanned color and whether it was smooth and rich or made rough from outdoor work back in Texas. Those lovely, dark eyes would benefit from black eyeliner, he thought, and possibly even some mascara on the boy's exceptionally long lashes.

It was indulgent of him, but what harm did it do to fantasize a little? He could even imagine Harley's sweet, sleeping head resting on that favorite pillow he talked about.

"A truck would do you no good here."

"Yeah, I figured that out. I work moving furniture, but they don't let me drive, thank god. I'm not ready for that, not yet."

That was a full-time job for sure, people were always moving in the city. Moving in, moving out...moving on. He'd seen so many people come and go. "You must be...very strong." And wasn't that a delicious thought?

"Yessir. You wouldn't think so, given that I'm on the short side, but I'm a little ox." Harley's smile was warm and gloriously happy.

"You're marvelous company, Harley. I'm glad you stopped by my little table. So kind of you to bring me the water." His bottle was empty, it was just what he'd needed.

"You looked like you could use a drink, and I was looking for an oasis. You seem like you're a good one."

"An oasis. I like that. It's usually quiet in my corner of the club." Winter liked it that way.

"That's spiffy. I love that you have your own corner." Harley's eyes went wide as a couple of their more flamboyant members sauntered by. "Will you look at that? I'd be scared to wear eyelashes that big."

Winter watched them for a moment. "They wouldn't suit you anyway. A little mascara would be more than enough for you." He glanced back at Harley, trying not to look as shocked as he felt to have said that out loud. "If that were your thing."

"You think so?" Harley tilted his head, eyes moving like they were trying to see his own eyelashes. "Never thought about it, to be honest. I'd try, I guess. Why not?"

The rational part of him said no, but there was no denying the jolt of electricity that ran up his spine.

No, Winter.

Except he wanted to. He really, really wanted to. "You'd try it? Will you try it for me?" That was a mistake. Now he had to hope the boy said no.

But he was hoping harder that Harley said yes.

"Of course. Do you have some?" No hesitation, no fear. Just yes.

Oh my god.

"I...no, but..." Now what? His whole night had just gone off-script. He put a hand in the air and waved toward the bar and one of the staff members hurried his way.

"Hey. What can I get for you, Master Winter?" Drew smiled at him, ready for whatever he asked for. Winter knew the staff would get him anything he needed, but this might be a tall order.

"A nice, new, black mascara, please. And an eyeliner."

"I think I can do that." Drew gave a nod and disappeared toward the back of the club.

He shrugged at Harley. "We'll see, I suppose."

"We will. That was cool, though. That you can just ask." Harley's eyes rolled. "I don't have that—gift, I guess? Never have had. Does make for some amazing stories though."

"I'll tell you a secret. It's not a gift; it's just a membership fee, and a little bit of seniority." He leaned back in his chair, watching Harley. "Tell me one of your stories."

"I was at a Cody Johnson concert, front row, and he walked to the edge of the stage. He reached down, I reached up, and we couldn't make it." Harley snorted. "We couldn't reach. Short shits."

He chuckled, though he hadn't the foggiest idea who Cody Johnson was. He'd find out, though. He had Spotify, and one of the boys had taught him how to use it. "Cody is height-challenged as well, I take it?"

"Bull rider. So yeah. Me? I roped in college, but I didn't want to lose a finger, so I quit."

"Bright boy. Where did you go to—"

Drew arrived with two brand-new packages, one eyeliner and one mascara. "I thought you might like a mirror. That one's mine, so I'll come around and get it later."

"Very thoughtful, thank you, Drew." Mascara and eyeliner required a steady hand, so he took a breath and pushed his nerves aside, again. Harley had his mind racing. "Sorry. Where did you go to college?"

"Tarleton State. It's in Stephenville, right outside of Fort Worth."

Okay, so yes. Texas.

"Scoot your chair this way, please. Nice and close. More light." He opened the makeup and looked over the eyeliner first. "You're sure you want to try this?"

"Sure. It washes off if it's terrifying, and what if we like it?"

I will like it. What if you do?

That "we" was killing him. Dear god. He was going to need another drink.

"I have to...touch you. If that's all right." His fingers hovered in the air, the eyeliner in his right hand, and he refused to let them shake even a little.

"I'm not scared. I don't bite." Harley eased right into his hand.

He liked to, but this was hardly the moment to say so. He cupped Harley's jaw in one hand and carefully—reverently —drew a simple line under each eye and blurred it just a bit with his thumb. He took his time adding the top line as well, extending it just a little beyond the corners, just enough to frame those dark eyes properly. To his credit, Harley didn't move, or even blink much, and when he was done, Winter sat back and had a look at his work.

He was captivated. And he wasn't even finished yet.

"Would you like to see?" Winter picked up the mirror, holding his breath as he handed it to Harley.

"Oh, wow." Harley turned side to side, eyes huge. "I look like a...like someone from a magazine."

Winter pretended not to notice all the eyes on them. He was the one being watched for a change, and it felt strangely right for once. The eyeliner felt like it belonged in his fingers, and his mind was suddenly filled with images of Harley with smoky eyes, winged liner, mermaid shadows...it had been such a long time. "I think it's beautiful. You were made for makeup. Are you ready for the mascara?"

Harley's cheeks warmed, and it was a lovely expression —a mixture of pleasure and arousal. "I am. Eyes open or closed?"

Harley's question proved the boy was more than just along for the ride. Harley was curious. Interested. His heart sped up a bit as he opened the mascara. Drew had found a nice thick one that should make those long lashes pop. "Open, please. It's probably difficult with all the lights and dry air but try not to blink."

He worked a little faster this time so Harley didn't have to keep his eyes open for long. "I don't have a blotter, which would make this look a little cleaner, but this looks very nice. I think you'll like it. I hope you do." Winter finished up and closed the mascara. "Go ahead, pick up the mirror."

Harley did as he was told, looking closely, blinking as he did. "I don't hardly look like me, but I totally look like me. How cool is that?"

"It's possible you look more like you." Winter put the mascara away. "More like you know yourself privately. Inside."

Harley nodded, and Winter didn't think he even realized it. "Like if I was in the Matrix movie, right? Less moving guy and more—fancy."

"That's right. The way you'd look if someone hadn't taught you what was expected...if you could just wear whatever made you feel good." A little voice in the back of his head told him to be careful, but he hadn't had a night like this in a long while and it felt so good.

"Yeah, I hear you. Like if you don't have to stress it, you could be anybody." Harley seemed hypnotized for a second, pupils huge in those dark eyes, then he shook himself, licking his lips. "That's a sweet little fantasy."

"It is. You can indulge in those fantasies here, Harley. That's what this club is for. Something to think about."

He glanced up to find Oliver standing a few feet away. "Come on over." He gave Ollie a wave. "Come see."

Oliver leaned on the table and looked at Harley. Winter was enjoying the look of awe on Ollie's face. "Look at you, sweetheart. Wow. You're beautiful."

"Mr. Winter here did it. He gets all the credit." Harley lifted his face so Ollie could see.

"No, indeed. You were beautiful before I talked you into eyeliner." The words were out before he knew it, bypassing his better sense. *Damn it.*

Harley blinked at him, blushed a deep, deep rose, and then he got a smile. "Well, thank you, sir. That's...sort of amazing to hear."

It's rather amazing I said it. If only you knew.

"Do not put your mask back on and smudge that gorgeous look," Ollie said, then took Harley's hat off and fixed his hair. "Keep that in your pocket too. Oh, you look so good!"

"Let me see!" Jesse bumped hips with Ollie and looked Harley over. "Oh. My. God. Cowboy. That is amazing."

Harley looked down, and for the first time Winter saw a hint of nerves, but it was forced away with a bright smile. "Winter did it. He made me up."

"All right. Shoo. It's gotten much too loud over here." Winter waved his hand at Ollie and Jesse."

"Sorry, Master Winter. We'll be at the bar, sweetheart." Ollie squeezed Harley's hand and as they left, all the other curious eyes moved on too.

"We lost our oasis for a moment there, hm?" He dared to touch Harley's knee, just gently. "I apologize. I certainly didn't intend all that attention."

"That's just fine. I did sorta forget that there was a party going on. It felt like you and me and nothing else."

"It did, didn't it? What a wonderful experience." Winter pulled his hand back reluctantly. "I enjoyed it very much."

"I did too." Harley looked where his hand had been. "Your hand is warm. I can still feel every finger."

Winter licked his lips and tried to reply, but he didn't know what to say. Whatever was happening here, it was time to stop it. He knew better. He just couldn't...do this again.

"Harley, it's been an absolute pleasure." He stood, it was time to go home. "But, I'm afraid it's past my bedtime."

"Oh." Harley blinked a couple of times, then he stood as well, holding out one hand. "Have a good night. Be careful going home."

Winter swallowed but took Harley's hand and shook it, pretending he could ignore the warmth in the boy's grip. "You too. Enjoy the rest of the party."

"Yes, sir. Goodnight." Harley stood there by his table, expression quiet and a bit confused, picking up Drew's mirror. "I'll take this to the bartender to give back to the server."

"Thank you." Winter pushed the mascara and the eyeliner toward Harley. "Keep those. Goodnight." He headed straight for the coat check before he changed his mind. It would be too easy to do.

He did look back once, and Harley was moving away from his table toward the bar, mask and hat back on.

He knew himself, and he knew what he could stand and what he could not. Harley would stay in New York a little longer, and like every little bird he'd fed and taught and cared for, he would fly away. It was what they did.

He'd be alone then. He was alone now. It was just better this way.

Winter pulled his coat on and left the club, the heavy doors closing solidly behind him.

4

Harley headed to the bar, handed the mirror over, bought a beer, and then found a place to prop himself up and people watch.

Obviously he'd fucked up but good. He wasn't sure how, but he was embarrassed that he had. He thought he'd been friendly, open-minded, not bitchy at all, but maybe he had said something stupid.

Whatever it was, he felt exposed and a little like a hick, so he hoped Ollie would show up so he could say his goodbyes and head home. Take a long, hot shower, jack off, and crash.

It was a great fucking plan.

"You put your mask back on!" Oliver asked when he did finally resurface. "Lost Master Winter, huh?"

"Yeah." He left like he'd been stung. "Having fun?" *You mind if I go home? I feel stupid and ridiculous.*

"He left? Well, what the hell? He's...touchy. He's here all the time but...nobody spends any real time with him; he's a loner, you know?" Oliver leaned on the wall next to him.

"Ah." So, he was supposed to pretend the dude hadn't

touched him, he guessed. "I didn't mean to upset him, for sure."

Still, he didn't want to try and pretend that he wasn't weirded out. It hadn't been anything like anything he'd ever experienced before. It was like riding a rollercoaster, climbing and climbing and then swooping down, and then when it stopped, his heart was beating too fast, and he realized none of it had been real.

Oliver shrugged. "Actually, I hope you did a little. Maybe it will wake him up. All he ever does is sit there. They say he used to be way more interesting. More fun, you know? It's too bad; he's not bad-looking even if he is older. Gray hair isn't my thing, but some guys are into it."

"I thought he was hot." But the mixed signals had been a lot. "I think I'm going to finish this beer and head home, buddy."

"Aw." Oliver gave him a pouty look. "Did he ruin your night? Are you sure? I'm sorry. I should have stopped you from going over there, it's just...people don't. Much."

"Don't pout, butthead. He just...was giving out signals, and now I feel a little like a dumbass." He sipped his beer, letting it cool his hurt feeling.

"Well, if he led you on that wasn't nice. I'm sorry." Oliver hugged him. "I wanted this to be fun for you."

"I'm having a ball. Seriously. This is the most fun. I just need an attitude adjustment." He had misread something. He hadn't committed murder. "This place is wide."

"As wide as some places are tall." Oliver winked at him. "You have your key? I won't be late."

"Do you want to share a car? I can hang a little longer, people watch." He wasn't a quitter, and he wasn't going to go home like he was a whupped dog even I he wanted to.

"Yes, I do. How about a dance or two and then we'll call

it a night? You want to?" Oliver poked him playfully and took his hand.

"Hell yeah! You and your sparkly tube top are going to shine under the lights."

"It's not a tube top! It's a corset, sweetheart." Oliver led him toward the dance floor. "And I want to see your pretty eyes. Please?"

"They make them for boys? I thought they were for Ren Faires and Halloween. Cool." He did as Ollie asked, shoving his mask and hat in his pocket, because what would it hurt?

Oliver rolled his eyes. "Hello. I'm wearing one. They make them for everyone! You'll see them all over the club on a normal night. They're kind of a thing here."

He was right; Ollie lit up under the dance floor lights, sparkling like a Mardi Gras disco ball, and blinding him every so often.

Harley just let himself dance and laugh, the tiny buzz he was riding allowing him to let loose.

Oliver bent to his ear to be heard over the music. "Whatever with Master Winter, forget him. But you need to think about this look. It's good on you."

"Thanks, man. I feel...sexy as fuck." And he didn't even want to get laid. He liked just feeling like he was having fun in a safe space.

Oliver laughed and spun him around. "You're a new man, Harley! I love it!"

"Am I?" He was just Harley, having a little out-of-body fun. It was good for him, he thought.

"Well, I have never heard Hardworking Harley say 'sexy as fuck'." Ollie laughed and shimmied to the music making his corset sparkle.

He hadn't thought it a ton. He'd more thought he was just...a dude.

"Aw. Look at you. Don't think so hard, sweetheart. Just dance!" A wave of people joined them as the next song started, and pretty soon they were surrounded by bodies moving like waves on a beach.

He let himself have that, let himself breathe and dance, and just be.

5

Harley slept most of Saturday, between the booze, the dancing, and the work week, but finally the bass of Ollie's music dragged his happy ass out of bed.

He threw on a pair of cotton trousers and a ratty t-shirt before heading out to the front room. "Hey, you! Morn-evening!"

"Well look who's up! Oh...poor baby needs some coffee." Ollie went right to the kitchen and started putting on a pot. "You want some eggs? I could fry a couple of sausages for the hangover."

"I'm less hungover from the booze than the dancing, but hell yeah." He'd offer to help, but Ollie was strict about his kitchen. "How's you?"

"Bored. I don't have to work tonight, and I don't have anywhere to be... I might go back to the club later. Right now though, food sounds good." Eggs appeared and sausages and a big frying pan. "How did the makeup remover I gave you work? It looks like you got it all."

"Yeah, thank you." He'd never done face stuff—he washed it, he guessed. The shampoo ran down over it in the shower, and he totally washed behind his ears, but that was it.

"You'll get used to it. That was fun. You looked great." Ollie pulled two mugs out and set them by the coffee maker. "I'm serious, Harley. It worked on you."

"Thanks." Too bad he didn't know the first thing about how to put it on, and he wasn't sure he wanted to watch a bunch of YouTube videos on makeup. That might be a little too much.

Ollie looked at him sidelong. "Are you going to wear it again?"

"I don't know. I mean, I don't really know how, you know?"

"You can learn how. Or I can do it for you. But you should practice."

"Practice." He didn't know. Part of the hot part of it was having Winter touch him, see him, and what if that was the deal? What the fuck would that mean, exactly? He didn't know that he wanted to understand that.

"Breakfast for dinner." Oliver split up the eggs and sausage and set the plates on the tiny kitchen table. "Fix your coffee and sit. Do you want toast?"

"Are you making some for you?" He wasn't making work. "And that smells amazing. Thank you so much."

Damn he was lucky that Jackson needed to be in Italy.

"I could eat bread all day." Oliver popped some bread into the toaster. "You don't sound like you're into practicing. Am I pushing? I do that. I push. It makes Jackson crazy."

"No, I just... I don't know. It felt fabulous last night, though. You don't wear a mask every day."

Ollie sat with him while they waited on the toast and crossed his legs. "Here's a hard question for you, sweetheart. Was that the mask? Or is this the mask?" Ollie raised a manicured eyebrow and drew a circle in the air in front of Harley's face. "Something to think about. You don't have to answer me. Just eat."

He didn't even know if he wanted to think about that. He wasn't sure he wanted to think at all. So he ate, and everything tasted like it was supposed to. Comforting. Normal.

The toast popped up and Oliver brought it back to the table with the butter, then changed the subject. "I could eat eggs every meal. Is that weird?"

"Nah. Eggs are cool, cheap, and you can use them for all sorts of shit." He was a fan, when he got right down to it. "Mine's potatoes. I love 'em. Masked—I mean mashed, baked, French fried, tater totted, potato chipped. I am a fan."

"Masked potatoes!" Ollie laughed. "There are no bad potatoes, but I think that one is my new favorite."

"Shut up." He cracked up at himself. Lord have mercy, he was a dipshit. Good thing Ollie thought he was funny too.

"One could call that a Freudian slip, hm?" Ollie waggled his eyebrows.

"I know, right? Shit marthy, good thing I'm not easy to embarrass, huh?" Because if he was, he'd have died a thousand deaths already.

Maybe three thousand deaths.

Oliver smiled. "It's a good quality. Keep that one."

"I'll do my dead-level best." He chuckled, leaning back and stretching tall, listening to his back pop. He did love a day off.

"So do you miss Texas?" Oliver took a bite of eggs and sausage and picked up his coffee.

He thought about that. Really thought. "I miss TexMex. I miss some of my buddies. I miss my pop, but he's just a gravestone and a bit of green. I miss who my mom used to be..." *Come on, try harder.* "Oh! I miss Dr Pepper everywhere and bluebonnets and tubing and good barbecue."

"Aw. Texas sounds nice. Sounds like it's become a good place for you to visit. Are we making a New Yorker out of you?"

"Right now, I'm loving it here. I have a good place to live, a job that keeps me busy and tired, and there's so much to do." It wasn't like if he lost this job, he couldn't go get another one. There wasn't one factory, one honkytonk, one Walmart to shop at.

Oliver narrowed his eyes. "We'll see, Hardworking Harley. We'll—"

Oliver's phone rang in the living room.

"Oh. Sorry." Oliver popped up and hurried to get it. "Hello?" That "hello" sounded curious. "Oh, it *is* you."

That was followed by a long silence before Ollie spoke again. "Well, I'll have to ask him. I don't know how he's feeling right now. I think you did. I'll ask, okay? Okay. Bye."

Oliver walked back into the kitchen and sat slowly. "So... that was Winter Love."

Oh. God, Winter Love? That name was getting better and better. He was praying that the middle name turned up to be spectacular. Still—it seemed weird that the man would call Ollie. "What—What did he want? Is he pissed?"

"I honestly don't know. Why would he be pissed? He asked me for your number." Ollie shrugged. "I told him I had to ask you first."

"I don't know. He just seemed so freaked out, you know?" In his experience, last night's wigged out often became this morning's pissed off. Angry made things way less your fault. "And sure. I mean, I wasn't pissed or wigged."

"Okay. I'm going to let you finish your dinner and then

send it to him. I got the feeling he really wanted to talk to you. Like, soon." Ollie chomped down his last bite of toast.

"Sure. I'm willing to make friends." Why not? It had been part of the most fascinating night in his memory. What was incredibly unnerving and unusual last night had mellowed into fun and exciting.

"Well, I'm glad you're good with it. I'm a little freaked. He's never called me before." Ollie rolled his eyes. "I mean, I see him every weekend but...wow."

"Do you not want me to call? I mean, if you are into him, I'll totally back away." He didn't play that.

Oliver's eyes went wide and he laughed. "Oh my god. So not my type. I told you, sweetheart, I'm not into gray hair."

"No?" He thought Winter was hot. Like whoa. "I just wanted to make sure. I'm not an asshole."

"Of course not! All done?" Oliver reached for his empty plate. "You want something else?"

"No. No, thank you. I'll do the dishes since you cooked." He stood up, then unlocked his phone. "Put his number in? I'll text him."

"Oh, that's sneaky. I like how you just took control there. Sexy." Oliver winked and set their plates down on the counter, then typed numbers into his phone. "I may add something more fun to my coffee. Interested?"

"Sure. I'm not driving." And it was Saturday. That was a moral imperative, to have a shot. "Hook me up."

"Right on." Ollie pulled out a bottle of Bailey's and started to pour. "Say when."

He listened for three glugs, as he got the water started. "When."

"Very nice." Ollie giggled as he filled his own mug. "I hate doing dishes. You are the best roommate ever. Thank you."

"Anytime. I don't mind at all. Handy, since I cain't hardly cook." And what he did cook involved grills, which apparently weren't a big option here.

"See? We're a good team." Oliver was suddenly right next to him and kissed his cheek. "As much as I am dying to be a fly on the wall for your phone call, I will go do my nails and stay out of your hair. But don't think I'm not going to ask all the questions later."

"Use the lilac with the glitter. It's Easter season." He thought that was adorable, and Ollie was good at it.

"Yeah? You like the glitter, huh? I think that's a great idea. See you in a bit." Oliver gave him a finger wave and left the kitchen.

He wiped his hands off, texted Winter with *Hey, you. It's Harley. You have a decent day?* and then went to finish the dishes.

Mr. Winter Love would either text back or he wouldn't.

Either way, he'd have a story for Ollie in a few.

6
_____

Oliver had been quite right to refuse to give Harley's phone number to him without permission, but Winter did not like waiting. He would wait, and he'd do it patiently, but he'd wanted to be the one in control of the timing of this conversation.

This felt right though, that the ball should be in Harley's court, that Harley should be the one to decide when and if they'd talk again. He'd been horribly rude the night before, he knew it, and he deserved a little time to chew on his own thoughts.

He'd just decided to take a shower when his phone vibrated on the bathroom counter and he picked it up and read the text message, as relieved as he was anxious that it was Harley. He quickly made a new contact with the number so he didn't lose it and simply put in Harley, since he didn't know the boy's last name.

Yet. He was determined he would. Soon.

But what to do with this text? Had he had a decent day? No, it hadn't been decent; he'd been angry with himself since before the sun had come up. How to reply? "Just fine, how was yours"? or "Miserable, I'm so sorry." Or what he really wanted to know... "Can I see you again?"

He decided texting wasn't his strong suit. But he did send one.

It's very kind of you to contact me. Might I call you?

The response came quickly, gratifyingly so, in fact. *Surely. I'm home & having coffee.*

That was wonderful and awful. He pulled on his robe, thinking that a cup of tea would help settle his nerves, stepped into his slippers, and called Harley as he made his way to the kitchen.

"Hey there. How's it going? You okay?" Harley sounded —warm. The man's voice was simply naturally warm.

"Am I—" He took a breath and tried again. He'd already decided he was going to get directly to his point so that he didn't lose his nerve. "Hello, Harley. I'm sorry if I've interrupted your evening, but I appreciate the phone call. I am anxious to talk to you about last night, and to apologize for my awful behavior."

"Okay. I accept your apology, and I hope I didn't do something to upset you. If I did, it was an accident."

"No, Harley. You were perfect. Beautiful and sweet. You were honest and I...was having trouble being honest with you in return, which is what you deserved." Harley's comment about the feel of his fingers was intimate and had stirred something in him he hadn't been prepared for. "I left abruptly without explanation, and it was rude of me. I hope I didn't upset you too much."

"I was...worried I'd done something wrong, is all. I'm still super new to, well, everything here." Harley's laugh was self-deprecating. "But I'm learning."

"I can understand that feeling. You didn't do anything wrong, I assure you. I know you're new, and I will be more sensitive to that in the future." Winter wasn't sure there should be a future, but he wanted Harley to feel comfortable coming back to the club at the very least.

"Good deal. We just finished having breakfast for supper here, and now I have coffee." Harley's chuckle bounced inside Winter. "We are living large, I tell you."

It sounded as if Harley was drinking his kind of coffee: one spiked with a little something. "I enjoy breakfast for dinner. Did you have eggs or pancakes?"

"Eggs and toast and these little sausages. They're like breakfast sausage with hot dog outsides."

Winter hummed. "Mm. I like those. The nice thing about eggs for dinner is they're easy to cook. No fuss. I was just debating what to do for dinner myself. You may have made up my mind for me."

"How do you take your eggs?" Harley actually sounded interested.

"I like them scrambled well. Even browned a little. But beyond that, I'm just happy to eat them. You could scramble in ham or sausage, cheese, vegetables, make it an omelet, whatever you like. If they're fried, I like them sunny side up over toast. Runny centers if they're poached. Did I miss anything?"

He rolled his eyes. He knew he was embarrassing himself. The boy was going to think he'd forgotten how to have a conversation. *Listen to you. The boy didn't ask for a dissertation on eggs.*

"Mmm... I like hard-boiled ones too, with a little pickle, onion, celery, tuna and mayo." Harley chuckled softly. "And I just ate, but I could murder a bacon, egg, and potato taco right now."

"A taco. Oh, I remember tacos. I haven't had one in years." They just didn't feel like something you had alone.

Tacos were probably every day where Harley came from, but in his world, tacos were a party food. Something you had with people. And tequila.

"No? Really? I love tacos. I think it's probably genetic, though. Do you... I mean, do you go out to supper ever?"

No, he didn't. Taking oneself to dinner alone was the most depressing endeavor imaginable. "No. Not...well..."

Wait. Oh dear. Was that a dinner invitation? Or just a question? *Damn it.* Was the boy inviting him out to dinner?

"That is, I enjoy eating out. I just don't often have the occasion to do so."

"Oh." There was a pause. "Wanna go get tacos?"

"Yes." He kept himself from overthinking by answering before his better sense could kick in. He was hungry. He would have tacos with Harley.

Oh. He should probably say something more than just "yes".

"Do you know of a place? I'm afraid I haven't the foggiest idea where one can get tacos."

"I do. I know of tons. I work all over, so I get to eat at lots of places. Give me an area, I'll find us a restaurant and meet you."

"Oh. Well, I am in Chelsea, but I can meet you anywhere." There had to be a place to get tacos in the neighborhood. Perhaps in Chelsea Market. He hadn't been through there in a long time.

"There's a good place in Chelsea Market on 9th. Los Tacos. I can totally meet you there."

"I would like that. Very much. I will meet you there shortly." Los Tacos. What a perfect name. Right on brand. His stomach gurgled hungrily. "I'm looking forward to seeing you."

"I am too. I'll see you in a few. Thanks for calling. I was thinking about you."

He waited for Harley to hang up first.

I was thinking about you.

Was he really going to allow himself to do this again?

Well, not in his house sweater, he wasn't. He took his tea to the kitchen, then hurried to his bedroom to change, finding casual clothes suitable for evening tacos rather than nighttime club wear, and shoes he could walk comfortably in farther than the trip to the corner for a taxi.

It was a Saturday night, and Chelsea Market was busy. Plenty of people wandering, eating, shopping. He found Los Tacos and looked for a place to wait for Harley that was out of the way but still visible. It wasn't easy, but he ended up near the sign on the wall with the menu.

He wasn't inconspicuous, but he was out of the way. He took a breath, allowing himself to relax a little, think a little. It was just tacos. Harley was a nice young man. And for all of that Harley was a grown-up too and had been the one to make the invitation. He hoped it wasn't a pity dinner.

Harley wasn't hard to spot either, at least Winter didn't think so, with his dark jeans and button-down shirt, leather jacket, and that obviously well-loved ballcap. Harley found him and headed straight over with a wave and a smile.

That smile was so sweet and genuine, all he could do was smile back. "Well, hello there. I hope your trip across town wasn't too frustrating." The East Village to Chelsea wasn't direct unless the L train was running.

Harley sat with him. "No, sir. It was fine. You been waiting long?"

"Not at all, and the people watching has been extraordinary. But you look better than anyone I've been watching."

That earned him a deep blush and a warmer smile. "Thank you. Do you know what you want? I'm happy to go order for us."

He couldn't take his eyes off Harley, so sweet. Lovely. "I haven't the vaguest idea. Would you order? Just get me whatever you think I should have." He pulled out his wallet. "On me."

Harley shook his head and stood with another of those smiles that went right to his eyes. "Oh, no. I invited you. That means it's my treat, right? I'll be right back."

I suppose so. He was almost embarrassed that he'd pulled out his wallet. Almost.

He watched Harley in line, and every so often their eyes would meet and one of them would smile and then Harley would blush all over again. Harley stepped up and ordered, pointing here and there like he knew exactly what he wanted, which only made him more endearing.

Harley headed back over with two Cokes. "They have Mexican Coke here! I love that. We're close enough that I can hear our number. Do you like guacamole?"

"It's been some time, but I believe I do. Is Mexican Coke very different from American Coke?" He'd never heard of such a thing. But Harley's excitement was adorable.

"It so is. Mexican Coke is made with real sugar, not corn syrup. And the bottles are cool too." Harley sat and grinned at him. "I am a guacamole fan, but I got two with it on the side, just in case."

He picked up his Coke and took a sip. It was sweet, but then he wasn't a Coke drinker, and all soda seemed sweet to him. He didn't hate it though, and he took another sip, then gave Harley a nod. "Very nice."

"It's not something I want every day, but it's a good treat. I drink a lot of water at work because I'm humping my butt."

He imagined Harley, sweaty and working hard with all those lovely, lean muscles popping in his arms, and decided he'd best not let himself fantasize while sitting here with the boy; he was very likely to embarrass himself. But what a lovely thought for later, in the privacy of his own bath.

He'd best concentrate on repairing the damage he'd done the night before. "I have to say, Harley, that I'm surprised you wanted to have a meal with me tonight."

"Really? I thought we were getting along pretty well for a bit last night, and you were nice enough to call." Harley gave him a serious look. "Life is too short to hold onto stuff that hurts. I want to live every single second I have with people I enjoy being with. I like you, Winter Love. I think you're interesting." Then Harley's head tilted. "That's our number. I'll be back."

Winter stared after Harley, stunned at the boy's honesty. He was right, life was short, and it wasn't until he'd brought that water over last night that Winter started to realize how dull his own had become.

He caught Harley's eyes on the way back to the table and as soon as Harley had set their food down, he caught the boy's hand. "I like you too. I'd use your full name for emphasis as you did but I don't actually know it. I'd like to though. I'd like to know a good deal more about you because you are also interesting to me."

"Harley Nathaniel McBride, from San Saba, Texas, born and raised."

Harley Nathaniel McBride. He liked that. It had a ring to it.

"A good, strong name. Very nice. I don't have a middle name. I took my own name when I left home, and never felt the need for one." Middle names were family names, and he didn't have any family.

"Like you just made your own name up? How cool is that?"

It was one of the best decisions he'd ever made and also one of the scariest. "I made it up. And when I finally decided to stay in New York, I made it legal."

"That's cool. I never even thought about doing something like that." Harley pushed over three tacos. "Chicken, pork, and beef. I went by Nathan when I was a freshman in high school. It so didn't work. I'm a Harley."

"I agree; you're most certainly a Harley." He scrutinized the tacos and picked up the beef one first. "These smell wonderful." He took a bite and savored it, enjoying the strong flavors, the warm beef and the cool sour cream. All he could do was nod with his mouth full. "Mmm."

"Rock on." Harley added hot sauce and chowed down, the groan almost sexual.

"Delicious." He took another bite, less interested in talking for the moment while he enjoyed his dinner. Something about all of this was just perfect. Harley, tacos, this ordinary, yet extraordinary place in Chelsea Market he would never have gone to on his own in a million years.

The Coke was perfect with the tacos, cutting the grease and the heat, and he got it. He suddenly got it, why Harley moaned like that.

He picked up the chicken taco. "This was such a good idea." And he meant more than the food. He hadn't felt this real...this confident and relaxed in quite some time.

He finished the chicken taco, and started in on the pork, which was juicy and spicier, and he found himself sucking the Coke faster.

"You want another one? I'll grab you one?" Harley was licking his fingers off.

"Oh, no thank you. I am quite full." That didn't stop him

from taking the last bite of the pork taco, though. He smiled at Harley as he finished chewing.

"So, that was a total win. I bet I look like a boa constrictor that ate a sheep." Harley patted his belly with one hand.

"The elephant inside a snake." He remembered every book he'd ever read as a child; books had been his best friends. "The Little Prince, have you read it?"

"Yeah, my momma's the school librarian. We read a lot." Harley chuckled softly, and there was a wealth of emotion there. "One of the very first things I did when I came here was go to the main library and gawk."

"Harley." He sat up and a warm rush of excitement coursed through him. The coincidence was astonishing. "I am also a librarian...at the main branch. I work mostly in the archives. I've been there for many years."

Harley blinked, the expression of surprise and happiness like a sip of sunshine. "No shit? How fun is that? I bet you've seen so much—all the people and books and things."

"I have seen and read a great deal. The archive brings in all kinds of interesting people." Winter didn't believe in fate...although he was starting to think he should believe in something.

"That's too cool, man. Seriously. I love a library." Harley leaned back in his chair. "And you're like in THE library."

"Now you know where to find me." The club, his work, all that was left was his apartment, and...well. That was the one place he hadn't offered yet. "You should feel free to use my account if you want to check anything out."

"Oh, that's sweet. Right now I'm on a Johnstone kick, and I'm using my Overdrive account through Texas."

"You like electronic books, hm? I have an e-reader and

it's handy for traveling, but I still prefer the feel and smell of a book." He liked browsing the stacks, people watching, reading bits of this and that as he wandered. It was the experience of the library that he enjoyed most.

"Well, right now I'm living in someone else's place, when you get right down to it. So, my phone is my lifeline there, but I hear you. There's that whole—I can read all the books! —thing."

Winter laughed. "So it is. How do you know Jackson?"

"We were in Boy Scouts together. His family moved when he was a Junior in high school, and we've kept in touch." Harley chuckled, rolling his eyes. "I'm like the silly country mouse that never left home, so when I got the chance, I did it."

"I'm sorry things became awkward with your mother. I'm sure you miss her." The boy had said she'd married a preacher, so awkward was probably an understatement.

"Yeah... It was...well, you know, I'm not in the closet. I'm not a huge rainbow flag guy, but folks knew." Harley sighed softly. "It's different when your people decide you're going to hell."

"Personally, I plan to enjoy my slow descent into hell. You and I have much in common, don't we?" He took the last sip of his Coke.

"We both like men, books, tacos, and our names. So yes."

"Those are the simple things, Harley. I think we may go a little deeper than that." He stood and started cleaning up. "Would you care to—" He shouldn't be so nervous. He took a breath and started over. "Would you be my guest for a nightcap?"

Harley stood, hand sliding into his for a second. "I would like that, very much."

He squeezed Harley's fingers for a quick moment before they disappeared again and the two of them finished cleaning up after themselves. "Excellent. It's an easy walk, and I'll make sure to get you a car to take you home later so you'll be safe."

"No worries. We'll figure everything out, I have faith." Harley sent a quick text, then looked up with a smile. "I don't know if Ollie would worry, but if he does, I thought I'd tell him where I was."

"That's responsible of you." He was fairly sure it was just a hello sort of check in as opposed to a safety check in, but either way this was New York City, and one couldn't be too careful.

"I try. I like to know the rules of the space I'm in." Harley chuckled softly. "Which I guess is a nice way of saying, if I do something wrong, I want to mean it."

He chuckled too. "Let's walk, Harley." Winter offered Harley an arm. "Thank you for dinner. That was fun."

"You're more than welcome." Harley took his arm like it was easy, even though Winter knew it couldn't be something Harley was used to.

That made it more meaningful, and he tucked Harley's arm to his side as they stepped outside. "Lovely night. I'm sure you're used to more sky and stars, but there is something to be said for a city street at night."

"It's a whole new world, that's for sure."

Winter glanced over to see if Harley was being sarcastic, but he was smiling, eyes searching the neighborhood with interest.

"I've traveled quite a bit, and I've been in lots of cities, but New York is unique. I love to visit Paris and Rome, Amsterdam, they're all interesting places but I'm glad I live here." He'd do whatever he could to convince Harley to stay in New York, but he knew the risks. Many young men didn't like to stay put.

"I've been all over Texas and to Mexico and New Orleans, but this is the first place I went...wow, you know?"

"Oh, I don't believe that. Really? New Orleans is a wonderful place." There was a reason he enjoyed Mardi Gras.

"It is. I used to go a lot, then...well, I had a weird experience, and I haven't been back."

He glanced at Harley, wondering if he'd get an answer if he asked what that meant. He was curious, so he decided to try. "Weird?"

"So...it's embarrassing, a little. I got my palm read, and the lady freaked me out, telling me I was cursed and all. She wanted money, and I know it was a con, but...it was scary. I was stupid."

They turned a corner, and it was only a few steps to his building. "Psychics can be unnerving. What exactly was your supposed curse?"

"She said I'd lose everything, that there was a demon chasing me and making me do evil, perverse things." Harley shook his head. "I'm a butthead, but I'm not evil."

"No, Harley. You're not evil." They climbed the steps to the front door and Winter pulled out his keys and unlocked the door. "You're just queer. But there are lots of people who think they are the same thing."

"Yeah. Trust me, this I understand on a bone-deep level." Harley winked, eyes twinkling. "If I was evil, I'd have stayed in San Saba."

He laughed. "So true. Go on in, I'm at the back of the building and up two flights."

"That's not bad! I'm in a fourth-floor walk-up. I tell you what, by the end of a long day at work, I'm pooped."

He didn't mind the couple of flights, he needed the exercise, but four would be a challenge. He followed Harley up the steps but squeezed by him when they reached the top so he could unlock his door. All three locks.

"After you. I wasn't expecting visitors, so you'll forgive the disorder. Not that it's terribly orderly even when I am expecting someone." He hadn't expected anyone but repairmen in ages. Years maybe.

"I'm crazy excited to..." Harley walked in, eyes wide, taking in the books and the knickknacks, the art and glass and pottery and furniture. God, was it horrifying? Off-putting? Ridiculous? "Oh, man. This looks like a *home*."

Winter closed the door and locked it. "It is that. This is the living room. My study through there is much more comfortable." And less cluttered too. God, he was embarrassed, but there wasn't any point to hiding who he was from Harley.

"It's great. So much to explore. All the books!" Harley clapped. "And you have a study? I've never met a person with a study."

"I call it my study. It's a den I suppose. It's where I spend most of my time." He led Harley down the short hall to the study. "I love it during the day especially. It gets so much light and there's a little balcony outside those doors. You'll have to see it in the daylight sometime." He turned on his desk lamp. "What would you like to drink? Brandy? Glass of wine? Irish cream?"

"Irish cream. I've never tried brandy or very much wine. Just Boone's Farm, you know?"

"Boone's Farm? Is that local? Have a seat. Irish cream it is. Over ice?" He gestured to a soft leather couch at one end of the room, then went to his small bar behind his desk.

Harley sat with a soft sigh, wiggling in. "Please, and it's

the stuff high schoolers drink at bonfires. You know...three buck Chuck?"

"Ah yes." That made him laugh as he poured two drinks. "I'm old enough to remember when it was two buck Chuck." Not that he ever drank it himself, but it was popular for sure.

"How old are you? I'm twenty-five in March."

So young. He handed Harley his drink and paced back to lean on his desk. "I'll be forty on the fifteenth." Less than two weeks away from the end of one decade and the beginning of another.

Harley's eyes went wide. "So soon! I'm glad I know. I will buy you a cupcake or a cronut or a...a...what are those Italian desserts that are so sexy... Oh! Cannolis!"

He did enjoy a cannoli. "You're very sweet. Thank you. But I don't usually celebrate my birthday."

"No? Can I ask why or is that not my business? I mean, obviously it's not my business." Harley blushed, and it was surprisingly charming. "But I guess I mean, do you not want me to ask?"

"You may ask anything you like. If I don't want to answer I'll simply say so. But in this case it's just a very mundane answer. The day I was born doesn't mean anything to anyone but me. The people I was born to didn't care, and very few people since have either. Birthdays aren't fun to celebrate alone." And he'd had a lot of them now too.

"I care!" Harley stood up and came right to him. "I know I don't know you, but how could anyone not care? That's awful! I will celebrate you, I promise."

How ironic. He should correct Harley, who in fact knew him better at this moment than most people at the club. Better than anyone but the older members anyway. He hadn't told anyone the story about changing his name or talked about his birthday; he hadn't had anyone in his home that he cared about at all in far too long.

And he'd had no interest in celebrating forty years until just this very second.

Instead of ruining a perfect moment with all of that weight, he touched Harley's face, fingers gliding along a stubborn chin, and looked into the boy's lovely, deep, dark eyes. "You're too good to be true. Thank you. I would like that."

"Me too." Harley leaned into the touch, just the slightest bit. "You have my word."

He didn't pull his gaze or his hand away, instead he encouraged Harley and flattened his palm to cup the boy's cheek. "What do you suppose is happening here, Harley?"

"I think we're figuring each other out just a little." Harley sighed softly. "I swear, you got the warmest hands."

Figuring each other out. Maybe a little, but Harley was such a mystery to himself that he was still a mystery to Winter too.

He led Harley back to the couch. "Can you tell me more about that fancier Matrix guy you talked about? The fancier you."

Harley tilted his head. "I can try... I hadn't thought about it much until last night. I—You want to see something?"

Harley grabbed his phone and showed him a picture from last night. The makeup was smudged, there were hints of glitter from the party, and the look would have been perfect if Harley's lips had been swollen from kisses or Winter's cock.

"You're beautiful in that picture." Winter sighed. "It looks like you enjoyed the rest of the party."

"I was going home, but Ollie asked me to stay and dance.

I came home and crashed hard, but it was fun. It wasn't what you and I were doing, though."

He nodded. The energy that he and Harley shared was extraordinary, the connection undeniable. He'd felt like he'd been watching Harley bloom. "You enjoyed what you and I were doing. Do you want to...try again?"

"I do. I want to... I felt... I don't know, special is a good word, but it's not it, exactly." Harley huffed out a breath. "I want to try with you."

His pulse sped up, heart beating hard like it had last night. He wanted to help Harley understand, find the real boy inside that strong body. "I want that too. I have everything we need in my bedroom, if that's not too forward." He felt his chest heat and tried not to blush, but an invitation into his boudoir was forward, even if his intentions were more innocent than they sounded.

Harley caught his gaze. "I promise not to do anything you don't want. I'm a good guy."

Be still his beating heart. Here he was worried this young man would think he was an old lecher and instead Harley was promising to protect his virtue. If only the boy knew there was little he didn't want. "I am also a...good guy. I never want you to feel uncomfortable, and I hope you can be honest with me about that."

"I will. Uncomfortable isn't always bad, but I'm smart enough to know the difference." Harley winked at him. "In fact, I can think of a lot of really good things that aren't exactly comfortable."

He raised an eyebrow and let himself smile. "You'll have to tell me all about them at some point," he teased. "Come on then, bring your drink."

"Yessir." Harley snatched the glass up and followed him. "Your home is like a treasure trove."

"It's hopelessly cluttered, you can say so. I'm not a packrat, but there are some things I don't care to part with." Objectively, he simply hadn't had any reason to part with most things. He lived alone, ao he didn't need room for anyone else.

Winter led Harley across the hall and around a corner to his bedroom. This room was far less cluttered, his bed was neatly made, but the heavy furniture was a bit too imposing for the room's size. He'd moved here from a larger space a decade ago, and he'd just never replaced the set. His dressing table, however, was perfect for the space, full of storage, and fitted with a full-length mirror. "This is my room. Have a seat at my table there."

"This is amazing." Harley sat and sipped his drink. "That's a mirror that has stories, I bet."

"Yes, indeed. Some lovely young men have sat in that seat you're in. They've all moved on now." He pulled a makeup cape and a couple of soft cloths from his closet.

"They have? I'm not going to say I'm sorry they're gone, 'cause I'm not."

"You are quite the sweet talker, aren't you? You look like you belong there. I don't miss them anymore." He draped the cape over Harley's shoulders and tied it in place. "This will keep the makeup off your nice shirt."

"Thank you. It's my one of my best two. The other one is white and not taco-friendly."

"Mine was in jeopardy for a while there, but I think I escaped without a spill." He pulled his own chair up close to Harley. "So. Do you have ideas? Is there something you'd like me to try? Or should we just...see what happens?" If Harley had thoughts, or wishes, he wanted to know them.

"I don't even know what to try. You just...do your thing. I'm here with you, and I'm not scared."

"I'm glad. There's nothing to be scared of. I will look after you." Winter pulled a drawer open and lifted out a box, found what he was looking for and got to work, starting by cleansing Harley's skin and applying a gentle moisturizer.

"Foundation evens out your skin, makes it like a blank canvas for me to work on. You can close your eyes or keep them open, it's up to you, and I will let you look in the mirror as we go along."

He got right to work, taking Harley's chin in one hand and a sponge in the other.

Harley stayed very still, eyes on his face, the expression somehow quiet and curious at once.

He took his time, studying the natural curve of high cheekbones, the hollow of Harley's cheeks, the height of the boy's brow. He only asked Harley to close his eyes long enough to cover eyelids and eyebrows. "Have a look."

Harley looked, tilting his face back and forth. "I look like a doll, a little. It doesn't feel bad though. It feels almost soft."

"Mhm. You're not a doll, though. You're a man. People have accused me of wanting to play with dolls... I assure you, I don't." He turned Harley's face back to him. "Shall we make some magic?"

"I like magic." Harley searched his eyes. "Where did you learn about this stuff?"

"From other people. I met a makeup artist who was headed to New York, and we traveled together. After that, I would experiment with it on myself, and I learned a lot more. Then I started making up my friends, eventually my lovers."

"Oh. I don't think I ever met anyone that did makeup for a living. Ollie does his own nails though."

"Ollie is talented. He cares about his nails, and his hair." Ollie cared about his figure too, and Winter wondered how much Harley knew about that. "There are many makeup artists in New York, given all the theater and movies that are made here. It's a very creative town."

"I know many people that carry boxes and pianos. I moved a harpsichord yesterday." Harley winked at him. "That took creativity."

"My goodness. It must be worth a fortune. I'm impressed. I'm not sure I'd want to be responsible for something like that." Not that he would be able to lift it if he wanted to. He'd leave that to boys like Harley who were actually as strong as they looked.

"It's a good job. I worked at a factory before this, loading trucks. My business card says Professional Pack Mule."

He laughed. Harley was just delightful. "Oh, that's quite a calling." He applied concealer and blended it, then pulled out his eyebrow pencil and got to work. Harley's brows had a very nice shape, but he wanted to extend them a bit and fill in here and there. "Perhaps I'll hire you to help me clean out my apartment someday."

"If you want. I think it's charming, though. Honestly."

"Thank you. I'm very comfortable here to be sure." He grabbed a brush and his color palette to set Harley's eyebrows and to use as a bronzer. He couldn't even pretend this wasn't turning him on; he loved this, always had, and the fact that Harley was beautiful without makeup made him that much more alluring with it.

"So, do I look different?" Harley sipped again, then licked the whiskey off his lips.

"You look just like you, only...more. But I haven't gotten to your eyes yet. That will be another minute. How do you feel about lip shades? Lip gloss?" The eyes were the best part. He would only do eyes most of the time, but since

Harley was so willing, he decided to see how the boy felt about the full treatment.

"Does it feel sticky? I don't think I'd like sticky, but I'll try."

He thought about that. "Sticky? Not really. Heavy maybe, at first, but it is something you get used to. Let's see how you like the look. It's easy enough to take off. A gloss or a shimmer would be lighter, we could start there. But first... your eyes." His favorite part.

The dark gaze was warm. "Yeah, that was...that was cool last night. Different."

"It was. I was so taken with your curiosity and your willingness to trust me." And Harley's lovely smile, dark eyes, strong shoulders...round, tight backside. "I still am."

"You're making my belly shake inside." He could feel Harley's blush, warming the sweet face.

"Is that a good feeling?" Winter slowly put everything away except his eyeliner and mascara.

"It's exciting. New. Do you like dark eyes?"

"I like all eyes, but yours especially. Dark eyes are warm, and they like a dark eyeliner. There's so much I can do." He was going to keep it simple tonight though, a line that would complement Harley's bone structure and make his eyes look bigger, but not detract from the boy's naturally handsome face.

"Thank you. I wanted blue eyes so bad when I was growing up, but I look just like my mom."

"I think everyone wants a look they don't have at some point. Different hair, different eyes, different height, something. We're all made just right as far as I am concerned. Be still now, please." He leaned closer to Harley with the eyeliner, close enough to smell fresh soap and aftershave. "Did you shave for me?"

"Mmhmm. Just for you."

He didn't try to hide the goosebumps, but he paused for a second to wait for his hand to be steady again.

Just for him. That answer deserved a kiss, but he didn't dare. When Harley said they were learning each other, Winter hadn't realized just how much he'd already learned. It appeared that everything was new to Harley. He hadn't been clear then on how far *everything* went. He thought he understood now, and with that knowledge came a responsibility he hadn't expected to be carrying.

Though he was more than pleased to do so.

"Sweet boy. Thank you."

Harley winked for him, then those eyes closed.

He slowly drew precise and practiced lines around Harley's eyes, and the room went quiet except for the sound of them breathing together. It was a little different than the club the other night, that intense silence. Harley's skin took the liner like a dream. "You were made for this. As an everyday look I'd go much simpler than this, but because we're playing a little...well, do you want to look, or shall I do the mascara first to complete your look?"

"You should complete it. I want to see it all done." Harley's voice was husky, low. "Should I open my eyes?"

"When you're ready." He capped the liner and dug out a thickening mascara that should make Harley's long lashes positively lush.

Harley blinked his eyes open, expression making Winter smile. "Am I gorgeous?"

"You are." He went in with the mascara wand, and it didn't take much to make Harley's lashes thick and dark. "Wait until you see."

"I'm a little nervous." Harley chuckled. "I feel fancy without even looking. Like a movie star."

"Give me your hands then, before you look." He took both of Harley's hands and held them, gently, but firmly. He was nervous too. He would understand if Harley didn't care for all the makeup, but he wanted Harley to at least like it, if he couldn't love it. "And look when you're ready."

Harley glanced at himself, then stared, eyes going wide. "I don't—I don't know what to say. I look like...not me, or lots of me, or... I don't know. Like I—It's..." Winter heard the softest whisper. "My eyes are so big."

"Your eyes are the best part," he whispered back, leaning close to Harley's ear. He turned Harley to fully face the mirror and stood behind him. "Do you recognize the lovely soul in that mirror, Harley?"

"I don't know..." He leaned toward the mirror. "I look like a familiar stranger, like someone I'd want to look at."

He decided against lip color; he wasn't going to do anything more right now. Harley was taking it all in, and he didn't want to interrupt. "And how does it make you feel?"

"A little confused in my chest, yeah? I mean, this isn't who I normally see. Can you imagine what folks would say back home? But I can't stop looking. I don't want to stop." Harley glanced at Winter in the mirror. "Is that wrong?"

"No." He smiled back at Harley. "Look all you like. It's you after all, so you're not being rude by staring." He took Harley's makeup shawl off and started putting things away. "This is just my first try at what I thought might work for you. You should think about what you like and don't like, maybe want more or less of...this is just a beginning. Just fun."

"Okay." Harley chuckled softly. "It's surprisingly intimate. Having you decorate me."

Decorate was a good word. And insightful word. Winter

came back over and looked at Harley in the mirror. "It felt like foreplay."

"Yessir, it sure did." Harley's eyes were sparkling. "My whole body thought so."

He bent and kissed the top of Harley's head, then breathed in deep. "Mine too."

"Can I kiss you? Is that too forward?"

Harley wasn't just curious; he was brave too. Winter tried not to let how hard his heart was beating show. "No. I'd like that."

Harley turned to face him, those lined eyes staring into his as their lips met, the first kiss almost chaste.

Almost. He lingered over it longer than he would a chaste kiss, and he couldn't stop himself from tasting Harley's lips with the tip of his tongue as he pulled away. "Mm. So, are you as new at this as you are with eyeliner?"

"At kissing? No. No, not quite. I'm new to being as open, but I'm not a virgin."

"Good to know. I wondered for a minute, you...feel new." He didn't ask Harley for permission; he just took another kiss, fingers sliding around to catch the sweet boy's nape.

Harley moaned and leaned forward, hands landing on his thighs. They were hot, almost feverish, and Winter's muscles clenched in a rush of passion.

The things he wanted to do to this beautiful young man.

He stepped back, guiding Harley to his feet. He wasn't a tall man himself, but he was taller than Harley, whose strong body seemed to vibrate and rumble like an engine as he held it.

Harley searched his eyes, and Winter wasn't sure what the boy was looking for, but obviously Harley found it. The kiss Winter got was almost blistering.

He met that heat with his own, turning off his mind and

all the alarm bells sounding in it. He didn't want to listen, he wanted Harley. He spun them, and it wasn't three steps to his bed, where he backed the boy against a tall bedpost.

Harley groaned, one hand landing on his hip and dragging him in closer. Winter felt the heavy erection, hot against his thigh.

Winter grunted and gripped one tight ass cheek with his fingers, rocking with Harley so they could really feel each other. "Do you want this, Harley? Do you want me?" He felt breathless and his voice was deep.

"God yes. I'm hungry for you." Harley cupped his cock through his jeans, thumb stroking him, base to tip.

The touch was unexpected, and the rush of sensation and need interrupted him, made him moan and lean into Harley's hand. He worked open the buttons of Harley's shirt with trembling fingers and kissed the bare skin under the boy's collarbone.

Harley sucked in a quick breath, and he smiled. So responsive. So eager.

Once the shirt was free, he pushed it down and off, tugging it free of Harley's wrists. He leaned back a bit to take in the patchwork tan—the darker arms and neck and paler torso of a man that had spent a lot of time working outdoors. Haley's skin was smooth, and Winter ran his fingers from shoulders to waist, feeling the muscle ripple at his touch. "So lovely."

"Thank you. I want to see you too." Harley reached for his shirt. "Please?"

"Of course." He dropped his arms to his sides and let Harley do as he pleased, though just the thought brought his nipples to stiff nubs. They rubbed against the heavy cotton of his dress shirt, making him shiver.

Harley worked his buttons open with nimble fingers, stroking and petting every inch of skin he bared.

His chest was fuzzy, where Harley's was smooth, though the hair was light in color. He didn't have Harley's stunning abs either, but he was fit; he cared about his shape and spent some time in a local gym with a trainer. He had no one else to spend his money on but himself, after all.

He was paler than Harley too, and felt himself flush at the gentle attention.

"Mmm...pretty." Harley eased his shirt off, slowly working those callused hands down his arms.

He shrugged. "Not as pretty as you." Winter kept his eyes on Harley, focused on the heat between them and nothing else. "I was worried bringing you into my bedroom would be too tempting. But it's not the bedroom at all. It's you that's too tempting."

"We're both adults, and I want to make us both feel good."

"That's what I want too." Once Harley got his shirt off he went right for the boy's belt, opening it easily.

The jeans were looser than he would have expected, and the weight of the belt dragged them down to mid-thigh. Oh, that was pretty—tiny hips, muscled thighs, and a line of glory leading to what promised to be a lovely cock.

He focused on that little line, tracing it from Harley's navel to the edge of his briefs. He pulled the elastic toward him and dipped his fingers below it, watching Harley's gorgeous eyes as he caught that hot cock in his fingers.

Harley's eyes widened, then went heavy-lidded, sultry. Winter did love a responsive boy.

"Why don't you remove the rest of your clothing, *petit*?"

"Yeah, the boots are a thing, right?" Harley sat on the

edge of the bed and pulled off his cowboy boots, setting them carefully aside.

"They are, and jeans. I'm a fan of that belt too." He watched Harley put everything down neatly, much more patiently than most men the boy's age who usually just tossed clothing aside.

"Yeah, thanks. It's my good one. My work belt is way thicker, sturdy."

"Thick and sturdy, hm?" He slid his fingers along Harley's cock again, through the briefs, then pushed them over Harley's hips, setting the heavy erection free. "Tell me what you like, Harley. I'm open to anything. Do you prefer hands or mouths? Do you want my cock inside you? Do you want to take this slowly? Or maybe you don't want to answer questions and leave it to me."

His questions were barely above a whisper, meant more to tease than to start some kind of discussion. That they could have later, as pillow talk in the half-light. He opened his own belt, then kicked off his shoes.

"I—I bet you'd like me on my knees, blowing you and looking up at you." Harley bit his bottom lip, the first sign that he wasn't perfectly confident. "I want your cock, but it's been a while. I haven't done that much."

His cock filled and his balls grew heavy at Harley's offer. "We'll...save that then," he said, voice thick and low. "I believe you're right about...looking up at me with those gorgeous eyes." He reached for the bedpost to steady himself. Perhaps Harley would believe it was so he could remove his pants, instead of compensating for a sudden weakness in the knees.

"I'm all over that. I like to suck." Oh, thank god. That was a delicious bonus.

"I admire your enthusiasm. I'm admiring a great deal

about you just now. I'm going to make you feel so good, Harley." He finished undressing, stepping out of his jeans and boxers and folding them as Harley had. "I'm rather fond of fellatio myself." He wasn't quite that pretentious, but the word amused him.

"I would worry about you if you were anti-blow job." Harley slid down to his knees, lips brushing the tip of Winter's cock, teasing the hell out of him.

He caught Harley's cheek in one hand, suddenly breathless. "Oh god. Harley. You're so beautiful."

"No one's ever said that to me before. Ever." Harley held his gaze, nuzzling into his hand.

That was so hard to believe...though coming from where Harley had, he did believe it. "Then everyone on earth is blind."

"That's okay with me. You see just fine." Harley kissed his palm, then turned to kiss the tip of his cock.

He inhaled sharply. "Yes, *petit*. I see you...as you are."

Harley smiled for him, then took him in, his cock disappearing into that heated mouth, inch by inch.

"Oh dear god." Need filled him head to toe, making him groan and sweat. He was grateful for the bedpost to hold on to, and he pet Harley's hair with his free hand. "Your mouth...so hot."

But it was the look in Harley's eyes that made him so achingly hard, made his balls draw up. He stared into them, not too shy to let Harley see what he was doing. He rocked a little onto his toes and back, feeling every inch of Harley's rough tongue and wanting more.

Harley's groan vibrated all along his shaft, and then that tongue slapped him, sending electricity through his entire body.

"Fuck, that's good." Winter didn't think he'd be able to

hold off too long and he didn't mind; he wasn't out for a trophy. Harley's mouth was heaven and he just wanted to enjoy it. He tugged on Harley's hair, watching his cock slide past those pretty lips.

Harley stared up at him, letting him in, letting him see into those dark eyes.

He wanted to keep this one, teach this one, share his bed and his home with this beautiful boy and, in this particular moment, none of that worried him. Right now he could believe that Harley was his and take that lovely mouth while losing himself in Harley's adoring eyes.

So he did. He rocked a little harder, and raised an eyebrow, asking if it was all right.

Harley's eyelids lowered, and he cupped Winter's ass, pulling him in deeper, asking for more.

Winter certainly had more, and he gave it up readily. He groaned as his cock hit the back of Harley's throat, but he trusted the boy to stop him if he went too far. His balls drew up, and he lost control, gasping on the edge of his climax. "Harley...petit..."

Harley swallowed, squeezing him and taking him in deep, nose buried in his curls.

"Oh... I—" His eyes crossed, and he gripped the bedpost hard as his orgasm overwhelmed him, moving through him in one dizzying wave after another. He was sure he'd said other things, but he couldn't be sure given the blood roaring in his ears.

Harley took everything, every drop, humming deep so that the aftershocks went on and on.

He allowed himself to stay in the moment and float, enjoying pleasure that was just shy of too much. He took a breath and tugged on that short, thick hair. "Harley. Merci, petit."

"Mmm..." His cock left Harley's lips with a pop, and Harley licked his lips.

"You weren't just being coy; you really do enjoy that, don't you?" He tried to catch his breath, but the smudged makeup at the corner of Harley's eyes took it away again. "So lovely."

"And you're fucking sweet."

He got soft kisses all the way up along his belly as Harley stood.

"Mmm." He pulled Harley in and kissed him, tongue sweeping through the boy's mouth. He turned his hip against Harley's stiff prick to give him some friction.

Harley opened up, pushing a soft, hungry little sound into his lips, tongue sliding against his. As they kissed, Winter moved them to the side of the bed, because he longed to see Harley stretched out in his sheets. He slipped a hand from Harley's round ass to circle that thick cock again. "Lie back, petit. Let me take care of you."

"Oh... I'd like that, a lot." Harley eased himself down, abs rolling, and that was incredibly erotic, watching those muscles.

"I would as well." He climbed over Harley and took another kiss, getting one more good look at those deep, sex-smudged eyes and then slowly kissed his way down, stopping to circle Harley's navel with his tongue.

Harley actually quit breathing for a second, and that was adorable.

He continued on, nuzzling into one hip and then the other, breathing in Harley's scent, and caught up Harley's balls in his hand. "I want you to feel good, petit. As good as you made me feel."

Harley shivered, that sweet, curved cock beginning to leak, to leave a little pool of need on that flat belly.

He started at the base, licking and kissing and tasting lightly until he reached the head, where he lapped up that slick little pool.

"So hot." Harley's voice was a harsh, rough moan. "Damn..."

"Yes." Winter lapped at the head and took the end of Harley's prick into his mouth, tongue gliding through the slit for another taste.

Harley barked out a sharp cry, thighs and belly going tight as he rolled up and curled over Winter's head.

Dear god, nothing was more honest and real than a reaction like that. He decided not to push Harley back down, instead allowing the boy to do whatever he pleased, and let the head of that delicious cock slide farther into his mouth.

Harley groaned, fingers ghosting over his hair, as his hips rocked in tiny jerks.

"Mmm." He did enjoy a needy lover. He stretched out flat and reached up to massage one pretty nipple as he started to move, each time taking Harley in a little deeper.

"H-harder," Harley whispered, then squeezed Winter's fingers tighter around that nipple.

Lovely, *naughty* boy.

He pinched hard and swallowed Harley's cock into his throat.

His boy went wild under him, shooting and filling his lips without any hesitation.

He lingered while Harley came down a little, then kissed his way back up. He gave Harley a little push, watched him tip back and land in the pillows. God, he felt so full of himself right now, like he could light a match and blast off for the moon.

"Damn…" Harley smiled at him, the grin goofy and baby-headed. "Thank you."

"It was my pleasure, petit. I promise you that. Thank you, as well." He took a kiss, then settled on his side, fingers roaming over Harley's chest. He'd enjoyed Harley's reaction to nipple play—to just one firm squeeze, honestly. They were going to be able to have so much fun.

"Do you need to get home, or can you stay for a while?"

"I can stay until you're ready to kick me out. Tomorrow's my day off."

"I won't be 'kicking you out'. Or asking you to leave. I will make you breakfast tomorrow, and we can eat on the balcony and watch the birds. Or I can bring it to you in bed and we'll just watch each other."

Harley cupped his jaw, bringing him close for another kiss. "Those are amazing ideas."

"I'm glad you think so." He rolled onto his back and held an arm out. "Come, let me hold you."

"That sounds wonderful." Harley cuddled right in with a soft little groan. "What an amazing night."

He kissed Harley's forehead. "A stunning night, with a stunning young man."

The young ones always went away eventually, but he was sure Harley was staying, at least for tonight.

7

Harley woke up, confused for a minute as to where he was. It didn't take long, because the imprint of Winter was everywhere he looked—books, knickknacks, that amazing, heavy dresser-table-thing.

He sat up and stretched, then went to the bathroom to do his business before sliding back into bed beside Winter. He caught sight of himself in the mirror—and he looked... well-loved. His lips were a little swollen, his eyes messy and smudged.

It was weirdly hot.

He smiled and snuggled into Winter's back again.

"Mmm. Good morning, petit." Winter had only just woken up; his voice was low, husky.

"Mornin'." He kissed the back of Winter's neck. The soft short hairs tickled his lips, making him smile.

"What a treat, waking up to you." Winter stretched and tucked his arm close. "Did you sleep well?"

"Like a rock, yes, sir. You're warm." He let his eyes close, let himself float.

"You're quiet as a mouse. I barely heard you breathing." Winter didn't seem to be in a hurry to move either.

"No one's ever accused me of snoring." He chuckled at himself. Like he'd ever spent the night with a dude naked before.

"They would be lying, for sure." Winter sighed and rolled to face him, then one finger reached out and touched his temple. "Look at you. Aren't you beautiful in the morning-after, petit."

He felt himself flush, going hot as fuck. He'd felt that way, seeing himself in the mirror, looking like—shit, he didn't even have words. "Thank you."

"You make me feel..." Winter took a deep breath and shook his head. "I suppose I don't have words for it. Happy and...apprehensive."

"Apprehensive? Did I do something?" He couldn't imagine what he could have done, but it might not have dick-all to do with him.

"No, no. I told you I didn't have the right words... I'm sorry. I...you'll find I'm not the most optimistic person. Perhaps that's a better way to put it. Part of me wants to lock you in so I know you'll...stay." Winter sighed again. "But don't listen to me, you've known me for such a very short time. I'm so dramatic."

Ah. Someone had walked out on him. Dammit. "Hey." He kissed Winter's forehead. "I got you. Whoever it was, sucks. And not in a good way, huh?"

Winter's fingers brushed his cheek, and he got a sweet but sad smile. "So, do you prefer a savory breakfast, or a sweet one?"

"I love food. Seriously. I love to eat. I'd tell you I loved to cook, but my mom wouldn't let me in the kitchen." His mom was fierce about what men did and what women did. It was a thing.

"Well then. I will allow you in mine, and I have something else I can teach you." Winter kissed him softly. "We've only scratched the surface I think."

"Mmm..." He smiled so hard his eyes crinkled. "I have to warn you. Ollie doesn't let me in the kitchen either."

Winter laughed happily. "Oh my. That's not a good sign, is it?"

"I'm not dirty or anything. I'm just...clueless, and I don't want to piss anyone off."

Winter blinked. "Goodness, I never imagined you'd be dirty. Not anywhere but here in bed, anyway." The surprised look softened into a smile. "I specialize in clueless. What did you know about makeup before yesterday? Hm?"

"Just that girls painted their eyes with colors." He kissed the edge of Winter's smile.

"I rest my case. But I promised to make you breakfast, so the lessons won't start today." Winter sat up on one elbow, watching him. "I'm very glad you stayed."

"I'm very glad you offered." He dragged one finger down along the center of Winter's chest.

"Do you think Oliver is worried about you?" Winter did the same to him, finger gliding through the channels between his muscles.

"No. Oliver is spending time with a guy. He does whenever the dude is free." He wasn't sure Ollie was getting what he needed, but that wasn't for him to say. They weren't that close.

Winter frowned. "Hm. Someone from the club?"

"I'm sorry, I don't know. I didn't even know that Jackson had a boyfriend until Ollie told me."

"Poor boy. Jackson is in good hands, don't worry. And

Ollie is a big boy, hm? So, I will worry about you, and I won't keep any secrets."

"I don't have a lot of them. I just try to tell the truth, you know?" He just tried to be real, even when it was hard.

"Me too. There are some things that are more difficult to talk about than others, but I don't have secrets." Winter sat up slowly with a soft groan. "I am going to make you coffee and something to eat, petit. Shall we have it in bed, or out in the sunshine?"

"Whatever makes you happy. I want to hang with you, sir, talk to you, have coffee and tell stories about our favorite cartoons."

"Have you a favorite?" Winter slid out of bed and pulled on a light robe, then went to a closet and brought one back to him.

"Thank you, and Dexter's Laboratory. I loved his accent. I used to pretend to be a boy genius all the time." He slid into the robe with a happy hum. "Soft. Thank you."

"A boy genius. I can understand that." Winter adjusted the robe on his shoulders and fussed with his belt, neither of which needed doing. He thought maybe Winter was looking for an excuse to touch.

Harley stepped right into Winter's space. Winter didn't need an excuse. "Good morning."

Winter wrapped around him, pulled him in with a soft sigh. "Mm. Hello there."

Oh.

Oh, he did love that—the contact, the holding. That was like a drug, and Harley thought he could get addicted.

Winter ended the embrace with a squeeze and kissed his temple. "Come with me. You'll love the living room in the morning. So much light."

They headed in, and Winter was right. The room was a

treasure trove, and the light was glorious, warming the entire space.

"I'll start us off with some coffee." Winter went through a narrow doorway into the kitchen. It was tiny, with no room for a table, but it was clean and Winter moved around it easily. "Then eggs and bacon, toast and jam...we'll have a little feast and then talk about plans for the day. A movie perhaps, or a museum? What have you seen since you've been here?"

"I've seen a ton from the window in the truck, and I've seen a bunch of amazing homes." He would never cease to be amazed by how an ugly building could hide amazing insides. He loved that. "And I've walked everywhere in my neighborhood, explored all the things I can. That's one of my favorite things here. There's endless things to look at."

Compared to his hometown of three thousand people? He could watch and look for eighty years.

"Have you been to the Metropolitan Museum of Art? Have you seen the view from the top of the Empire State Building? Have you wandered through Tribeca or Little Italy? These are things you need to do. I know you said you've seen the public library." Winter scrambled eggs as he talked and put a frying pan on the stove. "Do you like mushrooms? Peppers?"

"I love them. And not yet. I must have been waiting for you, so we can go together."

"That must be the case." Winter smiled at him, then went to the fridge and pulled out veggies. "So we'll go. How do you feel about chopping these?"

"Show me how you want it, and I'll figure it." He could cut his own meat up, surely he could manage a mushroom.

Winter sat a cutting board on the counter and put half a pepper on it, then slid it over to him. "We only need about half of this, and then you can start on the mushrooms. Do you know how to hold a knife? Like this. Start here, rock it back toward you." Winter showed him, then set the knife down for him to pick up. "Watch your fingers."

He wasn't good at it, but he didn't cut himself, and Winter didn't fuss at him for being slow, so it was actually fun.

In fact, Winter kept busy and didn't seem in any hurry at all. Bread for toast appeared on the counter, bacon went into the oven, and then Winter set a mug of coffee down in front of him. "How do you take your coffee, petit?"

"At work, black. When I'm fixin' to enjoy it? Sweet and creamy."

Winter chuckled and kissed his cheek. "Let me sweeten that up for you then." Winter slid the mug away and doctored it.

"Mmm..." He took a drink, groaning at the taste of the coffee. God, that was perfect somehow.

"This all looks good. I think that's enough mushrooms. Slide everything into the frying pan, please? Be careful. I've got the pan warming."

"Just put them in?" Harley did as he was asked, the sizzle making him smile.

"Good. Now you can sit and relax with your coffee, and I will make you your breakfast like I promised." Winter winked at him. There wasn't any room to sit in this tiny kitchen though. "Try the big chair in the living room. The one by the window. It's my reading chair."

"Excellent." He bebopped over and found the chair, curling in happily. "Oh, Winter! This is heaven."

He picked up the book next to the chair, curious to see what was on the reading list. The hardcover copy of *The Big Sleep* had a library barcode on the spine.

"It is, isn't it? There's a little table that unfolds, so we can eat at that." The smell of bacon was already filling the room.

"Neat." He opened the book and grinned. His grampa had loved this movie. "Phillip Marlowe, huh? Good taste."

"Back when books had cards in the front with names, that card had my name on it dozens of times. There are new copies now, so I took that one home for good." Winter came in and set up the card table, then pulled over a second chair. "Some people have comfort food, comfort slippers... I have that book."

"Yeah? Mine is *Territory* by Emma Bull. Not a classic, but I love it. Tombstone meets magic."

Winter looked at him, head tilting. "I haven't read it. I suppose I will have to check it out of the library. Soon."

"You can borrow my copy. I brought it from home. It's in my backpack." He had brought everything he could carry, which had ended up being jeans, shoes, t-shirts, and books. That, his phone, and his laptop was all he needed.

"You could read it to me." Winter disappeared into the kitchen again and he heard plates rattling.

"Sure." He'd never done that before, but that didn't mean he couldn't do it now. "I'd love to."

"Good. I'd like that." Winter sat a plate and a fork down for each of them. "I just need to get the toast."

"Here, let me get it. I'm not broke." He hopped up, ashamed of himself for being a laze.

"No, Harley, sit. Please. It's my pleasure, I assure you." Winter didn't let him help, stepping between him and the kitchen door.

"Are you sure?" At Winter's nod, he went back to sit. He wasn't used to being a lazy butt.

"Today. I promised." Winter ducked away and came back

with toast and jam, balancing his own cup of coffee. "Eat, petit. While it's hot."

"It smells so good. How did you learn to cook?" He dug into the eggs, humming happily. He loved having folks that made things taste yummy.

"I taught myself. I watched cooking shows on TV, and I read food magazines. Now I watch YouTube videos. It's been a lot of trial and error. But even you can make breakfast. I'm sure of it."

"Well, I am the King of Pop-Tarts and buying doughnuts." He winked over, then scooped up more eggs with his toast. So yummy.

Winter gave him a serious look. "Oh, no, petit. No more of that. Look at how fit you are; your body deserves better. You need to eat real food."

He didn't know what to say. He liked his sleep more than he liked dealing with getting to a diner for breakfast, especially since he ended up grabbing whatever he could find for lunch. Supper, though, that he had down. He had pizza Wednesday and Thursday, he bought Ollie supper on Monday and Tuesday, and Ollie cooked Sunday. Fridays and Saturdays were crazy flexible. "Yeah, I guess I should add in cereal to the mix, huh?"

Winter huffed, grinning. "I don't believe you've taken my advice to heart."

"I did!" He winked over. "Cereal is healthy. I like Frosted Mini-Wheats the best."

"Awful processed stuff. So much sugar. It's fortunate that you work off the calories on the job." Winter was enjoying his breakfast, eating well, sipping his coffee. "You'll see. You eat all your eggs, and you won't be hungry for hours."

"I love eggs." He chuckled at himself. "Who am I

kidding? No one's ever accused me of being a picky eater, and these eggs are amazing."

Winter's eyes locked on his. "That's a good boy." The words were simple, but the look on Winter's face was anything but. After a couple of seconds, one of Winter's eyebrows arched slowly. "Hm?"

His head tilted, as he tried to work out what he needed to say. Obviously he was supposed to respond with something, but he wasn't sure what, so he rested on a lifetime of training on being a decent human being in public. "Yes, sir. Thank you."

Polite was hardly never the wrong thing to be.

"Ah!" Winter smiled like a kid who'd gotten just exactly what he'd wanted for Christmas. Pure joy. "You are wonderful. Wonderful!" Winter took his hand and kissed it, then flopped back in his chair, looking so pleased.

Harley had no idea why he was wonderful but go team him! He beamed over and finished his breakfast feeling like he was a hundred feet tall.

Winter watched him and sipped coffee.

Harley finished his coffee, not sure what he was supposed to do, so he let himself relax for a second. He would do dishes, since Winter had cooked, but he hated that whole nervous energy shit, and Winter seemed relaxed too.

Man, he was comfortable. He so didn't want to leave and have to face the real world again.

"Suppose we clean up, then spend a couple of hours at the Met? Then I'll send you home to freshen up so you can meet me at the club. Sundays are quieter. Or is that too much of me for one weekend?"

"I could come for a little while, absolutely. Tomorrow I start at seven so we can get to the site by eight. We've got a law firm to move." He was bonded, so he got the teams with the important, heavy, or crazy delicate. It meant that he made the better money, got the better hours, and he worked with the same guys, for the most part.

"Yes, of course. I forgot. Well, let's see what time it is. Perhaps the club isn't the best idea. Still, you'll need to eat dinner." Winter stood and started picking up dishes.

He jumped up. That was his cue. "Let me do dishes. You cooked. That's fair. Tell me about the club? I mean, like, all I know is that there were lots of guys and you."

Winter was so much more than a 'guy' already. He was like...a fascination, magic, someone that he wanted to zip open and snuggle in and learn everything.

Wait, was that gross?

Not literally.

In a purely mental, wrap up in Winter's soul sort of way.

There, less serial killer, more obsessive interest. Go him.

Winter gave him no argument about the dishes, just carried things in and set them on the counter. "Well, the club is a safe space for anyone who identifies as male and queer. I think that's the most important thing to know. It's welcoming. It's not elite. Membership is required, though everyone is entitled to bring guests as they please. The membership is diverse in every way imaginable, and there are a variety of interests, kinks, fetishes."

"Yeah? Wow. I went to one deal in Austin once. That was fetishy. A rubber ball? We were sixteen and terrified." He'd been scared and overwhelmed and embarrassed. Totally.

"Oh my. That sounds like a trial by fire. Did you enjoy it?" Winter poured himself more coffee.

"Hmm...is it weird to say I don't know? I was so friggin' scared, not to mention I'd never imagined that sort of thing outside of movies." Hell, he'd been ninety percent sure some of those folks were literally vampires. "I was grateful I didn't pee myself, cream my jeans, or pass out."

Winter chuckled. "I'm sure you were. Well, I don't recall ever attending a rubber ball at the club, but there might have been one I decided to pass on. I go to many others though. I'm fond of the holiday parties, the leather nights, ropes and bondage, uniforms, corsets...other things I attend largely depend on my mood."

"Uniforms? Is that like when the soldiers go and dance?"

"No." Winter shook his head. "That's men in uniforms doing naughty things to each other. Or you."

"Oh!" Okay, he was a dork. "At least I know the tube tops are corsets and they're not only made for girls. Ollie was super clear."

"Oh, Oliver knows how to wear a corset, doesn't he?" Winter got a faraway look for a second. "Mm. Stunning. I could watch him all night. I'm very fond of corsets."

"They're real sparkly." He didn't know how he'd be able to have his nipples all whoa out there, because they were sort of stupid sensitive, and really, he wasn't sparkly, but he guessed Winter would be pretty in one.

"Sparkly?" Winter looked confused.

"Like the glitter and sequins and all? You know?" He waggled his fingers. "*Sparkly!*"

"Oh! You're talking about what Oliver was wearing at the Mardi Gras party. Yes, that one was quite...lustrous. But they're not all like that, petit. In fact, I'd venture to say most are not."

"Lustrous is a fab word." And totally described Ollie. That man was lustrous all over the damn place. "That was the first one I'd seen."

"It's exactly how I think of Oliver. And, lustrous is one of my favorite words. Dolorous is another. Mellifluous.

Lugubrious. I love adjectives that end in o-u-s. I'm sure you can appreciate words, having grown up in a library. You remember Jesse? I think of him as voracious."

"And loquacious." But damn fun to dance with.

"Indeed. Quite." Winter kissed his cheek. "Harley, I think you might be a figment of my imagination. You're much too...right to be real."

"You never know. I have terrible taste in movies, and I can't swim." Harley winked at him. Also, he wasn't incredibly good at going to school and shit.

"I don't have much interest in swimming myself. Movies, on the other hand... I don't know. I'll have to think that over." Winter handed him a towel as he finished up the dishes.

"Yep. I am a huge fan of weird B movies. Huge. The weirder the better."

"We'll have to watch one together sometime for me to truly evaluate how terrible your taste is."

"You name the time, I'll be here with *Attack of the Killer Donuts* and *Electric Boogaloo*." He thought he'd start easy.

"Oh my. I think perhaps I can verify the poor taste just from the titles." Winter shook his head. "Shall we get dressed and go out?"

"Let's do this, gorgeous." He intended to have a great fucking day.

8

Harley headed upstairs to get dressed to meet Winter at 'the Club' where he hoped Ollie could help him get. It had been a great day, but he needed a shower and a shave and to pray he had one more clean shirt.

He arrived home to the sound of a vacuum cleaner. Oliver had all the cushions off the couch, and was bent over, cleaning in the corners of the upholstery with a pointy tool.

"Did I miss the memo about cleaning day?"

"Hm? Oh, sweetheart, you're home!" Ollie stood up and it took Harley a second to recognize him fully. Ollie was wearing a tight black...was that a corset? His waist was so tiny it made his shoulders look wide, and Ollie was a string bean. "Did you have an amazing date?"

"I—Yeah..." Why was Ollie wearing that to vacuum?

"Well dish, Harley! I want to hear all about it." Ollie was wearing black leggings too, that made him look almost curvy.

"We had tacos, really good sex, breakfast, and went to the museum. It was amazing." And he couldn't stop smiling.

"Well, no wonder you look so radiant. Good for you.

Master Winter is choosey. I'm so glad he chose you." Ollie took a couple of short breaths and chuckled softly. "Oh, I can't get so excited in this thing. I can't get a deep breath."

"I...do you—I mean, I've never seen you vacuum like this before..." And he would have noticed, in theory.

"Oh." Ollie blushed. "This is for Raymond; it's what he told me to do today. So."

"Oh. Is he...here?" He felt a little lost, but he was okay with that. Someone would catch him up, sooner or later.

"No. I'm just doing what I'm told." And looking positively cheerful about it. "Do you like it? It's a new one. Raymond gave it to me."

"It looks like it's tight. It makes your butt look great, though." He still wasn't clear on the vacuuming part, but if Ollie was okay, he was okay.

"Right? I think so too. It's harder to wear than the ones I usually do though." Ollie started putting back the couch cushions.

"Oh. There are different kinds?" Huh. Neat. "I'm not deserting you. I got to see if I have a clean shirt. I'm listening."

"Lots," Ollie called after him. "I have a bunch. Jackson has a few too. Are you going back out?"

"Just for a little while. Winter wanted to have a drink at the club where they had the party." He thought maybe Winter wanted to make up for Friday, honestly.

"He likes you, huh?" Ollie leaned in his bedroom doorway.

"He seems to, yeah. I like him." He started smelling his shirts. He had to take these to the cleaners.

"Are you that desperate for laundry?" Ollie shook his head. "I'd lend you something, but that pumped chest would bust out of my shirts. Why don't you see what Jackson left in his closet? You two are pretty close in size."

"I just need a dark t-shirt. I'm only going for long enough to have one drink." He hated to snoop, but one t-shirt was all he needed.

"Are you and Jackson friends? Of course he would loan you a t-shirt. You change and then bring me your laundry, and I'll do it for you. Laundry is one of my chores anyway." Ollie left the room and after a second he heard the vacuum again.

He wasn't going to make Ollie do his laundry. He'd take it to the cleaners like he had been. He didn't need folks seeing the state of his unders. Lord, he could just imagine.

Harley, did you know your elastic is unravelling?

Harley, tighty-whities? Honestly?

Harley, you have holes in the heels of your socks?

Harley, you have sweat stains. What would your mother say?

No thank you.

He opened the closet that wasn't his and searched for something simple, dark, and clean.

If he'd wanted a white dress shirt or a navy or gray suit, he'd have had his pick of the closet. If Jackson owned anything casual at all, he must have taken it with him to Europe. Obviously, Jackson wasn't wearing business suits on his extended vacation.

The only black thing he found was a garment bag toward the back of the closet and he zipped it open. It was worth a shot.

Oh, that was leather. He'd know that smell anywhere, and he wasn't about to borrow anything that smelled that expensive. Didn't mean he wasn't going to look, though.

He pulled out the bag, finding a fancy-assed leather vest

with buckles on the shoulders and a lace-up decoration deal. There was a shiny, tiny golden one on straps, too, and a red and black one with chains. Yeah, this was dress-up stuff. Not what he was hunting at all.

They were nice though. The gold one looked like the same shape as the sparkly one Ollie wore the other night... stiffer and tighter. The one with the chains was soft and fancy and it looked like it would fit like a dream.

Maybe he should try the dresser. Heck, he didn't hang up anything he owned.

"Lord, buddy, I just need a black t-shirt. I promise to keep up with my laundry. I was supposed to do it today, and I got all busy."

He started to close the garment bag and the gold thing fell off it's hanger to the bottom of the bag. When he reached for it, he knocked the whole bag to the floor.

"Motherfucker! Ollie! Come tell me how to hang these goddamn things up without ruining them!"

"Huh? Which things, sweetheart?" Ollie came in wearing bright yellow dish gloves. "Oh my. What happened?"

"I was snooping. I suck. Help me put them away so they're okay? I shouldn't have opened the goddamn thing." He would just wear a white t-shirt under his jacket.

"If Jackson's going to leave stuff unlocked it's fair game, that's not snooping." Ollie took off his gloves and helped him carry the bag over to the bed, then pulled the clothing out. "You did make a tangle here, didn't you?"

"There's all these fucking strings." He shook his head. "I'm supposed to meet Winter in half an hour, and I don't even know where I'm going exactly."

"Don't panic. I'll get you there. Are you going to wear

one of these? This one would look great on you." Ollie held up the red and black one to his chest. "Mmm. Pretty."

"No. One, they're not mine. Two, they're probably expensive. Three, I just want a t-shirt. That's all."

"Okay, sweetheart. Okay. I didn't mean to get you all flustered. I'm sorry." Ollie started putting the things back on their hangers and back into the garment bag.

"I just know me. I don't want to ruin anything, and these are special." And how would he explain it? *I was snooping and then I wore your fancy stuff and messed it up?* "I have nosy person's guilt."

"If Jackson left them here, they're not that important to him, you know. And they'd look great on you." Ollie hung the garment bag back up. "Come with me, I have a hundred dark t-shirts. Maybe something will work."

"Thank you. I just—I was going to deal with my laundry today, and instead I was with Winter." And now he was flustered and running late. "I need to find my Zen, man."

"Just breathe. You can text Master Winter if you're going to be late; he's not going to be mad or anything. You're not standing him up. And you can do your laundry tomorrow or drop it off on your way to work in the morning." Ollie opened a drawer in a brightly painted dresser and held a t-shirt up. "Try this one."

"Thanks." He tugged the t-shirt on, finding it tighter than he'd normally wear, but not so tight he'd bust it. "Does it look okay? Can you see my heart beating in it?"

Ollie's eyes went wide. "Damn, Harley. You better keep that one, it looks great on you."

His cheeks went all hot. "Thank you. You look amazing yourself. That doesn't look like a tank top at all."

Ollie laughed. "It's a corset. Like the ones in Jackson's

closet. Like my sparkly Mardi Gras one, only a lot tighter. You're adorable, you dork. Let's get you an Uber."

"I try. I just want to have a drink and tell him goodnight. Then I'll be home. I have to be in to haul shit in the morning."

"Hardworking Harley." Ollie pulled out his phone. "You need a ride. I got you."

"A man's got to bring in the bacon, right?" In the back of his mind, he could hear Jackson going 'mmm...bacon', even as far away as Rome.

"Or find someone to bring it in for him." Ollie winked. "Your ride will be here in five. Master Winter will make sure you get home, but I'm texting you the address..." Ollie's thumbs tapped confidently on the phone. "Right...now. There. Now you know."

"Thank you. I look okay?" He grabbed his jacket and zipped it halfway up, then he picked up his gimme cap.

"I don't know how you pull off being so adorable and so fucking hot at the same time." Ollie kissed his cheek.

"Thank you. I shouldn't be late. I'll see you in a bit." He gave Ollie a hard hug. Man, that corset thing was stiff.

Ollie saw him out with a wave. "Have fun!"

"Just having a drink and saying goodnight!" He bebopped down the stairs though, didn't he? Because he was a giant dork.

9

The imposing front doors to the club seemed to hold more excitement than Mardi Gras as Winter walked through them. He nodded to Deacon behind the bar and made his way to his usual table. Sundays were quieter than most nights, but it seemed as if there were more eyes on him. He felt like a new man, as if he'd somehow been reborn last night. Perhaps it showed.

He knew it was probably a fantasy, but he was allowing himself to believe that Harley wasn't like the others, that Harley wouldn't fly away one day like they had. It was another birthday present to himself.

"Rum and Coke, Master Winter." Deacon had walked the drink over himself.

"Thank you so much. Oh, Deacon, I'm expecting a guest; you can put whatever he wants on my account."

"Yes, Sir. I will do that." Deacon smiled and went back to the bar.

His phone buzzed about five minutes later. For a second, he knew—he simply knew Harley was canceling, but what he received was, *I'm here. Do I just come in?*

He forced a breath and swallowed the dread down. Honestly, who was he to doubt the boy? *Yes, come right in and tell the bartender you're with me.*

K!

It only took seconds before Harley walked in, heading straight for the bar to talk to Deacon, who took Harley's drink order and pointed to Winter's table.

Harley turned and smiled at him, waving. As soon as Harley got his beer, he headed right over.

He stood, warming as his gaze roaming over Harley's strong shoulders and flat abs, so evident through the t-shirt. "Look at you. I'm so happy you were able to come."

"Me too. I had to borrow a clean shirt." Harley winked at him and leaned close to him. "I totally have to take in my laundry tomorrow."

"You made a fine choice." Whether Harley planned to stay in New York or not, Winter wasn't going to allow him any room to doubt how much he was wanted. He caught the boy's jaw in his fingers and gave him a short but confident kiss, then gestured to a chair close to his. "Ah, laundry. Somehow it remains the bane of every New Yorker's existence. I am fortunate in that my building has a rather well-equipped laundry room, in addition to a service, which I pay for. You are more than welcome to bring yours by."

"Oh, that's kind to offer. I may have to take you up on that at some time." Harley leaned in, hands on his thigh. "Although when I'm with you, I'm not thinking about laundry."

He chuckled, because he liked the way Harley gravitated to him. "Rather the lack thereof, hm?"

"Only because I'm wearing a shirt two sizes too small." Harley's eyes twinkled in the lights. "Thank goodness I had clean jeans."

"That shirt is not too small. It fits you perfectly. I approve of this look." A server brought Harley his drink and set it down, smiling first at him, and then more flirtatiously with Harley before going back to the bar. "What are you drinking?"

"Jack and Coke. I was going to have a beer, but this sounded better." Harley winked at him. "So, tell me about your work week."

"Mm. Okay. Well, I work an eight to three shift with overtime until five if I want it, and only on weekdays. I work in the archives, which usually means I am helping people find specific pieces of information that they've requested electronically, or sometimes they've made an appointment to look at something I found for themselves. I love all the old books and maps, and I have a fairly good handle on what is there and what isn't by this point so I'm useful."

"That's too cool. I will be lugging boxes and furniture, which is less boring than it sounds. I think of it as a seven-hour workday."

"Think of it? Is it usually a longer day?" Winter sipped his rum and Coke and wondered what a Jack and Coke tasted like. He'd never had one.

"If we have a long one, I get Friday off. The bosses are anti-overtime unless there's no way around it. If I work overtime, it'll be the end or the beginning of the month."

Winter nodded. "Well, it sounds like you might have time for dinner this week. I would like to invite you to join me any time you wish."

"Yeah? I'd love that. Seriously. You want me to come to yours, or I could take you out?"

"You already took me out. It's my turn. But I was thinking I could cook for you too." He took Harley's hand.

"Oh? Cool. You just need to tell me which day, what

time, and what I ought to bring." Harley's smile just lit up the bar.

"No, petit. You will tell me which day, because it will be whichever day you are too tired to find yourself something healthy to eat. Or several days. I don't need notice; you can come to my home and I will take care of you." He couldn't imagine anything better.

"Oh..." Harley put his glass down and hugged him tight. "Thank you."

He breathed in deeply as he returned Harley's spontaneous embrace, feeling complete for the first time in a very long while. "It's my pleasure and my privilege, petit."

"You're amazing." Harley slowly sat back down. "So, I got home, and Ollie was vacuuming in one of those corse-set dealies and panting like a lathered horse."

Winter nodded. "Mmm. Chores. It was probably his training corset. I imagine that looked uncomfortable to you."

"I guess, yeah. He didn't seem comfortable, but he didn't seem unhappy." Harley shrugged one shoulder. "You should see the ones Jackson had in his closet. They were all fancy."

"Your friend Jackson wears a corset well. They are popular at the club. You and he are about the same size. Did you try one on?" He knew the answer; of course Harley hadn't tried them on. But he'd also found that Harley was highly responsive to the power of suggestion. It was one of his favorite things about the boy.

"Jackson's?" Harley shook his head. "God no. I mean, they're *fancy*. What if I hurt them? Can you imagine? It's bad enough I snooped."

"Nonsense. If you actually held one you would realize that you can't hurt them. Good ones are really quite sturdy, because they have to be." And Winter had to assume that if

Jackson left them behind they were not among his favorites in any case. Anything Jackson wanted to show off would have gone to Europe with him. "I wouldn't be concerned about that at all."

"I had Ollie help me hang them back up. I have to admit, I've never seen so many...parts."

"Some of them can be fussy. They're often difficult to put on alone. I'm sure Ollie would be happy to help if you ever wanted to try one on." Winter sipped his drink, trying not to spend too much time imagining Harley in a corset, in case that never happened. He had no idea where Harley might decide to draw the line. Harley probably didn't know either.

"Maybe. I don't know. Is that weird? It makes me feel...wiggly."

Well, that could mean anything. Did it make Harley nervous? Turn him on? Maybe it felt naughty or... "Don't you worry, Harley. You don't have to do anything you don't feel comfortable doing. You shouldn't, ever. Hm?"

"Oh, I don't know. I've learned a lot by doing things that weren't comfortable. Moving here. Learning to water ski. Hell, I was terrified to touch another man."

Winter understood that fear. He understood it in his soul. "I like your touch. It's kind, caring."

"There was nothing about yours that didn't set me off. Nothing."

"Would you like to dance, Harley?" He stood and offered the boy his hand.

"I would love to." Harley's hand fit into his, just easy as you please.

He waved a hand as they headed for the dance floor, and the music changed gradually to something much slower and more his speed. It was good to be him sometimes; there wasn't much he couldn't get here if he wanted it, and everyone knew him well.

Harley moved right into his body, fitting them together. The chemistry between them was ever-present, buzzing between them. "Can you feel that too?"

He nodded slowly. It was unlike anything he'd felt before. He'd been attracted to many, in love with a few, but he'd never felt so drawn to anyone. "I can. You're so alive, petit."

"I'm so glad to be. So glad you *see* me."

"It's not difficult. You're a very bright star." He tucked Harley in tighter and spun them. It was amazing watching the world unfold for Harley, one new experience at a time.

Harley's laugh was husky and happy, wrapping around them as they twirled.

"I hope to see you this week, but if you can't come by, I'd still like to invite you to be my guest here on Friday night."

"Can I have both?" Harley chuckled, stealing a kiss. "You make me greedy."

"Mm. You can. I hope you do." He slid one hand down to cup a perfect ass cheek and took another kiss himself.

Harley was firm against him, responding beautifully, but staying polite, not grinding or making it obvious.

When the song ended Winter led Harley off the dance floor. "You probably should head home soon and get some sleep, petit."

"Yeah, I probably should. I don't want to, but I have to bring home the bacon." Harley sighed softly, kissing him once more.

He knew better than to stand between a man and his job, but he let himself wish Harley didn't have to. "Bring home doughnuts. They're more fun."

"Pop-Tarts, remember?" Harley teased. "I hope you sleep well. Text me when you get home?"

"Right. Pop-Tarts. Nasty things. And you are very sweet to look out for me. I will text. You do the same, please?" He should have known when he invited Harley here for a nightcap that it would be difficult to say goodnight. He'd slept alone for...well, quite possibly years at this point; he couldn't remember, but tonight he didn't want to be by himself. "Do you have a ride?"

"No, not yet." Harley squeezed his fingers. "Tell me to go. I'm waffling with the urge to ask you for another drink."

"Hm. Funny you say that, because I was just thinking about how hard it was going to be to watch you leave." He gave Deacon a wave. "We'll take a car together, and I'll drop you off at home first."

"Are you sure? I-I'd love that." Harley blushed so dark, and the expression was blessedly sweet.

"I am very sure. I feel as though you don't want to go home alone tonight any more than I do, but as you say, you need your bacon. This way, I see you home safely, and we get a few more minutes together." He took Harley's hand. "Come along. Deacon has arranged a car for me."

"Thank you. This has been...it's been a momentous weekend."

Winter offered his arm as they left the building. "It certainly has, hasn't it? I'm not sure what made you decide I looked thirsty and to come sit at my table, but I am very pleased...very grateful that you did." He was a firm believer that the universe had a bigger plan, and while personal choice was certainly a factor, eventually two people that needed to be together would find their way to each other. He'd waited quite some time for this next encounter, and he could only hope that Harley didn't have another path to his future.

"You have the prettiest eyes—like with all the glitter and sparkle, yours were the right ones. I needed to take a chance."

If anything could prove his theory, Harley's words did. They climbed into the back of a black sedan, and he sat close to the boy, circling an arm around him. "Just that simple? I had the right eyes?"

"Well, I assume it's the heart behind the eyes that does it for me, you goof." Harley snorted, snuggling right in.

"I've been called many things over the years, but I don't think I've been called a goof before."

"No? It's not an insult. It's a term of silly affection, I promise." Harley leaned in harder. "But if you'd like me to not do stuff like that, just say. I'm good at trying."

"Not to worry. I took it as a compliment." He sighed. He knew he needed to let Harley go home. Winter needed to think, evaluate this, spend some time in his normal life to make sure this was as real as it seemed. It wouldn't hurt Harley to do the same. But Harley craved his comfort, that was clear, and he didn't want to let the boy go, either.

"Good deal." Harley squeezed his fingers. "I know that I have to go home, jack off wildly half a dozen times thinking about you, and sleep, but I don't want to have to, and I feel like a teenager."

That made him laugh out loud. "That is quite a compliment as well. Truth be told, I don't want you to have to either. And yet here we are, doing the right thing and being very adult about the situation. Damn it." He didn't deny himself the smile, the joy of being human. "I certainly don't want to be the reason you drop a million-dollar harpsichord tomorrow."

"Right? That would suck in a million ways." Harley chuckled, then moved closer to whisper. "I'm going to rub myself raw remembering your cock in my mouth."

Heat flooded through him, and need made his balls ache at those perfectly naughty words. If Harley was going to play that game, Winter wanted him to know precisely what he was up against. He cupped a hand firmly over Harley's cock and rubbed it through the denim. "I hope you do."

Harley's eyes went wide, and a tiny whimper escaped his boy. Oh, that was lovely.

"Your mouth was heaven, petit. So enthusiastic. You enjoyed that, didn't you?" The car turned a corner, and he recognized Jackson's neighborhood. They were getting close to Harley's apartment now.

"Yes..." Harley hissed, bucking into his touch. "I want to do it again."

His cock thought that sounded like a marvelous idea too, but Winter stayed focused on Harley. "I look forward to that." He nipped at Harley's jaw until the boy turned his head so he could take a hard kiss.

Harley opened to him, totally focused on their kiss. Those hips rolled, riding his touch with desperation.

The car came to a stop, and he broke off the kiss and pulled his hand away, doing his best to hide his own breathlessness. "You're home, petit."

"I want you...so much." Harley's expression was hungry, wanton. "I—Okay. Okay. Dammit."

He chuckled and slid out of the car so Harley could get out on the sidewalk. "I want you too. And there will be time for us. Do sleep well, petit, as I will miss you tonight."

"I will miss you. Bad." Harley met his eyes. "I can really come for supper after work?"

"Yes, any time. I would enjoy that." He gave Harley one more kiss, then slid back into the car. "Goodnight, Harley."

"Good night, Winter. Text me when you get home?"

"I will do that." He closed the car door but instructed the driver to stay put until Harley was inside.

Then he endured the short drive home that felt endless without Harley in his arms.

10

I s tonight okay? I miss you.

Harley looked at his phone, then erased the text.

That sounded fucking needy.

Not that he wasn't needy, because he was. He hadn't gone over on Monday because he'd worked 'til eight, and Ollie had been up 'til four a.m. talking to him. So he'd texted and told the truth.

Now it was Tuesday, he was getting off at four, and he wanted to see Winter. Bad.

Can we pls have supper 2nite? I miss your face.

There. Better.

Winter's response came back quickly.

I miss more than your face. See you tonight, mon petit.

Tonight. I'll go home, bathe, and head over. Fucking A! That was better than what he'd hoped to hear.

If you just happened to bring an overnight bag I wouldn't be mad at you.

Good 2 know. See u soon.

The guys were pulling up in his neighborhood, and he waved. "See y'all tomorrow. Have a good one."

Then he hopped out and headed upstairs. Ollie had apparently gotten 'spoken to' about keeping him up all night, and was sort of hiding, so he was glad the man was at work.

He jumped in the shower, not lingering because he wanted to get on with it, get over to Winter's, and touch that hot man.

When he got out of the shower there was another text waiting for him from Winter. *Don't worry, I'll make sure you sleep too.*

You're worth being exhausted for. Okay. Tomorrow's work shirt, jeans, briefs, socks, ditty bag. Then he put on his good jeans, a nice t-shirt, and called for a car, put his boots on, and wrote Ollie a note before he left.

At least this time he knew where he was going. And it was still light enough out that he could see more than headlights and gray buildings flashing by.

He was buzzing—he'd not even gotten a chance to jack off, because Ollie had needed to chat about everything, and then he had crashed and burned.

On my way. I got my bag with me.

I hope you like pasta. Winter sent him a picture of spaghetti boiling in a deep pot.

Oh, yum. *Yes please. We're pulling over now.*

He grabbed his bag, excitement flooding him. It was silly, but so true. He was like a goofy kid for Winter.

Winter's building didn't have a doorman, but the security guard let him in, called Winter, and sent him on his way. Back of the building, up two flights.

He didn't run, because he had worked all day, but he didn't toodle, either. Two flights of stairs was still nothing. The door was ajar when he arrived, and he could smell the pasta cooking.

"Come in, petit. I'm in the kitchen." Winter's voice was muted by all the books and soft furniture in the living room.

"Oh, I'm so glad to be here." He put his stuff down, locked the door, and took off his work boots before going to see his Winter.

"Oh my. Don't you look delicious." Winter came right to him and gave him a warm hug, and he knew Winter was really glad to see him.

"I've been thinking about this all day, and I didn't even drop a box." Harley grinned and squeezed Winter tight.

"Impressive, petit. I didn't plan anything fancy, just good, old-fashioned spaghetti and meatballs." Winter pointed to a tall stool. "Sit and rest. You must be exhausted."

"Spaghetti and meatballs sounds so good. I am not anti-carbs. I figure I work enough; I can eat whatever I want." He propped himself on the stool, admiring the lines of his lover's body.

"I'm very pro-carbs myself, and blessed with an active metabolism, even still." Winter pulled a heavy, lidded pot out of the oven and set it on the stove, trading it for a small tray of garlic bread. "Those are the meatballs; they are done and soaking up the sauce. I opened the leaves on my dining table in the living room so we can eat comfortably and not at that awful card table."

"Oh, you are amazing." His belly snarled. Those meatballs smelled good. "How was your work?"

"Oh, it was a good day." Winter smiled over at him. "I spent most of my time researching civil war era rosters for someone doing some sort of genealogy study. Lots of reading. Tell me about what you moved today."

"A gigantic wall safe. It was a crazy thing. From this insane condemned building to a fourth-floor walk-up."

"Those are ridiculously heavy. How in the world did you

do that? How many people did it take? I can't even imagine getting something like that up flights of stairs."

"We are a four-man team, with a driver and a spotter." He'd been freaked the fuck out by halfway up the third floor. "The worst part was the first building. It smelled so bad."

"All of that sounds awful. I'm glad that it's over. I hate to think what had been going on in a condemned property before you got there." Winter strained the pasta and put it back in the pot with some olive oil. Tossing it all together.

"What's the oil for?" He loved watching Winter cook.

"Pasta likes to get sticky. I prefer it not sticky. Also, it adds some flavor. What would you like to drink? There's soda in the fridge, wine in the living room. Milk. Water. Whatever you prefer." Winter put on a hot mitt and stirred the meatballs around. "Mmm. These smell so good. I hope you're hungry."

"Starving. Can I have a big glass of water and then try the wine?" He saw people drinking wine with food all the time. He was curious.

"There are glasses in that cabinet. Help yourself." Winter pointed with his chin, and pulled two big, shallow bowls from above the stove. "You can put two wine glasses on the table while you're at it, and silverware please. In that drawer under the glasses."

"Yes, sir." He could do that. "So...you have a lot of stemmy glasses. Do the shapes mean things? And forks and knives? Spoons?"

"White wine has the smaller bowls, the tall skinny ones are champagne. The little ones are for liqueur. Red wine, wide, round bowls. We're having red. And the silverware depends on how you like to eat spaghetti. Fork, knife, the larger spoons."

"I can do that." Big bowls. Forks. He didn't need a spoon. His belly was gnawing on his backbone; he was so hungry.

Winter brought out bowls of spaghetti and a couple of meatballs each. "If you'd get the plate of garlic bread, please. I left it on the counter." Winter pulled a bottle of wine from a cabinet next to the tiny fireplace.

"Yes, sir. I'm on it." He put the glasses and the silverware down, then went back for the garlic bread. "This smells so good..."

"I hope you like it." Winter opened the wine. "You don't know about wine either I suppose, hm? I'll teach you what I know. It's not much, but I can open a bottle and enjoy it."

"Sounds good to me. I just want to know what everyone is enjoying." And the glass clinking was so sexy.

Winter cleared a spot on the table for him to put the bread, then poured them each some wine. "Sit, sit, petit. Please. Eat."

"Oh, this smells like heaven." He sat and served himself some before passing the noodles over. "Thank you so much."

"You're welcome. I hope it's as good as it smells. I'm told I make good meatballs, but I don't know that I've ever served them to a Texan." Winter watched him, looking both serious and amused at the same time. Winter was clean-shaven and wearing an expensive-looking button down that probably had a tie over it earlier in the day.

"It's going to be great. I can tell." He waited for Winter to serve himself, and take a bite, then he dug in, groaning softly over the pasta. So good.

That seemed to make Winter happy, and he dug in too, curling his pasta with a fork and a spoon. "So what shall we try tonight, petit? Did you bring your book to read to me? Or shall we try painting your nails or try something new with your lovely eyes? Something else you might have in mind?"

"My nails?" He chuckled and held up his hands with their blackened and torn-up nails. He had a dozen-plus cuts and splinters and shit. At least they were clean. "There's not hardly anything to paint."

"Oh, petit. Your poor fingers. Let me see." Winter turned them over, inspecting them, handling them like they were fragile. "A manicure then. No paint."

"Okay. I don't even know what that means." He just wanted to make them both happy, when he came right down to it.

Winter laughed and held up his glass of wine. "Don't you fret, my good boy. Just let me spoil you. Cheers."

"Cheers." They clinked the glasses and he took a sip. It was strong—way stronger than he'd expected—and peppery. Weird. Not bad, but weird.

"This is one of my favorites. What do you think?" Winter took another sip, set his glass down and swirled up another bite of spaghetti.

"It's like—like that fabric, the Christmas fabric—" He closed his eyes and tried to remember. "Oh! Velvet! It tastes like velvet feels."

Winter smiled at him. "That's a very nice way to put it, petit. Rich. Dark. Strong. But do you like it?"

"I don't know. I don't *not* like it." He tried another sip, and this one wasn't as surprising. "It's peppery and makes the meatballs taste like pepper. Cool."

He worked on his plate, even taking seconds, because it was so good.

"Let's play a game that Jesse taught me once. He called it 'this or that'. I give you two things, and you choose between them and tell me why. Then it will be your turn. Sound like fun?"

"Sure. Sure, that sounds cool." He didn't have any secrets.

"Okay. Beach or Mountains?" Winter asked the question, then sipped his wine, waiting for him to answer.

"Beach, because I've never been to the mountains and the ocean is magical." That was easy. "Classical music or pop?"

"Pop? Do I know any pop?" Winter laughed. "Classical seems like the right answer here. Hmm. Vivaldi. Bach. Tchaikovsky. Music for a quiet afternoon." Winter swirled his wine. "Late night or early morning?"

"Mmm... I guess late night? I mean, I don't like them together, but I'm more likely to be up late than up early."

"Like Sunday night?"

His cheeks heated. "Yeah, like that. Uh... *Jurassic Park* or *Casablanca*?"

Winter leaned forward. "Well, that's not fair. *Jurassic Park* is brilliant, and *Casablanca* is a classic." Winter sighed. "Well, Jurassic Park then. Because it was exciting and funny and extremely entertaining."

"And dinosaurs, right?" The dinosaurs rocked. "It's all about the dinosaurs."

"And of course, dinosaurs. Texas or New York?"

That one was easy. "New York. Home was getting too small for me. I needed to be—not there."

He needed to be away from judgmental fucks that thought he was a filthy piece of shit.

"So, fruit or veggies?"

"Vegetables. You can have them with every meal. Leather or lace?" Winter winked at him.

"Leather. I mean, how often do you wear lace, but leather is sexy and smells good."

"I can provide you with lace to wear if that interests you." Winter winked at him. "Men wear it more often than you might think."

"Okay, I know I'm not a big shopper, but... I have bought my own clothes for a bit at stores. There's not a lot of lacy shit except for vampire costumes."

Winter chuckled. "Vampires. You're not shopping in the right places. Perhaps I'll take you shopping this weekend."

"You know, the fluffy neck ruffles?" He winked over, tickled. He had a little extra cash. He could go shopping. "Speaking of, vampires or werewolves?"

"Vampires are sexy. Werewolves are furry. Easy choice. Shall we clear the table?" Winter stood and started clearing dishes.

"Of course." He helped, then got to work filling the sink with hot water. "Your turn." He stripped off his shirt so he didn't get it wet.

"All right." Winter moved out of view and a second later was at his back, hands sliding around to rest on his abs. "Shoulders or neck?"

"Mmm...that depends on whether you're talking turn me on-ness or massage-ness." Because he had hot spots on his neck that made his knees weak.

"I think you know the answer to that question." Winter's hands moved over him, thumbs brushing over his nipples.

His lips popped open, and he fumbled with the dishrag. "Oh..." He went hard in a rush, and his belly went tight as a board. Yeah. He knew. "N-neck."

"Good boy." He felt Winter's cock against his ass as he drew a line from Harley's spine to his ear with a hot tongue.

"Oh damn..." His eyes crossed as he grabbed hold of the

edge of the sink. His arousal went from—well, not zero. He hadn't been at zero in a few days, but a nice thirty-five to eighty in nothing.

Winter kept exploring, kissing and nibbling along his neck. He figured the dishes were gonna wait when Winter started in on his belt and opened his jeans. "Do you always take off your shirt to wash dishes? Because I approve of this practice."

"I didn't want to get my shirt all—" He grunted as Winter managed to give him some room for his prick and stroke a nipple at the same time, shattering his thoughts.

Winter was solid against his back, and rock hard. "Wet?" Winter asked, cupping him through his briefs.

"Uh-huh..." He rolled up, begging hard. "I haven't come since you. I need bad."

He couldn't see Winter's face, but he heard the soft gasp close to his ear. "Petit. What a gift." Winter spun him so his back hit the sink and kissed him, teeth nipping at his lower lip, hands pushing his briefs down past his hips. "Touch yourself, petit. Show me how much you need."

His eyes rolled, because part of him said that was private, but the bigger part of him screamed with needing to do it, show off, let someone—let *Winter*—see him.

So he grabbed himself at the base of his prick, dragging his fingers hard along the shaft, then a hard touch at the tip to make him fly before going back down.

"Pretty petit." Winter licked his lips and palmed himself through his slacks as he watched. "So sweet. Saving this just for me."

"For you." Oh fuck him. He was burning alive, buzzing, and he had to spread his legs to make room for him.

"Do you want to come in my mouth, petit?" Winter

reached out and pinched a nipple hard, then slid a thumb over it to soothe it.

He whimpered and shot, the sensation, the words, the need—it was all too huge, too erotic, wonderfully over the top.

"Next time." Winter kissed him again, tongue pushing past his lips and gliding along his own.

He wanted to apologize, but his mouth was full, and his cock was recovering and he could do it in a minute.

The kiss ended naturally, and Winter leaned back, eyes twinkling. "You must feel better."

"Lord, yes, sir. Thank you. I'm sorry for shooting so fast, but you're so fine to me."

"Oh, Harley. Don't apologize, shooting was the point." Winter kissed his cheek. "And thank you for saying so; I haven't heard that in a while."

"That was incredibly hot." He brushed their lips together, then dove in again.

Winter moaned for him, accepting the kiss and letting him drive, letting him taste and explore. He dove in, one hand curling around the back of Winter's neck, holding on tight.

Winter caught him with an arm around his back and leaned into him with a groan, hard cock pressing into his thigh.

Oh, he wanted that. He wanted it bad. "How do you need me?"

Winter leaned back and looked into his eyes. "Your heavenly mouth, petit." Winter's hands moved to his belt.

He dropped to his knees, his own cock happy and proud as he got ready to suck that heavy prick.

Winter opened his fly and pulled out a swollen cock, watching him and stroking it a couple of times before touching the tip to Harley's lips. "Pretty, petit, on your knees for me."

He kissed the tip, then dragged his tongue over the slit. The flavor made him moan; the scent of Winter made him dizzy.

Winter groaned, and his eyes closed, head rolling back on his shoulders. He seemed relaxed but those hips arched toward him impatiently. "Sweet boy."

He wasn't sure if he was sweet, but he was hungry, and he wanted Winter to fly.

Winter caught his chin in one hand and pushed that cock past his lips. "I want you, petit. I want to come in your mouth, feel you swallow it all."

He groaned and opened up, his lips fastening around the shaft of Winter's cock and beginning to pull hard. This was the fiercest thing he'd ever done.

"Yes. God, yes." Winter rocked into him, gentle thrusts at first, but they grew harder and deeper. "Want...oh, petit. I want you."

He grabbed Winter's ass and tugged him in deep, letting Winter in all the way, swallowing hard around the tip.

Winter's cry echoed in the tiled kitchen, and his lover lost it, hips thrusting, breathing in short, sharp pants. Winter's fingers tangled in his hair and tugged hard enough to get his attention. He glanced up at his lover, so fucking turned on it hurt.

"Are you...can I..." Winter hesitated, hips going still.

He pulled back, let Winter's cock slide free. "Fuck my mouth. I need you."

Then Harley sucked that fat dick right back in.

"Oh, petit." Winter pushed in hard, hips moving, prick sliding in and out, over and over until the rhythm faltered, and he knew Winter was close.

He took every inch, finally opening up all the way, letting Winter move him, take him where they needed to go.

Winter's hand shot out and gripped the sink over his head and he made a low sound, part grunt, part growl. "Yes," Winter whispered, and seed filled his throat and coated his tongue. "Yes, Harley."

He took it, swallowing convulsively, hand clenched around Winter's hip.

Winter let him lick and love on him for a bit, and finally pulled back after the deep breaths grew less shaky. "You're my good boy, aren't you, petit. Thank you."

Harley groaned and nodded. He was totally capable of good, bad, wicked—he was easy. He just wanted whatever this buzz was.

"Come kiss me." Winter caught him under the elbow and helped him stand, smiling. "You are irresistible to me, Harley. I couldn't even let you out of my tiny kitchen."

"We can try every room..." He grinned over. "Damn, that was hot."

Winter grinned back and buckled his pants back up. "Mhm. And now you have dishes to do. Perhaps we'll try out the desk in the living room later."

"Ooh. I could handle that." He stole a quick kiss. "Let me do these, and then I'll come snuggle?"

"That sounds perfect." Winter ran a hand through his hair. "I'll find a movie perhaps. And my manicure kit."

They had kits? Huh. He had a nail clipper with a hook deal... "Sounds good. I won't be long at all. I promise."

"Take your time, petit. We're not on a schedule." Winter kissed his cheek and left him alone in the kitchen, but he could hear Winter humming in the other room before he turned on the water.

The dishes were easily, if not particularly dry-ly, done. God, those meatballs were yummy.

He found Winter in the bedroom, sitting up in bed in pajama bottoms, watching TV on a big screen Harley hadn't even noticed when he was in here before. "All done?"

"I am. I put the wine in the fridge with a little plastic wrap on the top. Is that okay?"

Winter chuckled. "That's not necessary with red wine, but it won't hurt, thank you. I'm surprised you found the plastic wrap. I hardly know where it is myself."

Ha, he doubted that. Winter's kitchen was nice and tidy, really. It hadn't hurt that it was under the sink next to the trash can.

"Get comfortable and come sit with me." Winter patted the bed next to him.

He nodded and stripped down, slid on a pair of loose, soft shorts, and crawled into bed with Winter.

"You came prepared. Will you be leaving for work from here tomorrow, then?" Winter inched closer, took his hand, and studied it carefully.

Oh. Had he totally misheard? "I—Did I misunderstand? I did bring my work stuff, but I can head home if it's easier."

"No, you understood me perfectly. I just didn't want to assume. It's most certainly not easier. I will sleep better with you here." Winter started rubbing lotion into his hand with a firm touch, starting with the wrist and working out toward his fingers.

Harley's eyes went wide, and a soft whimper escaped him. He'd never felt anything quite like that. He hadn't even known his hands were hurting.

"That's nice isn't it? People don't take care of their hands enough, especially not people who work with them every day like you do." Winter took his time, getting into every nook and cranny of his hand.

He didn't know what to say. He just sat there with his teeth in his mouth and let the sensations pour over him. He felt hypnotized.

Neither of them said anything for a long while. Winter massaged that hand until it was relaxed and loose and then put that one down and did the same thing to the other one. The quiet wasn't even weird. Winter was very focused and seemed completely happy.

The second hand was less shocking, but he found himself melted and breathing with Winter like it was natural.

"I'm going to clean up your nails, if that's all right with you." Winter's voice was soft and sort of floated to him.

"Uh-huh." He'd washed them, but it didn't matter. He was happy.

Winter laid out a wide cloth, then got out a clipper and a file to trim and shape his nails. "If you could have any job you wanted tomorrow, what do you think it would it be?"

Oh god, he hated this question. So many people had asked—his parents, teachers, friends—and he didn't have an answer. Maybe he was just stupid and lacking ambition. "Please don't be disappointed, but I don't know."

"Why would I be disappointed? You're young. You don't have to know. I was just curious." Winter caught his eye. "I'm sorry if that is a hard subject. I didn't mean to cause you any stress."

"It's just—everybody asks, and I never remember wanting to be a fireman or a cowboy or an astronaut or anything like that. Nothing I love to do is a job."

"So, a better question then. What do you love to do?" Winter switched hands again.

"Read. Listen to music. Explore. Watch movies." Nothing that was a job. At all.

"Reading can be a job. It's a great deal of my job, for instance. Also proofreading and things of that nature. Exploring could be a job too. You could lead tours in the city or a museum. The others are more challenging, but you never know what we could come up with if we thought hard enough." Winter winked at him.

He blinked. That was the first time anyone had ever said anything like that to him. "I—thanks. Thank you. That's good to hear."

"Do you play any instruments? Guitar, piano?"

"Yes, sir. I play piano. Took lessons since I was four. Momma insisted so I could play at the church." He enjoyed it a lot, and he was passing fair at it.

"You do?" Winter's eyes lit up. "Did you see the little upright in the corner in the living room? I bet you didn't, since it has books stacked on it."

"No." He started to chuckle. "I haven't really explored much more than you…"

Winter's smile was warm. "Mm. I don't think I'll apologize for monopolizing your time."

"No. No, I don't think I want you to." That would be a lie, anyway. This new thing—the buzz between them—was fiery and inescapable.

Winter put his hands down. "There. How do they feel?"

He held them up, opening and closing his fingers. "Amazing. I swear, they feel so good it almost hurts."

"Hopefully not quite." Winter put everything back into a little zippered bag and closed it. "They look much better. Don't worry, I left them sufficiently manly for you."

"You're amazing." He reached for Winter, sliding his fingers over Winter's chest. "How do they feel?"

"They feel...warm. Caring." Winter leaned closer, asking him for a kiss. "Affectionate."

"Affectionate is not strong enough. I'll have to try harder." He stroked around one nipple, knowing how good it felt.

"Mmm. Sensual. Bordering on erotic." Winter nipped at his bottom lip.

"Better. Much better." This time he took that little nipple and tugged gently.

Winter moaned for him, one hand sliding up his thigh. "Naughty boy."

"I know how hot that is." Harley knew how sensitive his nipples were.

"You're right, petit. It makes me shiver a little."

"Yeah." He rubbed the tip, his own body shivering like Winter was touching him.

Winter caught him by the nape and tugged on him, pulling his mouth close to replace his fingers. Oh, he could so do that. He moaned and opened up, tongue dragging over Winter's flesh, drawing it up.

"Mmm. Yes, petit." Winter leaned back in the pillows and stretched like a lazy cat in the sun. "That is lovely, but do we need to get you to bed? When do you need to leave in the morning? Earlier than I do I'm sure."

"I have to be out of here by seven, so not early-early." And he could lose sleep for Winter.

"We have a little time then." Winter drew long fingers through his hair.

"Mmm..." He hummed softly, the air vibrating between them, before he licked again.

Winter sighed. "Do you have any fantasies, petit? I would love to know them. Find out what turns you on, even if it's only thoughts."

Oh, that was hard to say, because nobody wanted to say something that his partner would think was nasty or evil or gross. It was like opening yourself right up and saying, here are the weird, wet bits. "That's kind of scary. I don't want to seem boring or like an axe murderer, either one."

"I've heard it all, petit. I belong to a kinky club, remember? I promise I won't judge."

"I like sucking, you know that. When I jack off, I think about that a lot. I think about tattoos and stuff—not just one or two, but a lot, you know?"

"Mm. Ink is nice. Getting them or being with someone that has them?" Winter just sounded curious.

"Less getting them, more having them. You know, being...sexual." Being someone different, being someone special.

Winter nodded. "Do you not see yourself as sexual?"

"I mean, I like sex, but I'm not the guy you look at and think, 'sexy'. I'm strong, but I'm short—if you're short, guys expect twinky, yeah?"

"Some do, that's true. But, if it matters, that's not what I see, when I look at you." He felt Winter's cock shift and press into his thigh as if to make a point.

"I'm glad." He didn't see it, but he didn't have to. Winter did. In fact, Winter made him see it in himself.

"I see endlessly deep, dark eyes. Mmm." Winter hummed and went on. "I see a strong body that works hard. I see capable hands, and thick, proud cock."

His cheeks were burning, but he couldn't stop his smile. "You made my eyes look like they belonged to a stranger. It was...something else."

"But it wasn't a stranger, it was you. That beautiful boy is you, petit."

"I felt like a stranger, a little bit. I felt like I didn't have to

—" He stopped, because he didn't have to follow anyone's rules, but he had still felt like he was following...different rules.

"Didn't have to what, petit? You can tell me. This is just between us. I hope you know that." Winter pushed him onto his side and rolled to face him. "These things are complicated for everyone."

"I was like someone—not different, but different. I don't know how to explain it right, but I felt...free, somehow?"

"Sometimes if we feel like someone else we feel like we have permission to do things that don't feel right when we're...just ourselves. Hm? We lose the chains."

Harley huffed out a relieved breath. Winter did understand. Thank god. "Yeah. Yeah, just like that."

"There's nothing wrong with that; it's wonderful actually. You can make up new rules. Your own rules." Winter's fingers were exploring gently while they talked, nothing sexual, just a warm touch.

"I like that you sort of hear me. I was thinking that— about the rules. I grew up with one set, and I have another set now, but...maybe there can be more than one."

Winter winked at him. "Yes, of course there can be more than one. But why make things confusing? Let go of the ones that don't work anymore. They can change as you want them to."

"I'm trying. I used to pray that god would forgive me for being gay. Now I figure that's bullshit. I'm not bad for being gay. This is me." And he'd never, ever said that out loud before. Never. Fuck.

"Correct. You are who you are. If god created you, how could he not love everything you are? It doesn't make sense. I have a complicated relationship with god myself, and I think that's okay too. We're each on our own journey. Your journey has brought you here to New York, where being gay doesn't define you; it's just one part of who you are. So now, you can hold your head high and concentrate on the person the rest of you wants to be."

"That's really hard, huh? I mean, being gay has been... like a defining thing." And he knew it. It had been a shameful secret. Then it had been a defiant thing, almost angry.

Winter sighed. "When your survival depends on something it's absolutely defining. But now you can live the way you want, so you have to take some time and listen to everything else your heart has been trying to say all this time."

He felt—young, strangely, because this wasn't a young person's issue, but still, he did. He found himself staring into Winter's eyes, almost dazed. "Do you think you can help me?"

Winter nodded. "I can help. You have to do the work because only you know what's in your heart, but I can help. I'd like to help."

"Thank you. I feel like I'm brand new again—I know it's silly, but it's true."

"It's not silly. If I'm hearing you right, you are in a way. You've gone from shame to anger to this place where you don't have to be either." Winter kissed his forehead and smiled. "I'm surprised you're not terrified."

"I'm probably too much of a dork to be terrified."

Winter laughed. "You were lucky. You had Jackson's place to go to, and Oliver is very sweet. And you're not a stranger to work, clearly."

"Lord no. I'm a point me and shoot me guy." He moved closer and inhaled deep, jonesing on Winter's scent.

"Mm." Winter took a lazy kiss. "Are you going to have dinner with me for my birthday Friday?"

"I'm going to celebrate your gorgeous ass off." He intended to make Winter's birthday the best ever.

"Flatterer. My ass has seen better days. But I am looking forward to celebrating with you."

"Your ass is perfect. Seriously." He squeezed it, just gently.

Winter laughed. "Perfect, hm? How is it you make me feel both so young and so old at the same time? Part of me genuinely wants to help you, and part of me feels like I'm just starting out and learning right along with you."

"I think that's okay. I like learning together." And he had no doubt there were things he could teach Winter. Like how to move a safe, and how to make dogs settle, even mean ones.

"Me too, petit. Especially like this." Winter pulled him into a deep kiss, fingers sliding down his side.

Yes. Just like that.

Harley was very afraid getting into bed alone again was going to suck.

11

Winter reread the text Harley had sent him at work earlier. It just said, "Happy Birthday" and "pick you up at seven". He asked what he should wear in reply, but the answer shed no light on whatever Harley's plans were. "Whatever you want," was far too vague for him to infer anything at all.

He put on dress pants, a shirt and tie, and his fortieth birthday boots, but now that he was looking at himself in the mirror, he wondered about the tie. Should he take it off? Something told him Harley wouldn't have one, but he rather liked a nice tie.

Would Harley like him in a tie? Truth be told that was all that mattered.

There was something about Harley that made Winter feel ten feet tall, seen, cared about. It was a heady sensation, but rather like looking down from a skyscraper—exhilarating but dangerous.

He did need to be careful. He knew how to be a comfort for Harley and how to light the boy up with a touch, but he knew nothing of Harley's story or background. Not really. He could misstep at any moment.

Hopefully not on his birthday, however. He never celebrated his birthday with anyone, and he thought the deeper questions could be avoided for tonight.

A knock sounded on his door, and Winter thought it sounded happy, eager. He shook his head at himself. He was being silly.

Of course, when he opened the door, he found his lover in his finest cowboy clothes, carrying brightly wrapped presents, a huge bouquet of flowers, balloons, and a cake box tied with a bow.

He smiled happily, Harley's thoughtfulness making him flush warm all over. "My goodness. Look at you! Look at all of this. So handsome. Come in, come in."

"Happy birthday!" Harley sang to him, handing him his flowers and balloons. The bouquet was beautiful—all different colors, with the scent of roses redolent in the air.

"Oh, Harley. This is magnificent. Your flowers are stunning. So cheerful." He hadn't held a balloon in— forever. He hadn't smiled this hard in forever either. He ducked around all the things Harley was still carrying to kiss the boy's cheek. "We should... I need to put these in some water. Come in the kitchen."

"Yes, sir. I'll put the gifts here on the table. The cake ought to go in the fridge until after our supper reservations."

"We have reservations? You didn't have to get gifts. You are gift enough, petit." But he was excited by the idea of opening presents. He pulled down a vase and filled it with water. "There should be room on the bottom shelf in the refrigerator."

"We do! We have to be there at seven thirty, so I've called for an Uber." Harley kissed his cheek.

"You're spoiling me, Harley. Reservations, an Uber, presents, cake..." The flowers looked so nice in the vase, and he put them on the table with the gifts. "Where are we going? Or is that more mystery?" He took the cake from Harley's hands and put it in the fridge.

"Wolfgang's Steakhouse. Is that okay?" Harley looked so worried.

"Wolfgang's. Goodness. What a treat!" He was almost embarrassed; Harley had only known him a short time and it was such a splurge. But he wouldn't ruin the boy's plans for anything. "Tribeca is fun to walk through as well."

"I wanted to celebrate you, and Ollie suggested this place, so I looked it up. I haven't had a steak in eons." Harley beamed at him. "And you look amazing, birthday boy."

He straightened up at the compliment and smoothed his tie. "Thank you, and you look gorgeous. Fancy shirt, fancy boots...so handsome. I'm proud to call you my date." Harley was clean-shaven; he loved a nice smooth face. "I can't believe you did all of this for me."

"You are important. You deserve it." Harley wasn't flattering, or if he was, it was absolutely hidden.

"Thank you, petit." He wanted a kiss, and it was his birthday after all, so he didn't hesitate. He cupped Harley's jaw and pulled him in.

Harley stepped right into him, holding on tight, kissing him like there was nothing else on earth he'd rather do.

"Mmm." The buzzer interrupted them, and he smiled and stepped away to answer it. "Sorry petit." He hit the button to respond, and the security guard told him their Uber had arrived. "Our car is here."

"Let's go celebrate!" Harley took his hand and led him out, a huge smile on his face.

The security guard nodded to him as they headed out. "Happy birthday!"

"Thank you!" He looked at Harley grinning. "Did you tell him it was my birthday?"

"It was a little obvious with the two-foot-wide happy birthday balloon…" Harley winked over.

Winter chuckled. "I suppose that's true."

They laughed and chatted through the car ride, through the line to the maître d', and all the way to the bar where they waited for their table to be ready.

"I have to tell you, I've been in my fair share of nice restaurants, but I've never been here. It's quite posh." Winter leaned close to his ear. "And feels laced with testosterone."

"That must be all the meat." That wink was wicked as could be.

Winter laughed. "I hear the portions are huge."

"Just laid out there for you to pick from."

"Pink…raw…"

"Are you gentlemen ready for your table?"

Winter blinked at Harley, so sure they'd been overheard.

"Yes, sir. Lead the way." Harley nodded to Winter and fell in behind him as he walked.

Such a good boy.

Their table was toward the back of the restaurant, and it was a bit quieter than the bar had been, which was nice. The host left him with the wine list, and someone brought over a gorgeous little boule on a small cutting board with a serrated knife and what looked like whipped butter.

"Mm. Fancy bread. Did you celebrate at fancy places for your birthday at home?"

"My dad used to take my momma to Houston for hers, yeah. It was always a big deal." Harley offered him a grin. "Momma made Daddy his favorite dinner and a big cake."

"And what did they do for you?"

"When I was a kid, there was always a party. As a teenager, bonfires. After she remarried? Not a lot."

Right. The preacher. He didn't know yet whether Harley had left or was told to leave, but either way, getting out was the right answer. Coming to New York was a happy event; he hadn't felt this alive in some time. "When is your birthday, petit? I want to be sure we celebrate. Tell me again how old will you be?"

"I'll be twenty-five on March third, so...what? A little over two weeks?"

Twenty-five. Good lord. He remembered twenty-five; it wasn't an easy or a happy time. But things got better. "Another excuse to celebrate! A spring baby."

"Yep. That's me. I loved having a birthday in the springtime when I was a kid—it's a great time to have a party." Harley chuckled softly. "And I like spring—when things start to grow."

"Spring is nice here, so we'll have to walk through the park a few times. It starts late... March is still cold and usually wet. Our spring doesn't really start until April, but then things turn green again quickly."

"I can't wait to explore. I was having fun before, but now with you? I'm excited."

Winter loved listening to Harley talk. He loved Harley's energy and optimism. The boy was the best birthday gift he could have received, and more than he could have hoped for. He was also beautiful and curious and sexually adventurous...it was a dream come true, really.

A steak dinner was like a cherry on top of an enormous banana split. Almost too much.

"So what are you having?" He opened his menu and had a look, realizing with some embarrassment that Harley was likely to spend more than he made in a day on this dinner.

That was a dilemma, and he'd have to give some thought to before the check arrived.

"I want the sirloin and the baked potato. I looked at the appetizers, but I only knew shrimp cocktail, so you should choose what you want." Harley chuckled and shook his head. "I'm not real knowledgeable about seafood yet."

"Goodness, I won't have room for an appetizer. But I'm going to have what you're having. With sour cream. I love sour cream on my potatoes." The steaks in places like this were big enough for three people. He'd be taking home a doggy bag as it was.

"Do you think it's okay not to have a vegetable? I mean, we have cake at home."

"It's my birthday. We could have nothing but cake and that would be okay." He laughed and set down his menu.

"Exceptional point." Harley beamed at him. "You have to pick the wine, though."

"I would be happy to pick the wine. Which is kind of a fruit, which is as good as a vegetable, so we're covered." He picked up the wine list, looking for something reasonably priced. He liked wine, but he wasn't a connoisseur.

Their server appeared as soon as he put the list down and he ordered a decent red table wine, then gestured to Harley to order dinner.

"I'd like a medium sirloin and a baked potato, please, sir." Harley seemed relaxed, easy in his skin.

"I'll have the same, please. With a nice char. Extra sour cream." He reached over the table and held his hand open, palm up, inviting Harley to take it. "Did you ever think when you moved up here that you'd be sitting here having dinner with an old man?"

"You're not old. You're beautiful. And no! I thought... Well, I didn't think. I thought I had to get out, and this was a great opportunity." Harley leaned in. "I never imagined I'd meet someone like you."

"I know just what you mean." He wondered if Jackson had expected Oliver to bring Harley by the club, or if that was something Oliver had planned on his own. He appreciated Harley's compliment, and the best part was that he believed that Harley saw him that way. He still worried the shine would wear off eventually, but it wouldn't tonight, and he planned to enjoy every second with the beautiful young man. "I'm glad you got out, and I'm happier that it brought you here."

"Me too. So, what else do you want to do for your birthday, sir? Besides open your presents."

That was easy. He knew precisely what he wanted. He lowered his voice with the hope that only Harley would hear. "I want to make love, petit. I want to feel you...inside." At the boy's wide-eyed look he added, "Only if that's something you think you would enjoy, of course."

"I want to. I think you'll help me...figure it." Harley's voice went husky and rough.

He nodded. "I will. I'm patient. I'll look after you, I promise." One of the advantages of being his age over Harley's was experience.

"I believe you, and you won't hurt me. That's not you."

He squeezed Harley's fingers. "Thank you, petit. That's the kindest thing anyone has said to me in a long while."

"Not enough people have been nice to you. That's what I think."

One had to give people the opportunity, Winter mused silently. He hadn't done much of that in the past few years. If not for Harley, he'd be celebrating his birthday at the club, having a light dinner without anyone knowing one way or the other and treating himself to cake or ice cream on the way home. "I'm difficult to approach, I think. Although you didn't seem to have any difficulty."

"No one told me I couldn't. You can't break the rules if you don't know them, right?"

He'd never told anyone they couldn't either, not in as many words, but he knew what he'd been doing. "I'm going to remember that and never ask what the rules are."

"It's a great plan." Harley held his hand tight.

"Tell me about work today. What did you move?"

"Files. Lots of classified files. I actually had someone try to get access, which was cool."

"Try to get access? You mean to the files?" Was that cool, or dangerous?

"Yeah. I told my boss, and the FBI came and everything. Never had that happen before."

"That sounds rather scary, petit. Did you feel safe?" Harley must have had a background check to be moving classified materials. "I think I would have worried about you had I known."

"Sure. Folks think they can do anything with money. My boss pays me, treats me good, trusts me, and I'm part of a team. I'm solid." Harley shrugged like it was nothing. "My integrity's worth more than someone can pay."

It never occurred to him that something as simple as moving things could put Harley at risk. "They offered you money? You did the right thing, but...what if they'd pulled a weapon instead of handing you cash? Maybe it's time to rethink this job." Harley was young, not from New York. Integrity was important, but safety was the priority.

"Oh, they texted my work phone. It wasn't like they offered me a twenty for the box. If they'd pulled a weapon,

I'd have explained that I'm not from here, and if they shot me, they'd best kill me." Harley fastened a confident look at him. "I'm not scared of dying. Bad folks are, so they don't understand a man that's not. But really? We work in a group. We want to be safe."

"All right, petit. It's not every day someone runs into the FBI. I care about you, so I want you to be safe. I'm not as brave as you are." Not at all. He had no reason to be afraid of dying, but he was afraid of people with guns.

"The FBI part was cool! They asked all sorts of questions and all. I felt like I was helping catch a bad guy, and my boss was tickled as hell." Harley's laugh filled the air.

"Sounds like we're having fun over here." Their steaks arrived and the server set their plates down, turning them just so. "I hear we have a birthday at the table, Mr. Love."

He grinned. They knew his name. How exciting. "Yes, thank you. One that ends in zero, in fact."

"Twenty?" The server winked at him.

"Close." They all laughed.

"Happy birthday. Enjoy your dinner."

He picked up his napkin and put it neatly in his lap. "That was spectacular. He even knows my name!"

"Well, it is an amazing name, isn't it?" Harley winked over, so obviously pleased with himself.

"It is. I chose it for myself, and I have been very happy with it." He looked at his steak, his mouth watering at the aroma as well as at how wonderful it looked. "This is so indulgent. I can't wait to try it." He would have liked Harley to take the first bite, but he suspected the boy had been raised with manners much like his own, so as the guest of honor he knew Harley would wait for him to pick his fork up first. He did, and his serrated knife cut through the meat as if it were butter. It tasted even better, and he chewed slowly, savoring. "Oh my."

"Yes." Harley beamed at him, before taking a bite of his own, closing his eyes as he chewed. That was a blissful expression.

They were several bites in before either of them was ready to talk again. "Have you tried the potato? It's perfect. Look at all the sour cream they brought me." He had a whole ramekin of it, topped with chives.

"You can just dip it in, bite after bite." Harley did just that, so playful, getting a forkful of mostly sour cream.

"That is exactly what I had planned." He cut himself a bite because he liked the skin, dipped it and took a bite. "Mmm. Do you remember the first steak you ever had?"

"Lord no. I probably didn't have teeth yet. Do you?"

He nodded. "I do, in fact. I was on my way from central Pennsylvania to here on a bus, and the man who sat next to me bought me dinner in Philadelphia where we both had to change busses. He was headed to Washington DC on a train, actually, and I think he saw that I was alone and short on money. I was certainly hungry. In any case, he bought me my first steak. I thought it was amazing, but this one is far better." There wasn't much more to that story. He'd assumed at the time that the man wanted something, but he hadn't. They'd eaten and gone their separate ways.

"Oh, that's cool. Kindness from strangers is the best, because there's nothing attached to it."

"I'd assumed there would be, and I honestly wasn't sure what I was going to do if it came to that, but it didn't. I was shocked, to be honest. I didn't know at the time that people just...did things for others without wanting anything in return. In a small way, that man set me on a better path I think."

"That's a good way to think about it. I've been pretty lucky, when it comes down to it. I've never had a lot, but I've always had enough."

"That's good. I was all right until I left home. But I left suddenly and didn't have anything in my bag but a few necessities." That was over twenty years ago. He could hardly believe it had been so long.

"Yeah, when I came here at least Jackson met me, hugged me, and introduced me to Ollie. I was scared, but not terrified."

He nodded. "I was... I don't know. I felt safer in some ways and less in others. I was scared, but I'd been scared at home too. New York was easier in a way. I could get lost in a crowd. Nobody noticed me, and I liked that. I still like that sometimes." He shrugged. "I like being noticed by you, though."

"I couldn't ignore you. No way. You're...so...beautiful."

He smiled, caught between flattered and embarrassed. He hadn't ever cared particularly if he was attractive or not, but Harley made him want to believe it. "Thank you."

"It's the truth." Harley grinned at him, stroking a long line along his thigh, teasing him, tempting him.

"Naughty boy. Eat your steak. What kind of cake did you bring me? Did you make it?"

"It's a chocolate-covered strawberry cake. I bought it from a bakery, because you will thank me for that." Harley snorted softly, waggling his eyebrows. "Can you imagine me? Making a fancy cake?"

Winter shrugged. "I can actually. I think if you wanted to, you could figure out how to do anything you wanted to. Cake included. Strawberry sounds wonderful."

"Maybe with practice." Harley didn't look the slightest bit concerned. "You deserve better than practice."

"I appreciate any and all cake." He winked at Harley. "This evening has been amazing already and we haven't even gotten to cake yet. I'm still working on my steak. Did you try the wine? It's very good." He picked up his glass.

"Oh! Cheers! Happy birthday!" Harley lifted his glass with a smile. "To you."

"Thank you, petit. Cheers!" He touched his glass to Harley's and took a sip. "What haven't I asked you yet? Is there something I should know that I haven't found the right question for yet? I want to know everything."

"Hrm..." Harley tilted his head. "My dog was named Penny, my horse was Jack, my best friend is Deborah Haney."

"Wonderful things. Do you still talk with Deborah? Does she know where you are?" He took another bite of his steak, so pleased with how perfectly it was cooked. He was going to have to think hard about where to take Harley for his birthday.

"She's in the service, overseas. We video chat every couple weeks. I told her about you last week."

"Did you really? How sweet of you. You must thank her for her service for me when you talk next. Has she been overseas long? Do you miss her?"

"She went in when she was just out of high school. She's a Marine, and she's tough. This is her second tour. She's a field medic and says they're sending her to nursing school. She's super-buff, and a little wild. She got me in trouble a lot."

He laughed. "That's what best friends are for, aren't they? Everyone should get into a little trouble in high school."

"Who is your best friend? Do you like animals?"

"I love animals. Birds especially, and cats. I haven't been

around a lot of animals though." Winter didn't have a best friend; he wasn't sure exactly how to say that without sounding pathetic. It wasn't, he just hadn't ever bonded that way with anyone. "You are my best friend, I think. There's no one I would rather spend time with. No one that understands me better than you do."

"Oh. I like that." Harley took his hand and kissed it. "I want to understand you, balls to bones."

"You're getting there." He sipped his wine, and ignored the voice that kept trying to tell him not to fall too hard, not to count on too much...that a birthday was fine to enjoy, but remember how every little bird he'd ever known had eventually flown away.

"Good." Harley ate another bite with a soft moan. "This is so delicious. No. No, it's better than delicious." Harley met his gaze, winked. "It's *yummy*."

"It's scrumptious." He grinned and took another bite himself. He was going to have to take half of this home with him; he had nowhere to put it all. "You're going to have to tell me what you want to eat for your birthday. I don't think I can find barbeque like you're used to, but we can get close maybe."

"I like lasagna for my birthday. My mom made it once a year for my birthday, and that's still what I tend to get."

"Oh. Lovely. Perfect." He made a great lasagna. He'd cook for Harley's birthday. Wonderful. "Garlic bread? Vegetables?"

"Garlic bread and salad." Harley chuckled. "That's a birthday supper."

"Okay then. That shall be your birthday. At my place. Do you want to invite anyone? Think about it. You could have some friends. It might be fun."

"Maybe Ollie. The guys from work have families and kids and all, but Ollie and his guy would be cool."

"That sounds nice. A sort of double-date? We could go out if you prefer, but I thought perhaps I'd cook." Ollie, but not the guys from work. It didn't take a genius to read between those lines. But that was fine. It was Harley's birthday, and he should feel comfortable.

"Oh, I'd love for you to cook, if you have time. That makes it more special."

As if he wouldn't make all the time in the world for Harley. "I have the time, and if I didn't I would find it. You are special and important to me, petit. And it's your birthday."

"No, sir. Today it's *your* birthday!" Harley chuckled, eating the last piece of his steak. "Oh. That was worth it."

"It was. I'm almost too full for cake." He winked at Harley. "Almost, but not quite."

"Give yourself a few hours and you'll want some." Harley pinked and leaned close, whispering, "I can help you work some off."

He didn't blush. Harley lying under him was going to be the best part of the evening. "I look forward to this strenuous, calorie-burning, and most satisfying workout."

"Good deal." Harley's gaze was fastened to his, the hunger written there clear.

"My good boy. So sweet. I'm going to treat you like gold. Like you're beautiful and precious. Like you should be treated." As if Harley were truly his own.

"I want you to treat me like we're going to be celebrating your birthday thirty years from now, at this restaurant, and laughing about how fun it's been."

"Oh, petit." That was a lovely thing to say, very kind. Harley was so dear. "Then that is how I will treat you." As if that could possibly come true. Thirty years. He could barely imagine thirty days.

"Excellent." Harley finished his glass of wine. "I'm all warm inside."

"Wine will do that." He was glad dessert wasn't part of the restaurant outing, because he wanted to get Harley home and feed him cake. He raised a finger, and the server was there in a second to take his plate away and get him a doggy bag.

Harley paid without a wince, and then they stood. "Birthday part one, accomplished."

"I'm looking forward to the rest, but this would have been enough by itself, petit." He looped his arm through Harley's as they left.

"I'm so glad you enjoyed it. That steak was amazing. I've never had better."

"I can't say that I have either." He kept Harley close as they waited for their ride, Harley's talk of the future still swimming in his mind. "And the potato, mm. Delicious."

"With extra sour cream for both of us." Harley squeezed his arm. "You want to know a secret? This was my first reservation, and my first glass of wine at a restaurant."

"Was it? I would never have known." It was true, Harley had worked out this elaborate plan like a professional. "Reservations are a skill you need in New York for sure. You've gone so out of your way for me, and I want you to know how much I appreciate it."

"I just—you deserve a birthday. You deserve to be celebrated."

Harley was so earnest, and it warmed him all over in a manner he wasn't accustomed to. Winter felt so emotional. He was...so touched. "It's already the best birthday I've ever had. I'm not exaggerating."

"And you haven't opened your presents yet!" Harley looked totally excited, as if the gifts were for him.

"I haven't. I can't wait." He wasn't used to receiving birthday gifts, he hadn't had one from anybody in years. Their car arrived, and he pulled Harley in with him. "You know I'm usually at the club tonight. This is so much better."

"Do you want to head over for a drink? I'll buy you one. I'm all yours until Monday morning." Now that was a present.

"I don't know. Do you think we should? One drink at the bar, maybe. I want to open my gifts and I... I want you, petit."

"Whatever you'd like. I'm here to make your wishes come true."

He thought about that. His wishes had nothing to do with the club tonight. He could ask Harley to go tomorrow. "No, petit. Let's go home."

"Sounds perfect." Harley's hand was warm and solid on his thigh.

He nodded. "It does." He put an arm over Harley's shoulders and watched the dark city go by out the window. Forty was outstanding so far.

———

12

Harley was nervous as all get out that Winter wouldn't understand his presents. He'd found a copy of his favorite book, *Territory*, and then he'd found some fancy makeup brushes that the lady at the store had said were special and all, so—

God, he wanted Winter to like them.

"Home sweet home." Winter opened the door and gestured for him to go inside. "Would you like a cup of coffee? I think I'm still too full for cake yet, so can we start with presents?"

"We can! You go sit, and I'll bring them to you, okay?" Harley was buzzing. Just seriously buzzing, nervous that he'd chosen wrong.

"All right." Winter went and took a seat in his favorite chair, kicked off his shoes, and put his feet up. "I can't wait to open them."

"I can't wait for you to open them too. Either. Whatever. God, I'm excited." He brought both the packages over, sitting close by on the ottoman.

"They're wrapped so nicely. Which one first?" Winter

reached for them, hovering his fingers over one and then the other and back again. "Does it matter?"

"Open this one first." Harley handed over the book.

"Very well." Winter took it and smiled as he started to open it, carefully popping open the tape on the ends and obviously trying not to tear the paper. "Oh, it feels like a book. It is! Oh...wonderful! I haven't had the opportunity to check it out yet. This is lovely. Thank you." Winter flipped to the back jacket and read it, then opened the book and flipped through a couple of pages. "I can't wait to read it."

"It's my favorite, so I thought I could share it." There was something intimate about sharing favorite books. It said things about your soul.

"I appreciate this very much. I think reading someone else's favorite book tells you so much about them, don't you?" Winter put the book down and picked up his other gift. "I can't even guess at this one."

"I hope you like it." He prayed he hadn't made a crazy misstep. It was sort of...personal.

Winter opened the wrapping as carefully as the book. "Oh." Winter flipped the box over in his fingers slowly, then opened up one end and pulled out the brushes, one by one. "Oh, my. Harley, these are beautiful. One for liner, blush and...the shadow brush is amazing. They're so elegant." Winter ran his fingers over the bristles and tried out the blush brush on his cheek. "They feel nice too. I just adore them."

His heart was pounding, and his cheeks felt like they were on fire. "Happy birthday!"

"It is, very happy. Such thoughtful gifts. I can't wait to use the brushes on your handsome face. Shall we go to the club tomorrow? I could make you up before we go. I would enjoy that very much."

"You can. I'm so glad you like them. The person at the store said they were nice ones." He didn't know much, but he could see that Winter was truly pleased.

"They are. They're special, like the man who bought them for me." Winter put his gifts down next to him on the ottoman, caught him by the nape and pulled him into a deep kiss.

Oh. He sank into the kiss, hands sliding over Winter's shoulders as they fed on each other.

Winter stood, pulling him to his feet without hardly breaking the kiss for a second and moved them slowly toward the bedroom, hands sliding over his ass. He followed like they were dancing, like this was the most natural thing on earth.

"I want to thank you properly for all of my surprises. Can we have cake in bed...later?" Winter's lips moved under his chin and down to his collarbone.

"Anything you want, lover. It's your birthday." Although this was spoiling him, not Winter, those kisses sending fireworks through him.

"We're lovers officially, then?" Winter asked, pulling him through the bedroom door. "I like that very much. I want to call you mine."

"Oh good. I want that. Us. I want to be an us." He knew it was probably too everything—too fast, too much, too soon —but he didn't care.

"We're an us. But it's nice to be clear on what sort of us we are." Harley's back hit one of the thick bedposts. "Lover." Winter took another kiss and pressed a thigh between his legs. Oh fuck, yes.

He groaned, rolling against that firm pressure, letting himself feel the burn a little more.

He got a low moan in response and Winter untucked his shirt and started opening the buttons. "Mon petit. My boy."

"That's really sexy..." God, he sounded like a dipshit, but it was true. It was hot as fuck.

"I'm glad you think so." Where Winter was usually pretty quiet and reserved he wasn't shy in the bedroom, and Harley knew he was wanted. Winter slid his shirt over his shoulders and ducked right to one sensitive nipple, battering it with a hungry tongue.

His toes curled, and he rocked up into that hungry mouth. His teeth sank into his bottom lip as he fought his cry.

"Mm. You like this?" Winter switched to the other one, hands moving over his skin.

"Uh-huh." He more than liked it. It turned him right the fuck on, but it felt weird to admit it.

Winter smiled and took a step back, watching him. "Finish undressing for me, petit. Slowly, please?"

"Sure." Okay, this was weird, and a little hot, but it was Winter's birthday, and he wanted to make his lover happy, turned on. Harley focused on the erotic feelings, stripping himself steadily, slowly.

Winter watched him hotly, eyes roaming over each newly-bared bit of skin. "So beautiful, petit. I love the way you move. All your muscle is so lovely."

Harley loved that, because when Winter said it, it didn't sound fake. It seemed like Winter believed it, and he wanted that to be the truth. "Thank you."

Winter undressed too, laying his clothing neatly on a chair, then stepped in close again, proud cock pressing into his hip. "You're the best birthday gift of all."

He beamed over, rocking against that heavy prick. It felt

deliciously naughty, sliding against Winter with a deep hum.

Winter moved them, and they both fell naturally onto the bed. He scooted up toward the pillows and Winter followed, with never more than inches between them. Winter caught both of their cocks in one hand and worked them together slowly, just enough to rev them both up a little.

He put his mouth to work, licking and kissing, tongue dragging on Winter's skin, helping with building their arousal.

Winter reached over him and came up with a bottle of lube. "I want to make this good for you. The best."

He watched as Winter slicked his fingers.

"I trust you." This he at least had done once. Sort of. It hadn't been good, but it hadn't been awful. He'd let Winter put makeup on him. In public.

"Thank you. I promise you won't regret that." Winter held his gaze and pressed a finger to his hole, tapping gently. "You're going to feel so good."

Harley nodded, because he believed that. He truly did. He forced himself not to tense, not to pull away.

"Slowly, petit. This is too good to rush." The intrusion was gentle, and he felt Winter spreading the slick around and stretching him carefully. Winter kissed him, then slid lower, lips finding his nipple again and sucking it up hard.

That caught his attention, and he blinked, totally trapped in sensation for a moment.

"Mmm." Winter hummed and moved even lower, kissing over his ribs, his abs, finally swirling a tricky tongue around the head of his cock.

"Winter!" His entire body tightened for a second, and he gasped, everything lighting up behind his eyes.

"Petit." Winter took his cock in, tongue scrubbing along his length and added firm pressure until he felt Winter's knuckles against his ass.

"Oh fuck... I... I don't know what to do!" He gasped out the words, not even bothering to be embarrassed by them.

Winter pulled up just for a second. "Breathe, petit. You don't have to do anything. Do whatever you want. Or do nothing at all. Just feel."

He huffed out a desperate little laugh. "Not helping." But he did listen and forced himself to stretch out, to feel.

"How do you feel?" What he felt was those fingers twist inside him and Winter's hot breath on his shaft.

"L-like I'm fixin' to shatter apart in the best way. Does that make sense?"

"Mhm. Not to worry if you do, you recover quickly, and I have all night." Winter swallowed him down again and he swore he felt those fingers hook inside him.

He felt a jolt of pure lightning, and he barked out a cry. Fuck him. What the hell?

Winter's tongue was busy and didn't let up, didn't even stutter. Winter didn't seem surprised by his reaction at all.

He waited breathlessly for that sensation to happen again, and when it did, he wanted to scream. Fuck him, that was amazing.

Winter released his cock and those fingers slowly pulled away. "That's it, petit. Feels good, doesn't it?" He knew the sound of foil tearing, knew what Winter was doing.

"So good. I want more." He needed more. Fuck, he needed everything.

"So much more." Winter's cock pressed against him, heavy and thick; the gentle pressure was almost maddening. "If anything doesn't feel good, petit, you tell me." Winter spoke softly but his breath was coming in soft pants. "I want you to feel good."

"Me too. I want us to feel good." He swallowed hard, like that was going to make room inside him.

"Mm. Yes." The pressure grew and his body began to stretch to accommodate Winter. "We will. Patience, petit, and breathe."

He inhaled deep, then blew the breath out in a long, slow motion. The burn slowly moved into something softer, something that he could breathe into.

Winter groaned—the sound was soft but strained. There was something so hot about Winter's careful control and watching little bits of it crack because of him.

He couldn't stop moving, shifting, sliding on Winter's cock and taking more and more.

It wasn't long before they were rocking together, Winter taking him in long, slow strokes and staring into his eyes.

Winter was inside him. Deep and heavy and heady— inside him, and it was so much bigger than anything he had ever felt before.

"So tight, Harley. So beautiful." Winter was flushed from his chest to his ears and seemed younger and stronger somehow. "My boy."

"Uh-huh." His toes curled and he let a deep, near desperate sound out.

"You want more, petit? I have more for you. Are you ready?"

"Ready. God, lover. Ready." He didn't know what he was ready for, but it didn't matter.

"Fuck yes." Winter pushed one of his knees up, opening him even more and as Winter's thrusts got faster, harder, that cock sank deeper inside and scraped against that spot that made him see lightning before.

Harley's head slammed back against the pillows, his hips snapping in a sudden, impossible rhythm.

His ears filled with their sounds—heavy pants and low moans, Winter's hot curses and his soft cries. Suddenly, Winter's hand was on his cock, working it with every thrust through a hot fist.

"Yes!" He'd never made such wild noises in his entire life. Ever.

Winter didn't seem bothered by them and wasn't shy about his own sounds either. Even their bodies made noise, skin slapping together as they moved. It was filthy and sexual and the hottest thing on earth.

"Harley." Winter's voice was rough, raspy. "Fly for me, little bird." Winter's thumb dove through his slit, and his cock hit him just right, deep inside, over and over.

Harley shot, and for a wild second it was like he'd left his body, like his world had shorted out and all that was left was Winter.

Winter groaned, hips moving fast for a bit, rocking both him and the bed. He felt Winter come, felt that cock swell and pump inside him, felt a whoosh of air as Winter exhaled heavily, and all of that wild energy evaporated, leaving them both panting.

"W-wow." He closed his eyes, the world spinning.

Winter didn't seem to have words either, he got a nod and Winter slid to one side of him. "Petit."

All he could do was nod and whimper. That had been amazing.

Winter moved away so quietly he didn't even notice until he got back into bed and slid a warm cloth over his belly. "So beautiful, my Harley."

"Mmm...happy birthday. Happy birthday."

"Ecstatic birthday. Jubilant birthday. You are... I feel so

good, petit. So...cared for. Thank you." Winter kissed him gently. "Thank you."

"You're more than welcome." Harley winked over, rubbed their noses together. "And we have two more days."

Winter chuckled, sounding relaxed, muzzy. "Thank goodness, because we have so much cake!"

"Mmhmm. Strawberries are fruit. Fruit is healthy."

"So we can have it for breakfast. Or a midnight snack. In bed." Winter's fingers slid over him, just a light, affectionate touch.

"Mmhmm. Anything you want, lover." He hummed, as satisfied as if it had been his own birthday.

"Right now I have everything I want. I don't think it will be possible to top this night."

"I'll have to work hard." And he was more than willing.

Winter was worth it.

13

Winter had intended to have a little cat nap, then get up and try some of Harley's cake. They didn't nap as much as sleep, and the sun was fully up when he opened his eyes again.

Small wonder. Harley had worked all day in his strenuous job and then was up late with him. And Winter hadn't a workout like that in quite some time. Add some wine to that and a heavy dinner, and sleep was inevitable.

He smiled at the way Harley was curled into him, not just staying close but holding on. He understood. He needed some reassurance too. Some comfort. And to know his lover was safe.

Harley was lovely like this—well-fucked and sleeping, the day's stubble on his jaw.

He knew how he wanted to spend their day, if Harley agreed, of course. He wanted to use his new brushes and make Harley up, take him to the club to dance and let it smudge and melt with sweat, then kiss him and make love again until it was all over him too.

But he was in no hurry, and he thought perhaps they

could go out first; he just wasn't sure where. Brunch and a walk, shopping, sightseeing, whatever his beautiful boy wanted to do.

Harley smiled in his sleep, stretching up tall, muscles rippling. So pretty. So strong and cut and in his bed.

He slipped away, covering Harley with his fluffy down comforter so the boy wouldn't get cold. The bathroom tile was chilly under his bare feet as he did his business and washed his hands. *You're a lucky man, Winter Love,* he thought, looking at himself in the mirror. Forty wasn't old, but it wasn't young either. Still, this was decidedly the most energetic he'd felt in quite some time.

He shaved and wrapped himself up in a robe, and went to make himself a cup of coffee, enjoy his morning. The flowers and the balloons were there, as were his presents, and it made his home festive.

He and Harley had only known each other a handful of weeks, but the boy was a solid presence already. There were constant traces of the boy everywhere now. Leftovers in the refrigerator, a jacket over a chair, a toothbrush in the bathroom. Even when Harley slept at his own apartment, there were things left behind, and now he had birthday mementos. And presents!

And this was starting to move into familiar territory. How familiar remained to be seen, and he wanted so much to give the boy the benefit of the doubt. If he sat here and thought about it too much he would eventually talk himself out of all of it before either of them got hurt; he could do that, but should he? Did he need to?

He didn't want to.

What he needed was perspective, and he wasn't going to get it watching his coffee brew and thinking himself into a corner. He pulled out his phone, hoping it wasn't too early for Clint. Surely his old friend had seen everything in the years he'd been running the club. At the very least Clint knew him well and would have something to say to him. Hopefully something helpful.

He hit call and waited, sure that if Clint didn't want to be disturbed, he wouldn't answer.

"Good morning, Winter Love. How are you this bright day?"

"I am officially forty, there's cake in my refrigerator and a beautiful boy in my bed, so I have no complaints." He smiled. Quite the opposite, he could only brag.

"Congratulations! You survived another birthday, very nice. Is this the young man that's living with Oliver now? I've heard decent things."

"Harley, yes. He's lovely. He thoroughly celebrated me last night with dinner and presents. I feel absolutely spoiled." Stunned and spoiled. Harley had gone to such trouble and all for him.

Clint chuckled softly, the sound warm and happy. "Oh, goodness. Did you go anywhere I need to be terribly jealous about?"

"Wolfgang's. We had potatoes. Harley asked if I thought it would be excusable not to have a vegetable, which was the most adorable thing. He let me pick the wine..." He sighed. "Oh, I like this one, Clint. He sees me."

"I couldn't be more pleased, dear friend. Oliver has very good things to say about him too."

"We're coming to the club tonight. I'd like you to meet him. I feel like I need... I'm very..." He sighed. "These young men can be hard to hold onto."

"I'd love to. Would you like a seat at my table? I'll invite Thomas and his boy."

He smiled at that. "Oh, that would be wonderful. Harley

is a Texan, so he might appreciate Sam, and he certainly could use some friends." Although even as he said it, he part of him protested, wanting to keep Harley to himself and away from all the people that could capture the boy's interest.

"Wonderful. I'll call Tommy, see if they have plans. One way or the other, I'm very much looking forward to seeing you, buying you a drink."

"Talking me off a ledge? Making sure I'm not making some horrible mistake? I worry, Clint." He had no regrets, but he'd been decidedly alone.

"Mistakes happen. You know that, but happiness does too."

He nodded. "It does. I know your librarian; he floats by regularly." He liked to tease Clint about his long-time lover.

"Yes. He and I have an agreement that makes for a lovely situation."

"I look forward to seeing you later, and to introducing you to Harley, who I hope will be my regular guest for a while."

"My fingers are crossed, friend. I will see you tonight."

"Thank you, Clint." He hung up the phone knowing full well there would be more of this conversation at a later time, but there was little point in asking Clint's thoughts regarding this relationship without Clint having seen them together yet, let alone about a boy he hadn't even met.

He finished his coffee and grabbed another one before Harley wandered in, snuggling into his back. "Mornin'."

"Mm." So sexy, his Harley. So sensual. Winter slid a hand along the arms that encircled his waist. "Good morning. How did you sleep?"

"Like a log that had amazing orgasms."

"Oh, that is a happy log. I can relate. Are you sore? I have

Ibuprofen in the bathroom." Poor boy would feel well used for the day, he was quite sure.

"I have a bit of a twinge. I sort of like it." Harley winked at him.

He turned and kissed Harley's cheek. "I have to confess, I like to hear that. Somehow it makes me feel...taller."

"Mmm... Kiss me good morning, lover." Harley's expression was one of pure joy.

"With pleasure." He caught Harley's jaw in his fingers and pulled their lips together, offering a lazy morning kiss.

Harley was minty-fresh, cuddly, and sporting morning wood. How pleasant.

"Would you like some coffee? We could drink it in the sunshine on the balcony and scandalize my neighbors with a snuggle." He didn't really think they'd scandalize anyone unless Harley went out naked.

Which would be nice, but even he had boundaries.

"Sounds utterly perfect. I mean it. You need another cup too?"

"I just topped mine off, thank you." He moved out of Harley's way. His tiny kitchen didn't make romance easy. "I'll go open the balcony doors."

He wandered through his living room and opened the doors, then found the balcony chaise cushions and set them out. They could share; he didn't think Harley would mind.

"Mmm... It's chilly. Can I snuggle?" Harley cradled his mug, sipping deep.

"Of course." He sat deep into the chaise and raised his knees, giving Harley a place to sit and access to snuggle against him. "There's a blanket there, too. Grab it."

"Yes, sir." Harley put his coffee down and got them arranged, covered and close together.

"Oh, very nice." He tucked an arm around Harley. "Later

today I want to try my new brushes out. What do you think? Before we go to the club?"

"Sounds good. They look different, hmm? Sexy." Harley rested hard against him.

"I adore them. They look so stylish. I bet they will feel good in my hand." He nuzzled Harley's hair, content just to sit and sip coffee. "The club is owned and run by a man named Clint; he's a friend, and I look up to him. He's invited us to sit with him at his table tonight."

"Yeah? That's cool. I'll have to wash my good shirt today and iron it."

"You can use my machine. I have a little stacked unit in the closet in the bathroom. But don't stress it; they're going to love you whatever you wear. Just show them your smile, and you'll be dressed up enough." And his eyes. Harley was going to be so lovely. "I bet Sam will wear his cowboy hat. Thomas likes it."

"Yeah? Is he real or an urban cowboy?" Harley didn't sound terribly worried, more making lazy conversation.

"Oh, very real. He's Texan, though I couldn't say where he's from precisely. And I believe he used to ride uh...horses. Broncs? In the rodeo."

"Wow. I'm not that kind of guy. That's...intense shit."

Winter agreed. Far too intense for him. But he loved to listen to Sam talk. "He had stories. He'll share them if you ask; he's a wonderful storyteller."

"Oh, that's cool. I bet you love stories too."

"I do. Of course I do, don't you? I love hearing people talk, hearing what they have to say, learning things I never imagined. What could I possibly know about the rodeo otherwise?"

"I've been to a bunch, but I always liked the carnivals

and the food and the concerts. I was less about the animals and all."

"I remember carnival food. Funnel cake. Corn dogs. Cotton Candy. I imagine that's the same nearly everywhere you go. What was your favorite?"

"Funnel cake is my favorite. My absolute favorite. Especially with strawberries on top." Harley made a face very close to an orgasm. "Guh."

He chuckled and made a mental note to find his boy funnel cake for his birthday if he could. "You and I are in agreement there. Though I don't remember strawberries being an option. I just remember the sugar. It got everywhere, all over your fingers, your face, on everything you were wearing. If you breathed in too deeply you would inhale it. And the dough was greasy and warm and perfect."

"Crispy. I love crispy bread. We should learn how to make that. I bet we could, together."

"Hot oil sounds dangerous, but then again you let me get a makeup pencil close to your eyes, so I suppose you trust me." He chuckled softly. Trust wasn't an issue; he was sure of that. "There must be some difference in funnel cake from place to place because I've never once had it crispy. It's always been soft and warm. We'll make both."

"Soft? Really? How weird, yet cool. I don't even know how you'd make it soft." Harley tilted his head, obviously thinking about that. "Although you could put everything I know about cooking in a thimble and still have room for string."

"Not to worry, if we try it, we'll know." He breathed deep, enjoying the morning air and his boy. He could get used to this. He shouldn't but he could.

"Mmhmm." Harley could snuggle with the best of them, the solid body heavy against him.

"Should we wander out this morning? Would you like a nice brunch? Or a walk in the park? It seems to be a lovely day."

"Sounds good—either of them. I brought jeans and a couple of decent sweatshirts." Harley kissed his jaw. "I love to do things with you."

"Mmm. I'm rather fond of doing absolutely nothing with you as well. Like this. You work so hard all week that it must be nice to just sit sometimes."

"Nicer with you. I have been sleeping through Saturdays though before I met you. This is better."

"Really? That tired?" Poor pup.

"Tired, but really, no one telling me to get up and do. I was having my little rebellion."

That was adorable. And wise of Harley to see it for what it was. He touched his lips to his boy's ear and whispered, "I will never tell you to get out of my bed on a Saturday if that's where you want to be."

"Mmm...if we're in bed of a Saturday, we could think of things that are way more fun than sleeping..."

"Mhm." He nuzzled under Harley's ear. Maybe he'd be wicked today and keep the boy buzzing a little, just to enjoy. Harley had waited days for him once without being asked, so some part of Harley must get off on the anticipation. It would be a treat to bring his boy to Clint's table feeling needy. "Without a doubt."

Harley tilted his head, offering himself over like a prize sacrifice.

"Suppose I make you a promise, but you have to wait until we get home from the club tonight, petit?" He slid a hand over Harley's hip.

"A promise?" Harley shifted against him. "What for?"

He drew a firm line down Harley's half-hard cock with his finger. "For keeping that pretty cock just like this all day."

Harley's lips parted, eyes going heavy-lidded, and Winter wanted to see them, painted and a little mussed.

"I will let you come any way you want tonight when we get home. Anything you want. How does that sound, mon petit?"

"Amazing."

Oh, that little rasp, the flash of hunger in Harley's eyes suited him to the bone. That was exactly right.

"Mmm. You like to be a little naughty. I am looking forward to our day even more now. Shall we start with some birthday cake? We never did get to it last night. We must have been...too busy."

"We were absolutely busy, in the best possible way." Harley nibbled his bottom lip, teasing him. Taunting him.

He happily took the bait and kissed Harley until they were both breathless, fingers gripping his boy's nape. "Let's have cake and take our stroll in the park," he suggested, barely above a whisper. "And then we'll come home and get ready for tonight. I have plans for those new brushes you gave me."

"O-okay." Harley blinked at him, eyelashes fluttering. "Anything."

He grinned. That was how he wanted his boy, floating on a kiss, on life, on him. And soon, on cake.

14

H arley was buzzing. Winter kept teasing him, touching him, making his skin burn.

It was maddening and, if he was honest, a little wonderful.

The little whispers and touches had driven him crazy all day long, and now it was late afternoon, and all he wanted, now that they were home, was a hard, deep kiss.

"Do you need to check in with Oliver, petit? Before we get ready to go out? Will he worry?" Winter's hands slid over his shoulders. It wasn't even a sexual touch, just an affectionate one but it still made him tingle.

"Mmm...he knew I was coming for the weekend. I told him I would be home after work Monday, most likely." He thought he'd see Ollie tonight.

"Good. I like that you keep in touch. We may even run into him tonight, but I wanted to be sure." Winter kissed his forehead. "Are you wearing your button down tonight? Do you wear anything under it? If so, and you pull it on over your head, you should do that before we get started on your makeup."

"No. Tonight I'm going to be a little more casual and unfasten a button or three." If they danced, it got hot on that floor.

"I approve. Are you ready to get started then? Anything special you want me to try?"

"No. No, I want to be however you can't stop looking at me." Hopefully that made sense.

Winter cupped his chin and smiled. "I hope you know that you're beautiful to me just as you are."

"But I want to be amazing. I want to be as bright as the others."

"I think once you meet subs like Sam tonight, you'll find you don't have to be bright all the time. But sometimes it's good. I love bringing out your lovely eyes. I will give you what you want, petit."

Winter picked up his new brushes and pulled him into the bedroom. "You sit. Take your t-shirt off please."

"Mmm...yes, sir." He wasn't sure if he got off on this or if he got off on how Winter got off on it, but either way, it worked.

Winter laid out the new brushes carefully, smiling at them, then pulled out his eyeliners and shadows. Winter fussed and fidgeted, putting the makeup cape on him, and settling him on the bench so his face caught the light just so. So many little touches, gentle caresses.

His cock was hard as a rock, and that dull ache felt so fucking deep.

"You have such a lovely color in your cheeks today and a sexy little bit of stubble, so I don't think I'll do foundation if that's all right with you." Winter gave his cheek a little scratch with his fingernails making a soft raspy sound. "I like this."

"Mmm..." Fuck, his nerves felt like shattered glass, and it made him lick his lips.

Winter knew. He saw it in that indulgent smile. Winter knew how he was feeling, all of it.

"Good. Be still now, Harley, love." Winter picked up his eyeliner.

Love. Oh, that sounded sweet. "I can do that."

He could totally do that.

"Good boy." Winter leaned close and got to work, the eyeliner going on cool and drying warm. He could feel the intensity of what Winter was doing, in every careful, deliberate stroke.

"I'm so hard..." he whispered.

"Are you?" Winter's fingers rested lightly against the bulge in his jeans. "Oh my. That's lovely, petit."

His lips parted, and he couldn't stop licking them.

"If you don't pull that tongue back in, I will find you something to do with it." Winter winked at him, then kissed him, tongue keeping his very busy.

He could be busy. He liked being busy...

Winter pulled away, removing his hand too. "Good boy. Back to work?"

"Yes, sir." His nipples were hard, his prick was like diamonds, and he was happy as a pig in shit.

Winter worked silently for a little while longer, using a couple of the new brushes to put on shadow and do something to his eyebrows. He noticed that Winter didn't like to talk much while he was doing this but seemed lost in his own thoughts.

"Do you want to see?" Winter asked finally. "Go on, look in the mirror."

His eyes looked so big, so rich with the gold shimmer on

them. He felt like he was staring at a movie star, or a rock star, or someone special. "I—wow. Look at that."

"Do you like it? You wanted bright." Winter stood behind him and looked with him, smiling over his head. "That gold loves the new brush, so smooth."

"It's so sexy." He didn't feel like himself, and that felt dangerous.

"It is sexy, isn't it? You look amazing. Just...amazing." Winter admired him with an adoring look.

"Thank you. I feel... Well, you know how I feel."

"I hope so. I hope you feel beautiful and wanted." Winter kissed his temple. "And I hope you're looking forward to your reward later."

"Yes, sir. I'm looking forward to dancing with you, to being with you." *Rubbing against you. Touching you. Needing you.*

"Good boy. We should get dressed now." Winter started putting away the makeup and tapping off his brushes. "These are such a treat."

"Oh, I'm so glad you liked them." He'd spent a fortune for them, and he'd never bitch, but it felt amazing that Winter loved them.

"I do. I like having new ones that are just for you." Winter closed the drawer in the vanity and opened up his closet. "I have to think about what to wear. What do you think?"

"I'm wearing light gray. Do you have blue or white or black?"

"I don't have white; it's never been a good color on me. I do have blue." Winter pulled a shirt out. "Navy? I also have black."

"You're beautiful. Let me see the black one?"

Winter showed him a black button down. It had fancy

silver buttons. "This is fun. It's nice to have someone care what I'm wearing."

"Oh, that's nice." Harley licked his lips again, wetting them. He was hooked through the balls. "Sexy man."

Winter smiled. "Black then. And my new boots." Winter found clothing and started dressing, but one eye was always on him.

Just what he'd asked for; Winter couldn't keep his eyes off him.

He changed into his good jeans, leaving the fly open as he tugged his shirt on. He wasn't above giving Winter a little show.

Winter's eyes landed squarely on his crotch without an ounce of shame. "Those jeans might be a little uncomfortable, petit. I'd apologize but...you're so handsome."

"I'm aching for you. Everyone will know." And he didn't hate it, at all.

"You're going to make quite the impression, and you might not realize it, but that will reflect well on me. You will have earned your reward tonight." Winter tucked in his shirt and slid a black belt through the loops of his pants.

Such a hot bastard. Harley tucked in, swallowing a moan when his fingers brushed his prick.

Winter slid into his boots, then went to the mirror to finger comb his dark hair. There was a little gray at Winter's temples and some more scattered throughout, but he wasn't what Harley would consider gray-haired at all.

It was hot, obviously, because he was following the guy around like a god.

"Are you ready, petit? You look so good. There will be some other handsome people there tonight, but you just remember that I only have eyes for you. Hm? You can be confident of that." Winter took his hand and gave him a light kiss.

"I believe it. You could have had one of them before. Now you have me." And that was that. Winter wanted him.

"Now I have you. And you, petit, have me. Hm? I'm yours too." Winter put his phone in his pocket, grabbed the apartment key and led him out.

15

W inter felt like a new man walking through the club's imposing doors with Harley by his side. His boy's very presence made him feel confident, younger, so proud. Harley looked beautiful and seemed happy to be out, even though he was sure the boy had to be a little nervous about all of this.

Clint had the most calming energy he'd ever been around, though, and he knew Harley would be able to relax soon enough.

The club was busy, his usual spot was open, but there were seats at Clint's table all the way across the room. He nodded to Deacon, whose eyes went wide.

"Hello, Sir! Hi, Harley! Master Clint said you'd be coming in. I'll let him know you're here. You both look amazing."

"Thank you, Deacon." He turned to his boy. "Would you care for a drink, petit? Or shall we wait until we're settled?"

"I'm easy, honey. I'll follow your lead." Harley gave him a warm smile. "I think that's the wisest idea, don't you?"

"You're a smart boy." Particularly given they'd be sitting

at a table full of Doms and their subs. He had never really considered himself a Dom, but he was quite comfortable in their company. They appreciated his appetites and even shared some of them, so they had plenty in common.

"Go ahead and sit, Master Winter."

Of course, to many of the subs, and to all the boys that worked for Clint, he was Sir or Master anyway.

Harley tilted his head, eyes curious, but he didn't question or complain.

"Come along, petit." He offered Harley his arm and moved to the back of the room, keeping his boy close. He could feel eyes on them, and he was sure Harley was aware as well; the boy was very observant.

Harley didn't shy away from it, but he did stay close, fingers firm on his arm, proving a hint of nerves.

"They have to look at you because you're so beautiful, my boy." He pulled out a chair for Harley, not giving a damn what anyone thought about it. He did as he pleased and always had.

"Thank you, sir." Harley kissed his cheek, the buss soft, sweet.

Clint's table sat eight, and so far they were only two, but he knew Clint would be along shortly. He didn't mind having a moment to sit with Harley. "I should think we'll run into your friends tonight—Oliver, Jesse—they're usually here on Saturdays."

"Yeah, I know Oliver likes to come out." Harley leaned into him a bit. "It feels like this place is just waiting to come alive, hmm?"

He nodded. "We're here a tad earlier than usual so we can talk a bit with Clint before he has to be the host and owner he is. Anything can happen here, and he's often called away for one thing or another."

"I can't imagine owning something this big. That's a ton of work."

"I imagine it is, though Clint doesn't talk about it that way. He's never mentioned it being work." Clint was rightfully proud of the club.

"Winter."

Speak of the very man. He stood. "Good evening, Clint. Were your ears burning? We were just talking about you."

Harley stood as well and offered Clint a warm smile.

"All good, I'm sure." Clint shook Winter's hand and gave him a smile in return.

"Always." Winter turned to introduce Harley. "Clint, I'm so pleased to introduce you to my Harley. Harley, this is Master Clint."

Harley held out his hand to shake. "Very nice to meet you, Sir. You have a great place here. It's beautiful."

He watched Clint, knowing the man well after all these years, and noted the genuinely pleased expression. "Thank you, Harley. I hope you feel welcome and comfortable. Please, both of you, sit."

Harley went for his chair this time and he nodded. "Thank you."

The temptation to say "good boy" was strong, but they hadn't discussed how they would address each other quite yet. That was by design; he wanted Harley to understand the dynamic at the club a bit better first.

Harley caressed his shoulder as he sat, the touch leaving tingles.

He gave his boy a fond look as Harley sat beside him.

"Harley, Oliver tells me you're a friend of Jackson's. Subletting his room. How do you like New York?" Clint raised a finger in the direction of the bar and gave a slight nod.

"It's fascinating, Sir. I have seen so many things—from apartments to folks to food. I've fallen in love."

It was a rare thing that made him blush, but Harley managed it, though he supposed the boy could have meant in love with the city.

Clint chuckled. "I'm sincerely happy for you. I see Winter has worked some of his magic on your eyes tonight. It suits you very well."

Harley's blush was the best type of rouge. "Thank you, Sir. He did. He's amazing."

Clint nodded and started to say something, but a boy arrived with his drink, and they exchanged a few quiet words.

He turned to Harley and took his boy's hand. "You're doing just fine, petit. Why don't you get us drinks? I'll have wine; Deacon knows my favorites."

"Yes, sir." Harley leaned close. "Do you want me to start us a tab?"

What a great idea. "Be my guest, love." Harley picked up on the formalities rather quickly. Such a bright boy.

Harley walked off, making a beeline for the bar. His boy had a lovely ass.

"He seems happy."

Winter glanced at Clint. "He does, doesn't he? I'm honestly over the moon about that."

"Another Texan, too? We're going to have to introduce him to Tommy's Dr. Sam."

Oh, Clint must be in a good mood, to tease about Sam O'Reilly, who had just recently received his PhD.

"I'd hoped they might be in tonight, but if not I'll be sure to give Thomas a call. I don't think Harley has quite the same fire as Sam, but we've only known each other a short time. You think he fits in though, don't you? That he's comfortable here?"

"He seems to be perfectly willing, and he is obviously smitten. I'm glad to see it."

He nodded. "He loves the eyes, the makeup. And we discovered it accidentally, it was a lovely moment. Unforgettable, really. We'll see how long he stays...like this. Mine." He had no reason to think otherwise of Harley, but he'd been close to this with so many younger men. He thought of it as being realistic, not pessimistic.

"I very much hope he's the exception to the rule, my friend."

"Thank you. I do too. Obviously." He winked at Clint.

"Master Winter!" Oliver appeared out of nowhere in a pink jacket and a feather boa. "Hello, Master Clint. I'm sorry to interrupt."

Clint shook his head and chuckled. "Apology accepted, boy. Everything is well?"

"Yes, Sir. Very good. Excellent. Master Winter, Harley looks amazing. Did you have a good birthday?"

"It was so good I'm not sure I'd mind never having another birthday."

Oliver looked horrified. "Don't say that!"

He laughed. "It was a wonderful day, and I can't imagine ever topping it, that's all. Silly Oliver."

"So...he's arguing with Deacon about payment, Harley is, I mean. He doesn't seem to understand that you have an account..."

He glanced at the bar. "Oh, sweet boy. That's my fault. Thank you, Oliver. Excuse me a second, please, Clint."

"Of course." Clint didn't seem the least bit concerned.

He made his way over to the bar and rested a hand on Harley's back. "Something wrong, petit?"

"Yes, sir. You said I should set up a tab, and Deacon here won't let me!"

"Oh, I see." He gave the bartender a meaningful look. "I know it's not customary, but let the boy run a tab for us, Deacon, would you?"

Deacon hesitated a moment and then nodded. "Yes, Sir. My apologies to you both." Deacon took Harley's credit card.

"There now, petit. Bring our drinks, please."

"Thank you, sir." Harley relaxed. "Thanks, Deacon. Seriously."

"You're welcome, Harley." Deacon reached across the bar and touched Harley's hand. "We're cool. I misunderstood."

"This is all real new to me. You rock." Harley grabbed the two glasses of wine and followed Winter back to the table, waiting for him to sit before handing him one of the glasses.

"Thank you, my sweet boy." He patted Harley's seat. "You're having wine too?"

"I thought beer and wine would make weird kisses."

He laughed. "How thoughtful." He clinked glasses with Harley. "The confusion over the tab is my fault, Harley. I'm sorry about that. We'll talk more after tonight." He gave Harley a smile and a wink.

"Sounds perfect. Cheers!" Harley sipped and hummed. "Tastes like a velvet jacket feels."

He could just imagine his boy in a velvet jacket.

And nothing else.

One of the younger Doms strolled over, a big smile on his face. "Mister Clint."

"Callum. You made it. Sam said something about a lecture out of town so I wasn't sure you would."

They exchanged a warm handshake and Callum took the open seat next to Harley. "Gentlemen."

"Hello, Callum. Where's your boy?"

"Raine?" Callum turned in his seat and pointed to the half-naked sub at the bar. "In the leather."

Winter chuckled. "Though not much of it."

"Well, he's floating, you know. He's comfortable."

"Very sweet." Raine was a firecracker of a man from the West Coast, a child star that had burned out in a rather amazing fashion, from what he understood.

"Callum, this is Harley. He's recently moved here from Texas. Harley, this is Master Callum."

"Pleased to meet you, sir." Harley stood to shake hands, offering Callum a smile.

"Another Texan? Is Sam going to convince you to turn this into a cowboy bar, Clint?"

Harley's eyebrow lifted, just the slightest bit. "Oh, no worries, sir. I'm not a cowboy, just your run-of-the-mill, blue-collar redneck."

"Run-of-the-mill you are not, petit." He slid his hand down Harley's arm.

Callum raised an eyebrow. "I can't say I've seen too many blue-collar rednecks with eyes like that, boy."

"That's because I'm lucky to have someone to make me special tonight."

"You are at that." Callum nodded. "Lucky and special."

Clint grinned. "Harley reminds me a little of Sam. There must be something about subs from Texas. They're so...direct."

He wasn't sure Harley was ready to identify as a sub, but he didn't correct Clint either.

Raine made his way over with a cocktail for Callum, something clear and sparkling with a lime in it, and a bottle of water for himself. Silently, he set the water on the table and knelt in the space between Callum's chair and Harley's.

Callum opened the water, handed it to Raine, then took it back and set it on the table again.

"Speaking of Sam, where are they? He said they would be here tonight. He borrowed one of my books."

"They'll be along. You know how Saturdays are." Clint shrugged, then seemed to share a knowing look and a grin with Callum. "They take their weekend sessions very seriously."

Winter had one ear on the conversation, but was focused more on Harley, watching as his boy took everything in. He really had no idea how their conversation and all of these new behaviors and people would sit with the boy. But this was his world, and if they were going to be together, this would have to be Harley's as well. Eventually.

Harley seemed to be soaking everything in, but he wasn't saying a lot, more watching with a sharp gaze.

"How is your wine, petit?" He slid a hand over Harley's thigh. It seemed like contact was important, to remind the boy he was fine, he wasn't alone, that he was cared for.

"Good. It's going to my head a little bit." Harley gave him a little half smile. "How's yours?"

"Delicious. The company is good too. Are you all right?"

"Lots to take in, huh?" Harley leaned over. "This is...new for me."

He nodded. "I know. But you're safe. These are good people. I will answer all of your questions. All of them."

"I'll have a lot." Harley leaned in, whispering in his ear. "Tomorrow, over a long, lazy breakfast. I'll make a list. Tonight, we're celebrating your birthday, and I'm being brave."

Good gracious, he felt as though his heart could just explode. He turned his head and caught Harley with a kiss. "Thank you, mon petit."

Harley stroked his cheek, just barely, but he felt the touch like fire.

As they sat and talked, plenty of people came to visit with Clint. Mostly the traditional Doms and their subs in varying degrees of dress, all kneeling for most of the conversation. Winter pointed to one lovely boy in a thong that left the sub bare-assed, crawling behind his Dom as they walked away. He grinned. "Seems as if Gil has been a bad boy."

One of Harley's eyebrows went up. "Well, that's something, I reckon."

A soft chuckle sounded behind him. "Now, you sound like home. Good lord and butter, we're fixin' to take over, Mr. Clint."

"Indeed, Dr. O'Reilly."

Thomas's Sammy came around and hugged Clint, the sub as free with his affection as anyone he'd ever seen. "Good to see you, Sir. You look good. Masters. Fellow Texan." Everyone got a warm smile, and Harley got a wink. "Mister, you want a glass of wine?"

Sammy was obviously flying four feet above the ground, and the boy's leather harness exposed why. The boy was sporting two black nipple rings proudly, a chain dangling between them.

"White, sweetheart. And water for yourself. Callum, would mind asking your boy to bring Sam's stool? His hands will be full."

"Of course." But Callum didn't even have to ask, the boy got up and bowed slightly to Thomas before heading for the bar.

Thomas gave Clint an equally warm hug. "Busy tonight."

"It is. It's lovely. Winter's come to introduce his new boy to us, the dance floor is filling, and it's always a joy to have you and Callum at the table." Butter wouldn't melt in Clint's mouth, but the teasing tone was clear.

Harley's hand landed on the small of his back, drawing his focus. Someone needed connection.

Callum stood up. "Where's my hug?"

Thomas snorted but was definitely amused. "Oh, I'm sorry. I'd assumed you were saving it for my boy."

"I have enough for the both of you." Callum hugged Thomas who laughed and shook his head.

"Winter, it's very good to see you. Happy birthday. Forty, I hear?"

"Shh. Let's not say that too loudly." He smiled though, because it was kind of Thomas to remember. "Thomas, this is Harley. He's new to the city and to the club, and Clint was kind enough to set this up so perhaps he could meet your Sammy. Harley, this is Master Thomas."

"Pleased to meet you, sir." Harley stood, smiled, and shook Thomas's hand, easy as you please.

"Good to meet you, Harley. Sam is always happy to talk with another Texan, and he's found his way in New York quite well. Tell me, is Harley a family name? Or are you named after the motorcycle?" Thomas gave Harley a wink.

"The motorcycle. Absolutely." Harley chuckled and grinned wide. "I look forward to meeting him, thank you, sir."

Thomas pointed over Harley's shoulder. "He's on his way back." Raine arrived with Sammy's stool and Thomas accepted it with a nod. "Thank you, boy. I appreciate the errand." Thomas set the low stool down and sat in the empty chair beside it.

Winter tugged Harley closer and whispered to him. "Master Thomas's boy can't kneel for long periods of time due to an old injury. The stool is his accommodation. They're an unusual couple in the best way."

"Oh, that sucks," Harley whispered back. "I'm sorry. I won't notice, promise."

"No, I didn't mean that. I just thought you might be curious. I've found Sammy to be an open book during our conversations. He's very easy in his skin. You're rather like him that way."

"Yeah?" Harley held his gaze, those beautiful eyes deep enough to drown in. "That's cool." Then his sweet lover whispered. "I still want you. Even just sitting here."

His eyes narrowed even as his balls grew tight. "Good boy."

Harley huffed out a soft little puff of air, and Winter knew Harley's balls had just drawn up as well. He was learning how much Harley appreciated praise, and he was going to have to be more deliberate about doling it out.

"Thank you, sweetheart." Thomas took his wine from Sammy. "You may sit for a bit if you like, or you could take Harley for a tour. Master Winter says he's new."

"Thank you, Mister. Master Winter, is it cool if we wander? I swear to bring him back."

Sam was so kind. Winter thought he'd make a great friend for Harley. "Would you like a tour, petit? I understand Sammy is an excellent tour guide."

"Yeah? Absolutely." Harley stood, smiled at Sam, pointedly not looking below the chin.

Poor boy. He supposed he'd consider it a win if Harley didn't refuse to come back. "Have fun boys. Take your time." Winter heard Sammy start talking as he led Harley away.

"You weren't exaggerating when you said he was new, were you?" Thomas asked, picking up his wine again.

"No. He's curious and brave, but no, everything

—*everything* is new. It's wonderful, but I worry. I haven't discovered where he might draw the line yet. I couldn't even say for sure where that line could be." He glanced at Callum and Clint who nodded in sync. "I'm trying to bring him along gently."

"Well, well. Winter, you and I will have to have a nice long talk." Thomas chuckled and shook his head. "As I have been in your very shoes."

"I believe you have, though I might have an easier time than you as I am more of a sensualist than a sadist." He winked at Thomas.

"Quite possibly. Though do you know that Harley won't need to go that far?"

"I am fairly certain he won't. I would know by now, I think. Still, I don't want to scare him off."

"If it makes you feel better, Winter, Sam lasted about five minutes down that hallway toward the playrooms before he bolted and left the club." Clint chuckled. "Harley's already beaten his record."

"Very funny." Thomas snorted. "True, though."

"And this is his third visit. He started at Mardi Gras!" Winter chuckled. Talk about a trial by fire.

"He came with Ollie to Mardi Gras, didn't he?" Callum asked. "That boy isn't exactly subtle. And they're friends. You can see how much Ollie cares about Harley when they're together. It's sweet."

"I hope Harley makes many friends. Enough to make him want to stay. New York is...big. But I think he's taking to it."

"I'm trying to remember what Sam's complaints about the city were when he first arrived. I remember he said that no one touched him here. No hugs, and you can see what a hugger he is."

Winter nodded. "I remember that myself." Though when he'd first arrived, no touching was a good thing. It had taken him a while to warm-up to people again.

Clint tilted his head. "It was good for us to have fresh ideas, new needs. We all grew."

"Don't let Sam hear you say all of that, because he's already got a big head." Thomas was teasing, he assumed. Sammy had never been anything but humble that he could recall.

Clint chuckled, but it was Callum that laughed loud. "That's O'Reilly for you. He knows his place in the world."

That was a lovely compliment for both Sammy and Thomas. He recalled a time when Sammy was far more timid, the newbie sub hiding under the brim of his cowboy hat, shielding his eyes, hard to read. Thomas had somehow managed to bring out the best in the boy, find his confidence, and Sammy owned that now. "It's rather remarkable, isn't it?"

Thomas somehow managed to look both humble and proud. "He is. Remarkable, I mean."

Winter thought his boy was as well, and was handling himself nicely for being out of his league. That did seem to be one of Harley's finer qualities—the ability to jump into new experiences.

He'd never been terribly brave; he liked his routine and didn't often step out of his comfort zone, but Harley was making him want to try new things too. He couldn't remember having more fun than he'd had on his birthday, and now, tonight, seeing his boy begin to belong.

When Sam brought his boy back to him, he was blushing dark, but smiling, and Sam wore a vaguely wicked expression.

Thomas patted the stool for Sam to sit beside him. "Was it a good tour, Harley? What do you think of the place?"

Good lord. Thomas was as wicked as Sammy. Winter held a hand out and pulled Harley into his seat.

"It's eye-opening for sure, but everyone was real nice." Harley chuckled softly. "And I got a hug from Ollie."

"Oliver?" Thomas turned to Sammy. "Is Raymond here tonight?"

"I believe so, Mister. Oliver was corseted to the nines. He looks amazing."

"Oliver wears a corset so well," Winter agreed. "Just beautiful." Hot, too. Not that Oliver was someone he coveted, he just liked to look. "Didn't you think so, petit?"

Harley nodded. "There are some in Jackson's closet. So fancy and complicated. I was scared to touch them."

"They're not scary, though some of Jackson's favorites were complicated." He put a hand on Harley's knee. He'd love to see the boy in a corset, but he needed to tread carefully, it had been a big night already. "One day you might like to try one."

"Maybe. I thought it was a tube top, when I saw them the first time."

He laughed. "Everything is so new. I almost envy you, learning all of this, trying new things. It's easy to feel jaded, to feel like you've seen it all. But I'm seeing everything new again with you."

"I don't mind learning new things. That's one of the reasons why I decided to come here. Having a bigger life."

New York was certainly bigger. The club, bigger still. "So tell me...of everything you saw, what was your favorite?"

"When you knew I needed a hand at the bar." There was zero hesitation, even if that wasn't what he'd been asked.

"You're a good boy, petit." He kissed Harley's cheek.

"Oliver pointed me in your direction, and I knew immediately what I'd done. I apologize for all of that."

"No. You fixed it. Thank you, sir. It's been a fascinating evening." Harley took his hand. "Are we going to dance tonight?"

"Yes. Yes!" He smiled at his lovely boy. He loved to dance with Harley. "I would love to. Shall we?"

"Yes, please, sir!" Harley stood and held one hand out to him. "If all y'all will please excuse us?"

Clint's chuckle made him blush and he rolled his eyes, but he couldn't help his grin.

"Dr. O'Reilly, you're already a bad influence," he heard Clint say as they left the table for the dance floor.

"Sam is a history professor. That's wild, huh? He's young."

Not as young as he looked. Sam was aging beautifully.

"People come from all kinds of professions. You'd be surprised. Thomas is in marketing at the Metropolitan Museum of Art. Callum books talent for a lot of the comedy clubs and some smaller concert venues. The couple dancing over there? They are gastroenterologists." Winter caught Harley around the waist and pulled him in, grinning. "I'm a mild-mannered librarian. Very under the radar."

"My librarian." Harley kissed his cheek. "All mine."

"Yes, petit. I am yours." He would take whatever was coming, even if it meant Harley eventually wanted to move on. He was too happy now, too committed. Too in love.

Harley followed his lead like he had done it all his life, letting Winter turn and sway and hold him. "My little love."

"Yes." Harley caught his glance. "All yours. I'm so happy, lover. I didn't know I could feel—"

"Feel?" Winter kissed him. "Feel, what, petit?"

"In love. I'm in love with you. I didn't think it was a real thing, but it is."

Winter blushed, heat radiating from his chest to his cheeks. He'd been in love a couple of times, but not like this. "I suppose it takes the right person—or the right combination of people—to make it real."

"It must." Harley pressed in close, holding him as they rocked on the dance floor. "Because it feels pretty damn real."

"It is. Very real." He nuzzled behind Harley's ear. "I want you to move in with me."

"You do? I'd love that. I promised Ollie three—two and a half—more months, but I would love that."

"I understand. I can wait, or...we can just pay Oliver. But that's entirely up to you, petit. I don't want to rush you." Rush. That was amusing. He hadn't planned to ask, it just popped out of his mouth. He was happy he had, but his apartment was old and cluttered, so small. He was going to have to donate a few—a few dozen—things.

"We'll figure it. We will. Right now, dance with me. Please."

"With pleasure, petit." Dancing with Harley was possibly the best birthday gift of all.

16

Harley woke up early and headed to make coffee and sit in Winter's favorite chair.

Last night had been an eye-opener. Like a hard-core one. Everyone had been nice, honestly, but Sam had taken him to a quiet little room in the back and had kind of schooled him.

Sam had shown him a cabinet of all sorts of cuffs and ropes and paddles and things. Then the man had given him a set of...hints.

Listen, man. This is new and weird, but there are a few things to remember. First, you and your man, y'all make the rules for you. Second, ask questions. Ask thousands of them. Ask the stupid ones, the hard ones, the weird ones. Third, let Winter help. These men, they're like rednecks with a winch when there's a stuck vehicle. They live for this shit. And fourth, in public, when you don't know what to do, remember your manners. It'll take you so far when you're lost in this world.

That was all good advice, it made sense, but he wasn't sure where to begin asking questions. Maybe the rules?

Maybe whether Winter owned any of the things he'd seen in that cabinet.

Maybe why that one guy was kneeling and what 'flying' meant. Was he high? Harley wasn't an innocent—he'd smoked pot, but he'd never done anything harder, and he wasn't really interested in that.

"Mm. Do I smell coffee?" Winter shuffled out of the bedroom in his fancy robe and slippers, looking sleepy, and happy.

"You do, lover. You want a cup? I was just being lazy and enjoying your chair."

Winter came straight to him and kissed him good morning. "You look so good in my chair. I'll get my coffee this time, and you stay lazy."

"Are you sure? It's the best chair." He snuggled back in again with a sigh.

"For now. Just look at you." Winter watched him, an adoring look in his eyes. "We can share it when I get back." He got a smile and then Winter ducked into the tiny kitchen. "You made a whole carafe! Excellent, we can take it slow this morning."

"I knew you'd want a cup, lover." Hell, he knew he'd need more than one.

"Or three!" Winter called from the kitchen and reappeared a moment later. "You make good coffee. How did you sleep?"

"Like a well-loved man. You?"

"Happily." Winter waved for him to scoot, sat, and pulled him back down onto his lap. One arm went around his waist to tuck him close. "And like I don't want to be very far from you today."

"Mmm... I approve." He nuzzled Winter's stubbly jaw, feeling warm and close, like he belonged right here.

Winter sipped his coffee and held him, just quietly, like there was nothing else he'd rather be doing.

He let himself relax fully, and he figured there was nothing better than this—being here, like all the way here with his lover. "Thank you."

Winter looked at him curiously. "For what, petit? I just woke up."

"For this, for last night, for you, I guess. For everything."

"I should say the same. And for this amazing birthday weekend. I haven't ever been celebrated like this. You've made it special. You're special." Winter tilted his head. "How much of last night are you thanking me for? Because the club visit must have been quite something for you."

"Oh, wow. I have so many questions. It was like three different times—that's common for bars, I know, but wow. The party, the time we were just there, and it was slow, and then last night."

"It's wonderful isn't it? Something for everyone. You can ask questions any time. As they come to you. It's fine."

"Sam said I should ask you anything, even if it was silly." He rested his cheek on Winter. "So I'm going to start with one I'm sure is silly. That one guy, the one on the floor there at the table? Was he high?"

"High? Raine?" Winter looked confused. "Definitely not. Callum, like every Dom I know, only plays sober."

"Oh." See? Stupid question. Still, Sam said to ask, so he pushed on. "I mean, his...person said he was flying, is all."

"Oh! Oh, no, Callum said he was floating. Floating is... when your endorphins have kicked in heavily, like after a scene. Or an orgasm. Only because the scene or session is usually a lot longer than an orgasm, the effects last much longer too."

"I understand post-orgasm goofies, totally." He chuckled

softly. He was sort of into the ramp up to orgasm himself, but that was just him. "I'm not sure I'd want to have to leave the house during them."

"It's difficult to really explain until you feel it yourself, but you don't think. You don't really care what others do either. You're focused on your Master. Laser focused."

"I don't understand, but I'm glad he wasn't stoned. I don't love the idea of him being out and about and not able to...function."

"Callum had a close eye on him and was taking very good care of him, I promise. Just like I would always take very good care of you."

He lifted his chin and kissed Winter's jaw. "Thank you. I'm... Sam said everyone was different. Like for everything. So we make our own rules."

"Indeed. We see what works and doesn't work for us. I can tell you that a lot of what you saw in the back rooms holds little appeal for me except perhaps to watch."

"Yeah, I reckoned there would have been a hint of whips and chains lurking around, but I hadn't seen them." Not that he'd been snooping, but he'd been here quite a bit.

"If I get the urge to spank you it will be with my bare hand, I assure you, and appropriate to the moment." Winter's grin was wicked and playful.

He rolled his eyes and nipped Winter's chin, playing back. "So, what's your interest in this whole thing, love?"

"Aesthetics, mostly. That's a broad view of my kinks. Makeup, clothing, leather, beautiful bodies, pretty bondage...and I like to watch. Everyone. Anything." Winter sipped his coffee.

"Huh." That made sense. He wasn't really sure he had a kink. He liked Winter a lot, he loved how Winter saw him—

but that was called being an exhibitionist, wasn't it? He wasn't sure he was that.

Whatever. It didn't matter, he guessed. He was him. That worked.

"That's all? 'Huh?'" Winter snorted. "I'm not sure what to make of that response, petit."

He kissed Winter's throat. "Oh, I was just thinking about me, honey, not you, and that it made sense. You do like to see things."

"I do. It's Sunday, and I think we should take it easy today since we both work tomorrow, but soon, I'd like to see you in some of those things. How would you feel about that? Next weekend?"

"I'm totally free next weekend." And he was willing to trust Winter too. "Is it okay if I don't have any? Kinks? I mean... I haven't given it a lot of thought. You? You, I can't stop thinking about."

"Darling boy, you like what you like, it's really that simple. A kink is really anything that gets you off. You most certainly have kinks, but there's no need for labels if you don't care for them." Winter winked at him.

"I do? Cool." He liked that idea. Him, having kinks. Who would believe that?

"Mm. Yes. Shall I name one for you? Or would you like to let it be?"

Oh, now he was curious. Like for real, honestly curious. "Can you? Name one for me?"

"Delayed gratification," Winter answered simply. "You enjoyed wanting all evening, that was clear."

"Yeah. Yeah, it's good, wanting, and then the actual orgasm is more than just rubbing one off, huh? It feels way more real, like we meant it that way." He'd never considered that there would be a name for it.

"Well, we did mean it that way." Winter winked at him. "You were most appreciative when I let you come for me."

"I was. I like that—when it's big, when it's not just a bodily function." Winter made him wiggle some. "And I did appreciate you, all the way to the bone."

"So, that's a legitimate kink, petit. And I am sure over time you'll discover others. It's nothing to be embarrassed about, obviously."

"Well, there you go. I get to belong." That didn't embarrass him at all. He loved the idea of finding a place where he fit in.

"I can't imagine you'd have had any trouble with that in any case. So that was your one burning question? Nothing else?"

"No, that was just the big one. I mean, Sam's nipples were pierced, Winter, and just out in the open where anyone could touch them!"

"Yes!" Winter chuckled. "Wasn't that a lovely thing? He is proud of his piercings. But no one would dare touch them, petit. Trust me on that."

"No?" Okay, that was pretty cool, when you got right down to it. He liked that idea, knowing that everyone was so respectful.

"No. Sammy belongs to Master Thomas. Just as Raine belongs to Master Callum, and, petit, you belong to me."

"Mmm..." That was a fascinating thought. "I'll be yours, no problem at all."

Winter's eyes sparkled in the sunlight. "Thank you, love. You make me happy. Though, I fear that you'll find something, somewhere, someone you want more than you want me eventually. Once you find your feet, discover who you're meant to be, it might not be mine any longer."

"I'm not that kind of guy. I'm steady as anything."

"You are a good boy, Harley. Just so...easy. So open. This weekend has been a dream. But tomorrow we go back to work, hm?"

What did that mean? Did that mean that all the things Winter had said were just for this weekend? That it wasn't really true? That would suck, especially since he'd meant what he'd said. Maybe this was, like, a game, something Winter put on and took off like a costume. He could do that, he guessed. At least he could pretend to until he figured it out. What had Sam said? If he didn't get it, just be polite. "Yes, sir. Totally."

"I will miss you. Unless, of course, you'd like to stay with me for a night or two. I won't tire you out for work, I promise."

"I'd love to."

Winter was wigging him right the fuck out, but he needed to just breathe and figure out what was what.

"You really were amazing last night. I hope you know that. Clint was very impressed with how comfortable you seemed. And I do enjoy dancing with you."

"Mmm...we dance together well." He sipped his coffee, telling himself to stay loose, stay easy. "I loved it."

"I suppose I got ahead of things asking you to move in. I'm sorry about that. I know you and Oliver are good friends." Winter nuzzled his temple. "You can let me know when you're ready. If you are."

Okay, this was weird. "Did I do something wrong? I mean, between last night and now? If I did, you can just tell me."

"Wrong?" Winter looked genuinely confused. "Not at all. You're perfect. What do you mean?"

"I just...last night you seemed like you were sure about

me. This morning maybe you have buyer's remorse?" Hopefully that made sense.

"No remorse, petit. No regret. I want you. But I know how young men are; I've been with quite a few, and it would be wrong of me to hold you to this when I know your mind can change. Youth is like that. It's not mean, it's just true."

"Oh, that makes sense." Was he supposed to say thank you? *Dear Winter, thanks for making it clear that I'm just one of a lot of immature, stupid guys, and that I'm too young to know anything real, but in fifteen years? I'll totally know things about people like me. Love, me.* "Do you want a warm-up? Mine's gotten cold."

"Thank you, petit. Yes, please." Winter handed him his cup. "Should we make breakfast? Do you have plans today?"

"All I'd planned was to be with you." He stood and took the mugs, heading to fix the coffee, roll his shoulders, and get his good mood back.

"That will make it a perfect day. Perhaps we can relax, read for a while in the sunshine. I have a brand-new book, after all."

"Sounds good to me. I'm totally into taking it easy."

"Good. Then I will take you out for some lunch. Perhaps we'll try the taco place again. That was fun."

"I love that place. Good food, honest—sounds perfect."

"I remember watching you walk into the market that evening and thinking about how much I wanted you."

"I was just tickled you wanted to give me a second chance."

"It is very unlike me to go hunting for a phone number. I would have given you many chances, if it had come to that." Winter took his cup of coffee and blew on it, then sipped it carefully. "Mmm."

"It worked out." He didn't know what to say, now, because he felt...unsure.

"Rather well, in fact." Winter seemed oblivious, like he had no idea Harley was losing confidence. As if nothing had changed in Winter's mind at all. "Should we get dressed? Take our books to the park?"

"Sounds like a plan." He leaned over, kissed Winter's cheek, and tried to let it go. He'd have to talk to Oliver, maybe. Later. Or Sam. Someone to help him learn the rules.

Because Harley was in over his head, and he didn't feel like drowning.

Nope. He was going to swim.

17

W inter handed off his coat to Ricky, who was working the coat check, and stopped by the bar to order his usual. Deacon was busy, so he waited patiently and had a look around the club. It seemed like a typical Friday night, with couples milling around, coming and going from the back hall. The dance floor was empty, but it was still early for that. He hoped to spend some time dancing with Harley later.

"Master Winter! Where's your boy?" Deacon was smooth and smiling as always.

"He'll be along. He had a challenging week at work so I told him he should take his time."

"Let me get your usual, sir."

He'd only seen Harley for dinner once, and although the boy did stay the night, it was up and out early for both of them the next morning. The poor boy seemed...less like himself. Tired, maybe. Stressed. Harley had a physical job to begin with, and the weather had been rainy and cool, which surely hadn't made it easier.

Weather was never an issue for him; he worked

underground essentially, and the archives were climate controlled. It was fifty-five degrees and forty percent humidity day in and day out for him. That never changed.

His cluttered apartment never changed. His seat at the club never changed either.

"Here you go. Do you need anything else, Sir?"

"No, I'm fine. Thank you, Deacon." He picked up his usual drink.

A Manhattan, which also never changed.

Harley was a big change, though. One he hadn't expected to come into his life, and one he hadn't expected to miss as much as he had this past week. That was dangerous territory, but there was nothing to be done about it. He understood his feelings for the boy, and he understood that logic and rational thinking were useless defenses.

But Harley was still his boy; that didn't seem to be in question, so he slowly sipped his drink, as usual, and watched people come and go.

Warm hands settled on his shoulders, a soft kiss brushing his ear. "Hey, gorgeous. I missed you."

He was startled for a second but, the touch calmed him and he smiled, turning his head. He wanted a kiss. Right now. "Petit. I missed you as well."

"Work was a bugger bear this week. I'm glad to be done with it. I got twelve hours overtime!"

He reached for Harley and pulled his boy into his lap. "You must be exhausted. Do you want a drink?" *You smell so good.*

"I want a kiss, lover, and then a margarita as big as my head."

Lover. How sweet was that? And his boy could be so direct. "I will happily kiss you, petit. Come here." He pulled his boy down by the nape.

Harley opened up, tongue sliding along his, the taste of peppermint barely there.

He hummed and deepened the kiss, not caring if it was fit for public consumption, they weren't actually in public, and he'd seen men do far more than kiss in this space.

Harley groaned and wiggled in his lap, tongue lapping at his lips.

"Mmm. My boy." He smiled at Harley as he ended the kiss. "You're delicious. I want to hear all about your week. Go and get your drink. Tell Deacon it's on my account, please."

"Yes, sir. Thank you, so much. Do you need another one yet?"

"No, petit. Thank you. I just got this one."

Harley kissed his cheek. "Be right back, lover. We'll start our weekend."

He watched the boy go, glad that he remembered to be specific about the tab this time. He planned to talk with Harley about some of those subtle things soon. He didn't think Harley thought of himself as submissive, and truthfully, that wasn't what he needed all the time. But here, their rules had to bend a little.

He loved the way Harley had said "our weekend". It was their time, after all.

Harley smiled at Deacon, and whatever his boy said, it had the bartender in stitches.

He watched curiously as Harley ordered his margarita. Now that his boy was here he didn't need or care to watch anyone else. Harley had all of his attention.

Harley wore jeans and a leather jacket, the dark hair just beginning to curl. He wasn't a tall guy, at all, but those shoulders were broad, solid.

Winter smiled as Harley made his way back to the table,

meeting the boy's eyes. "It looks like you and Deacon are getting along. And your margarita looks good."

"We were talking about drinks as big as my head." Harley's dark eyes caught the lights above the dance floor.

"That one is pretty close." He reached out and pulled a chair closer. "Sit, petit. It's good to see you." Harley was right where he said he'd be. Like always. Like every time they'd made plans.

"It's good to be seen, and I'm so glad to be here with you." Harley settled into his chair with a little wince that turned into a smile.

Oh. Was Harley hurt? "Take a nice big sip of your drink, and then tell me what hurts and why."

"Sorry, lover." Harley took a drink, humming deep in his chest. "Oh, that's nice."

"Deacon knows how to mix a drink. Clint had one or two backup bartenders, but Deacon is the only regular." He touched Harley's knee. "Sorry for what, petit?"

"Just being a titty baby. I'm okay. I just had a little run-in with a falling dresser."

Part of him said leave it alone, but he wanted to know what happened, and if Harley was his...he was allowed to ask. "What aren't you telling me, Harley?"

"I got a couple-three stitches. Nothing big."

He stared at his boy. "What? Stitches? Did you think I wasn't going to notice? Don't hide things from me, petit, there's no point."

"Well, I reckoned you'd see when you got me naked, but by then, we'd be naked."

It was difficult to argue with that logic, even if it did make him laugh. "Is it terribly painful? Was it expensive? Why didn't you call me? You should have called me."

"It aches some, it's covered by worker's comp, and it

wasn't my fault." Harley leaned toward him. "I have a story to tell you. So. The bosses tell us it's a volatile situation with a break-up and the cops there, everything. We're moving things out that are marked by this little bitty guy, and suddenly this mean-looking dude comes tearing out of the apartment next door, and the little guy screams and starts throwing things like the goddamn Hulk. He upended a chest of drawers over the railing and one of the drawers came out on the way down, smacked me on the thigh and tore a groove. The whole time, little Hulk is screaming and roaring. The cops arrest him. The mean-looking guy is crying. I got to go in an ambulance. It was wild."

He shook his head. It seemed as if Harley had a new story all the time now, and each one was more insane than the last. "Perhaps it's time to consider a new job, petit."

"Oh, man, I wish. Problem is I got no skills but reading and lifting. But they pay me more because I have a security clearance and no fear."

"You should have more fear; this is New York City. Let's see if we can't find you something else to do for work. You're smart, Harley, as I've told you before, you might be surprised what's out there." This job was dangerous. That was no good.

"Maybe. I'm open to things, you know that." Harley kissed the tip of his nose.

"Mm. Yes. Thank goodness for that." He winked at his boy. "How is Oliver? I haven't seen him yet tonight."

"I didn't see him at the apartment. He was mad last night though. All sorts of things were broken this morning." Harley's eyes rolled like dice.

"Oh my. Trouble in paradise?" That didn't sound good, Oliver and Raymond had been together a while. "I'm sorry to hear that. Hopefully nothing of yours was broken."

"Lord no. I don't have anything in the kitchen. He's got himself a wild temper. Tomorrow, he'll be wearing that corset, cleaning, and all...peaceful."

He grinned. "That's good for him. Peace. It's good for all of us, don't you think?"

"Yes. Do you think that it's... Do you think that the corset is why?"

"I think the corset is a big part of it, yes. And having purpose and chores... Oliver needs to know someone is paying attention. The corset is many things; it's different for different people. But he can't forget who he belongs to when he's wearing it, can he? Not as tight as he wears them."

"Right. I don't see how he vacuums like that." Harley winked and took a long drink of his margarita.

"There are many wonders in this world." Winter sipped his as well. "How would you like to take a stroll through the rooms and see what people are up to?" He liked to do that, see who was letting people watch, admire.

"Sure, lover. Sounds like a plan." Harley kissed his cheek and stood, holding one hand out to him.

They left their drinks—he didn't worry about them; no one would touch them—and he took Harley's hand. "We can just watch a little. Maybe you'll see something you like."

"What all do you like that we're going to see, or do I get to guess?"

"Well, if they're doing any bondage, I like that. Ropes, leather, doesn't so much matter. Sometimes there's entertainment in the one big room. Those are my favorite things. I don't stay to watch the more sadistic work, that's not really my interest. What did you like?"

"I didn't see anything in the back. We went to a lounge, had a water and a cookie, believe it or not." Harley winked at him.

Interesting. "He only took you to the sub lounge?"

Oh, Sammy, you little devil. Sammy didn't give the boy the full tour. Still, Harley was blushing when they got back, so he must have gotten an eyeful of something.

"Yeah. I mean...there were folks in there, and they were something to see."

"I imagine so, there are plenty of pretty men at the club." He'd make sure Harley got more of a look tonight. Why not? If Harley intended to be with him, the boy had better know what came along with him.

They stopped by the sub lounge, which was the first room they came to as they headed down the hall.

"This was the room. It's empty now, but it wasn't last week."

"No, and it won't be in another hour or so. It's early yet." He led Harley down the hall and poked his head into the exhibition room to see if anyone was there. "I've seen many couples working in here, some workshops too." There were a few couples milling around, but it wasn't clear whether anything was planned.

"Have you? What was the best one?"

"Well, that's a difficult question to answer. I've attended so many." He thought about it; he did remember one that he'd particularly enjoyed, and also learned a lot from. "A couple of years ago, someone taught us about wax play. Hot wax. It was fascinating and beautiful."

"Wax? Like candles?" Harley's eyebrow went up, but he nodded. "I've seen that on a movie."

"Yes, special candles, with special safe wax. I hope it was a good movie." Winter had no idea what movie Harley was talking about, but something told him it wasn't the kind of movie he was thinking about.

"I don't remember. I just remember a lot of hissing and

moaning and being embarrassed that I was watching it with other people."

He chuckled. "The hissing and moaning sounds accurate." A pair of subs being led on leashes by burly Doms walked by them and he took Harley by the shoulders to watch them walk away. "They are lovely in all their leather aren't they?"

Harley nodded. "Is it real hot, or do they have special leather for pants?"

"They're hot. It's a softer leather than some, but it's still the real thing. I've worn leather pants a couple of times, and I liked them, but it wasn't summertime, that's for sure."

"I bet your backside looks amazing in leather, but I hear you. Christmas clothes, right?" Harley winked at him. "But, honestly, they look like they are right where they want to be."

"I'm not a fan of leashes, personally. They're pretty, but I like to know a boy just follows me because he is supposed to." He winked at Harley and took a few steps down the hall.

"Good to know." Harley's laughter was soft, almost silent, but it was there, and merry.

"Master Winter, are you bringing Harley to the Shibari lab?" Jesse stopped and gave him a smile. "You should."

Oh, that could be fun. "Yes, perhaps. Thank you." He nodded to Theo, who nodded back and nudged Jesse into the room. Then he turned to Harley. "Do you want to try something new, petit?"

"Sure. I'm at your disposal all weekend. What do you need me to do?"

"Allow me to practice some knots on you. Very simple stuff. I think you might enjoy it." He stroked Harley's cheek with his fingers. "Do you know what a safe word is? You might need one."

"I do. Oliver and I talked about them. He said red and yellow are normal."

"Perfect. Easy." He took Harley's hand and pulled him into the room. The seating was arranged in pairs, two chairs facing each other, or cushions on the floor. There were two lovely cushions off to one side that he liked the location of. "Are you comfortable on the floor, petit?"

"Sure. It smells good in here. Spicy." Harley settled on the cushion, inhaling deeply. "Cinnamon and something else."

"Mm. I'm not sure, but you're right. Something warm, but I can't put my finger on it. Not vanilla..." It was relaxing, whatever it was. Soothing.

Winter nodded to a sub as a length of white bondage rope was set on the floor beside him. "Thank you, boy."

"You're welcome, sir."

Harley reached out, stroked the rope. "Oh...it's soft. That's good."

"Yes." He picked it up and handed it to Harley, loving how it looked in his boy's fingers. "Play with it if you want to. It's quite nice, has a good light weight."

"I like that it isn't rough. I don't love the feel of rough sisal people."

"Right, this is meant to be sensual, comfortable."

The instructor got everyone's attention and sat his own sub on a tall stool where he could be easily seen. He started with a single-column tie, very basic but eye-catching. "What do you think, petit? Shall we try it?"

Harley nodded, then whispered. "It's cool to talk?"

"Yes. It's absolutely fine to talk. You can ask me or Master Kelvin questions too, if you have any." He took Harley's hand and rested his arm just so, then started slowly wrapping the rope around his boy's wrist. He didn't have much interest in tying Harley up in general, and this was a simple knot he already knew, but he enjoyed the closeness and the sensory parts of the exercise. As long as Harley was willing to be with him, feel this, he was happy.

Harley watched with a curious gaze, and he had to wonder how much his boy was taking in.

He made sure there was room between Harley's wrist and the rope and then tightened the knot down and lifted his boy's wrist by the free end. "Not too bad."

"Dude." Harley grinned at him, wiggling his fingers. "Look at that."

"I like how it looks." Mostly he just liked that they were doing this together. "Have you ever wanted to be restrained? Sexually, I mean?"

"It's never come up, really, but it's sure pretty, isn't it?"

He nodded. It was pretty.

"How did it go here?" Kelvin stopped by and had a look at his knot. "May I?" That was to Harley, as Kelvin reached for his wrist.

He looked at Harley. "Do you mind if Master Kelvin has a look, petit?"

"No, sir. Didn't he do a fine job?" Harley held his hand up.

Kelvin looked the knot over. "This isn't your first knot, Winter. This is very pretty. Not too tight. Perfect."

"No, it's not. But it's his. And thank you."

"Lucky boy. Firsts are so much fun." Kelvin let go of Harley's hand and moved on to the next couple.

"So... Do you like this? I mean, you know how..."

"I like how it looks. I like the act of tying the knots. I know how because I've been to many of these classes over the years." He winked at Harley. "I don't feel a need to restrain my lovers. Not with ropes, anyway. Just with...words."

"Mmm..." Oh, that was a happy, interested little sound, wasn't it?

"We are a good pair, Harley, aren't we?" Kelvin started showing them how to do the double column, and he removed the knot on Harley's wrist as he watched.

"More than good, hmm? You and me. We're solid."

"I think so. I hope so. I do love you, petit. I struggle with that a bit, though, which has nothing really to do with you." He started threading the rope around Harley's wrists, lashing them together, and he felt like it was strangely metaphorical, given their conversation. He'd like to bind his boy to him, but he knew better. He didn't care for the hazards of Harley's job, but he knew he had to leave that decision to the boy. He wanted Harley to live with him, but Harley wanted to ride out his agreement with Oliver and he had to respect that too. The demands he'd made of lovers in the past hadn't worked out well for him at all. Little birds had wings. Clipping them was a mistake.

"I know you do. I'll just have to be steady. You'll learn."

Harley had a way of warming him in the sweetest way. He gave his boy a fond smile. "I'm an old dog, but I don't give up easily."

"I'm just stubborn as a mule." Harley winked at him. "Maybe even two mules."

Winter chuckled and finished his knot. "Can you out-stubborn that?"

"Not in my experience, sir. Not a bit." Harley didn't tense against the bondage, in fact he seemed easy, relaxed.

Harley's respectful 'sir' made his mouth go dry and he swallowed hard. Sometimes when Harley used the term he was just being polite, and sometimes it seemed to mean more. He wasn't never sure, and he didn't care. Respect was intended and that was enough for him. He ran his fingers over the knot, admiring the pale rope against his boy's tanned skin. "Pretty. How do you like that?"

"It's... I thought it would be weird, maybe scary, but it's not. It's... I don't know how to describe it, I don't think."

"It's trust. It's a physical symbol of trust. More than symbolic I suppose." Harley had put himself in Winter's hands. He didn't take that responsibility lightly.

"It is. I do." Harley leaned in to whisper. "With more than my hands, lover."

Winter kissed him, curling his fingers around the rope that bound his boy's wrists and tugging him closer. Harley went, groaning deep in his chest, opening for him.

He let it happen; he'd never cared who saw him, just as he'd always liked to watch. Eventually, though, Kelvin's voice cut in.

"May I interrupt?"

Winter broke the kiss off gently. "Of course. Show Master Kelvin your wrists."

He didn't miss the wince as Harley shifted back to his pillow.

Harley lifted his wrists, the white shocking against Harley's skin.

Not quite as shocking as the blood stain growing on his boy's Wranglers, though.

"Winter." Kelvin nodded his head at the stain.

He nodded. "Yes, thank you, Kelvin. He got stitches today. It looks like we've overdone it a bit."

"The knot is perfect." Kelvin left them and he took Harley's wrists.

"What haven't you told me?" He asked softly, making quick but gentle work of removing the rope.

"I'm sure they just pulled. I'll find a bathroom and rinse it out and tighten the bandage."

"No, you will not. We are going home." He reached a hand down to help Harley to his feet.

"What? I didn't even finish my margarita..."

Winter pointed to the growing stain on those jeans. Stubborn was one thing, foolish was another.

"We go home before you end up in the ER. Can you get up?"

"Of course." But by the time Harley was up, he was pale under the tan. "I think you're right about the drink. Can we go?"

"Mhm." Winter tucked an arm around the boy to give him something to lean on and sat Harley against a bar stool so he could call a car. "Deacon, can I get a towel please?" He was concerned Harley had torn the stitches open, but he'd settle for home first and then call for help if they needed it.

"Of course." Deacon looked down, and his eyes went wide. "Let me get you a car. One minute, Sir."

"Yes, thank you." He put his phone away and let Deacon handle it. "Clint doesn't like blood, you know. We'll hear from him tomorrow."

One of Harley's eyebrows winged up. "I didn't bleed on his floor. I didn't know I was bleeding. I'll totally wait outside."

Winter snorted. "I'm sorry, petit. That was mostly a joke. We'll probably hear from him, but only to see how you are doing."

Deacon gave him a towel and set out a glass of water. "In case you're thirsty, Harley. Does it hurt? What did you do?"

"He had an accident at work and has stitches."

"Oh, man. That sucks. Take it easy, okay?"

"Thank you. I will. I'm sure it just pulled some, you

know?" Harley shrugged one shoulder. "Shit timing on my part."

"There's never a good time to get hurt, petit. Let's go out and look for our car." The ones that Deacon called came quickly; they were usually on retainer with the club.

"Yeah. Still. I want to have a good weekend with you."

"We will have a wonderful weekend. We'll be together." He led Harley outside and straight into the waiting car.

He hated the way Harley was bleeding, and it seemed to take forever for them to get to his building and up the stairs.

"Let's get to the bathroom, petit, and get your shirt off. How are you feeling? You look so pale. Be truthful, please. Just tell me everything." He tried to keep calm, but he wasn't the stoic type. He was worried about his boy.

"A little tender. I want to get cleaned up and maybe fix this evening. It's been a rough day."

"We're home. We can make some tea and put on a movie, or read some of your book, or just snuggle on the couch." Once they made it to the bathroom, he helped Harley get undressed, removing his shirt and bloody jeans.

The bandage was soaked, and when he removed it, finding a line of stitches along the muscled thigh. A couple were popped, the blood moving sluggishly.

He frowned. He wasn't sure what to do. It looked bad, but he wasn't thrilled with a papercut so, maybe he wasn't the best judge. "That doesn't look good to me, Harley. Perhaps I will call for someone to come repair your stitches."

Harley winced and shook his head. "It's just sore. I don't think I want it touched a lot more…"

"Will it stop bleeding?" He found his sad little first aid kit. It wasn't much, but it did have gauze and tape, some butterfly bandages, Neosporin.

"It has to. I don't want to leak no more." Harley swallowed hard, like he was taking in a frog.

"We'll try. I'll put some pressure on it." He got a washcloth and soaked it in some warm water to clean Harley up. He was going to have to put his foot down if it didn't seem to want to stop. He knew that. He just...he knew how stubborn his boy was, and he really didn't want to argue.

"It's just a thing. I'm cleared to go back to work Monday." Harley kissed his temple. "Hey. It's good to see you."

"It's good to see you too." He sighed. "Though you should have been more forthcoming with what happened to you today at work. I ought to have known about this before it got to this point."

"I didn't think it would be so gross."

"So what? Something happened at work, and I should know about it. I need to know everything." That was how this worked. He took care of Harley; how could he do that if he didn't know everything?

"It really hurt." Harley seemed so embarrassed.

"Of course it did. It still does, I assume. My poor petit." He combed his fingers through Harley's hair and kissed him. "You can tell me, it's all right."

"Fifteen stitches to the inside, seven on the outside. I didn't pass out, but I wanted to puke."

That seemed rather significant, but he tried not to make a big deal of it and worry his boy more. "So brave, my boy. I'm proud of you." He spread some ointment thickly over the stitches before putting on new gauze.

"Thanks. I didn't want to just not be here with you. Especially not after my day."

"I understand. And while I appreciate that, please don't keep something like this from me again." He tried to be careful as he taped down the gauze. "Tomorrow I will run out and get some more of this."

Harley touched his cheek with trembling fingers. "Can we sit together for a bit? Then I'll make us a sandwich or something."

He took Harley's fingers and kissed them. "I'd like to hold you for a while. And if you're hungry, I will make sandwiches and you will stay off your feet. Hm? Let me get you something to wear."

"Thank you. For everything." Harley sighed for him but smiled.

He cleaned up, then brought Harley into the bedroom. "Pajama pants, do you think? Or shorts?"

"Either works. I'll try to not bleed on anything." Harley winked at him, obviously trying to lighten things up.

"Mm. Thank you. My living room already looks like something from a murder mystery, so we don't need to add to the aesthetic." He handed Harley his pajamas and once the boy was dressed they moved to the couch. Harley cuddled right in as if he was drinking in comfort.

Winter gave it to him, holding him close, smoothing fingers over his boy's skin. "I can help you, Harley. I can always help. I want to, in fact, because I care about you and the things you need are important to me. But you can't keep things from me. You can't pretend you're fine when you're not. You have to let yourself be vulnerable with me, so that I can see you. Really see you. And so that I can let you see me too." He didn't know a better way to say it, what he needed from his boy was...everything. He needed everything.

"I'm sorry, lover. I just... I wanted to have a fun night. I'd been looking forward to it. I—I know it sounds silly, but I miss you." Harley's cheeks were red as beets and hot.

"No, petit. That isn't silly at all. I missed you too. I didn't get nearly enough kisses from you this week and, although I've been alone in my bed for quite some time, it feels lonely without you next to me now. It's not silly. Unless we're both silly, in which case, it hardly matters." He smiled at his boy, trying to help them both relax.

"Right. I'm totally willing to be silly together." Harley chuckled softly. "I was scared. I'd never been in an ambulance, and that emergency room?" His eyes went wide. "I've never seen anything like that. I felt totally overwhelmed."

"They can be overwhelming, because they tend to be very busy in this city. But you've learned your lesson and you will call me next time, like a good boy, yes?"

"Even if you're at work? I mean, wouldn't that bother you?" Harley stroked his jaw. "I would have loved to have you there. I felt...like a yokel. Like a stupid redneck."

He loved the affection in that soft touch. It was new to him, sweet, kind, and also exciting. "You are neither, though I understand what you mean. I don't know that I would have felt less uncomfortable, but at least we'd have been together. So yes, at work. In the middle of the night. In the middle of anything."

"You can call me too. I know how to get around town. I will come help you whenever I can."

"Such a good boy. I will. If I need you, I will call you, I promise." He nuzzled noses with Harley. "Or, if I just need tacos."

"Mmhmm. Or if you're lonely in bed. I would be here, every day, for that."

He had to take advantage of that. "Then move in with me." He said it like he meant it this time. Like it wasn't a question as much as a decision made. "Move in with me now. Tomorrow."

"Okay. I have to keep paying rent for two more months. Is that cool with you? I gave my word that I'd do that."

"Of course. Pay rent. Spend the night with Oliver sometimes if you like. Just...live here with me." Now they were getting somewhere.

"Yes. I'll start right now." He felt it—how this tension in Harley dissolved, and he hadn't known it was there.

"Right now. That's it, petit. It's what we both need. Too many nights away makes us careless. Makes us worry."

"And lonely. It was so easy to learn how to sleep with you."

He nodded. "And lonely. Alone is okay. Lonely is miserable." And he didn't need any help with the rent, so eventually he could talk Harley into a different job. Maybe something at the library. Maybe something in the park. Maybe.

"Yes. I want all the nights, lover. I want to come home."

"Home, that's just right, petit." Home was where Harley belonged. Home was just how this felt.

Harley cupped his jaw, fingers stroking gently. "Home. Love."

18

The throbbing of his leg woke Harley up, and he slid out of bed, hoping that walking on it would ease the ache. It didn't—but at least he wasn't dreaming about the hospital, about the blood.

God. That had been intense. He'd seen a little girl come in with a dart stuck in her eye, a dude with a gunshot wound, and a scary homeless guy who kept chewing on his own fingers.

Nasty stuff.

Still, he'd survived it, hadn't he?

He limped into the kitchen and got himself a big glass of milk.

He'd survived it, got through it himself, like always. He was the most reliable person he knew after all, except maybe Winter. Maybe.

Winter made him soft inside, made him want to give himself over, somehow. It was weird and wonderful, and if he was honest, a little scary.

But he was moving in now, so it was a kind of scary he

was going to have to get used to. Good thing he was used to doing things that frightened him.

He leaned against the counter, pondering food. Was he hungry? Maybe he just wanted milk...

"It's too early." Winter wandered into the kitchen, mussed and sleepy, and reached for him sliding a hand over his abs.

"Too early?" He leaned in, letting Winter hold him.

"For work." Winter pet him, hands sliding over his skin. "Not that you will be going to work."

"No. It's not time. I'm hurting a little, huh?"

"Of course you are. I'm so sorry, my sweet boy. You need some ice and some Tylenol. The hospital didn't give you anything stronger, did they?" Winter let him lean, holding some of his weight easily.

"No. They said Tylenol should do it." He lifted his face for a kiss, begging for the connection.

Winter smiled at him first, then gave him the kiss he was looking for. "I hate that you're hurting, petit. But don't you worry, I'm going to take good care of you."

"You don't have to." But he loved that Winter was willing.

"Oh, but I do. And it's important that you allow me. You must." Winter looked at him seriously. "It's what I need."

"Yeah?" He frowned, trying to work that out. "I don't want you to think I'm weak or lazy, but..." He just wanted to set his load down a second.

"Oh, no, petit. You are none of those things. Accepting help, being vulnerable, is a measure of trust, that's all. And helping you helps me too. It...fills me up. Makes me feel taller. Do you understand?"

"I think so. I want to understand, but maybe not tonight. Now I just want you to hold me." That was the god's honest truth.

Winter nodded. "I'd like that too." Winter pulled an ice pack from the freezer, wrapped it in a dishtowel, then ducked under Harley's arm. "Come back to bed, love."

"Yes, sir. I'm all over that." He leaned, trusting in Winter to hold him.

Winter got him settled in bed with ice on his leg before he brought Tylenol and a cup of water from the bathroom. "Take these," Winter put them in his hand and climbed into bed with him.

"Thanks." He took the pills and cuddled in, sighing softly. "You okay?"

"You're hurting and exhausted and wondering if I'm okay? I'm fine, petit. More awake than I should be at this hour, but I'm not alone there." Winter's arms wrapped around him and pulled him close, encouraging him to lie against Winter's shoulder.

"No more lonely nights." He loved that idea, that this was their bed, their home.

"That's right. You're mine now. You belong here. It's good to belong, isn't it? I remember when I finally found that, it was almost hard to believe at first."

"It is, but I'm willing to believe in you."

"You won't be sorry. I promise you won't." Winter was real and solid and that sounded like a promise he could believe in too.

"I'm not." He took a deep breath, let it out.

"Is there something on your mind, petit? Is it your leg?" Winter slid a warm hand down his arm. "You're okay?"

"I'm okay. Have you ever held yourself so stiff that you're scared to relax, and you have to force it?"

"Not in a very long while. But I remember not realizing just how tightly I'd held things in until it all came out in a rather embarrassing, tear-filled rush. It wasn't an easy day, but the next one was better than the hundred before it."

"I'm sorry. I never ever want to make you cry." He would rather fuck himself up.

"Oh, no. Not you, petit. You could never, unless I'm just that happy. And don't be sorry, it was good day. Working through hard moments isn't a bad thing. But you don't have to be scared to relax, I'm here, you're in my arms. You're as safe as can be."

"I know. I know in my heart and soul. I just need my body to hear me."

"When your leg has healed a bit, I'll make sure your body understands too, petit." Winter's voice dropped to a whisper. "I will be very convincing."

"Mmm...promise?" He couldn't stop his soft hum for love or money. That whisper was everything.

"I will make you any promise you want me to, petit. Anything at all."

"Just give me a chance to learn all the rules, lover." He was good at fitting in, mostly, and he'd do it.

"We're making them up, remember? Sam's excellent advice." Winter's tone was gentle, soothing. "The club has some rules, but we only have the ones that suit us."

"Yes. I only care about suiting you. You're the one I'm with."

"You were made to be mine, Harley. I'm convinced of it. And everything I've learned that came before you, was preparing me for this. For you."

"Mmm...for me? Yeah?" He loved the way that sounded.

"Just for you, mon petit. My love."

"Yes. Yes, your love." He relaxed, his eyelids drooping. "Your own."

19

It had been so long since Winter had taken on a lover, a boy that was his, that he wasn't sure anymore what came next. Harley would be moving in; that was settled, and Winter would see that he was offered membership at the club, but beyond that, he was at a bit of a loss as to what he wanted their relationship to look like.

He was in love, that was easy enough to understand, but he needed more than love—not a lot more, but more. That worried him, in a way he had never been worried before. He'd met his other lovers at the club, almost exclusively, and they all knew—they already understood what was expected of them and they gave it to him without being asked. Which meant that Winter hadn't ever asked before.

And Harley, sweet boy that he was, hadn't ever been asked, not as far as he knew. If he asked for obedience, would Harley agree? If he asked for subservience, would that ruffle the boy's proud feathers? What if he wanted Harley to kneel for him?

He wanted to be the boy's sun, moon and sky. And he

was so close. But asking...would that be risking more than he was willing to lose?

He sighed and stroked his fingers through Harley's hair, watching his boy, soothing him back to sleep when his injuries threatened to wake him.

And he wanted Harley to kneel for him. He wasn't sure he could be truly, fully happy without that, or something reasonably like it. The outward show, the respect of his peers was more important to him than he wanted to admit, but he wasn't going to lie to himself or to his boy.

Harley nuzzled into him with a soft little moan, the sound happy and musical. Satisfied.

He liked that sound, the sound of a happy boy. That he understood and knew how to nurture. With Harley, that was the easy part.

Harley wanted to make him happy—he didn't really question that—and that delicious innocence that had intrigued him so was now a bit problematic.

He'd call Clint, except for the hour, and the fact that Clint would tell him what he already knew. If he wanted to play it safe, he'd leave things be as they were. But if he wanted to know everything they could be together, he'd take the risk.

Harley lifted his head, frowning. "You okay? You're all tense."

"Am I? I must have stiffened up sitting in one position for so long." It was a lie, he was comfortable as could be with Harley in his arms, but Harley had surprised him, and he didn't know what else to say.

"Ah. That sucks. You need me to rub your back?"

"You should be sleeping. We both should be."

"Mmm... I love sleeping with you. I'm going to bring my

pillow over too. I bet you love it." Harley was dozing, just talking randomly.

"You have a special pillow?" That was sweet. He hunkered down with Harley, pulling the quilt up over them both.

"Uh-huh. I brought it from home. It's the perfect pillow, and it's got a soft pillowcase." Harley snuggled in, cheek on his shoulder.

"Funny, the things we take with us when we leave for good. Right? The things we feel are important." He yawned, relieved that sleep might be coming for him too. Harley's presence was so calming, reassuring.

"Mmhmm...books, and the best pillow, and my favorite pair of boots."

"Yes. Books. Baseball cards. A horse figurine." And a few other things—a barrette that was his mother's. A pocket knife. The cash from his father's wallet. "So long ago."

"A horse figurine. Will you show me later? I'm going to buy a LEGO thing to make and add to your—our—house."

"LEGO." He chuckled. "Of course I will show you. It's ceramic. I painted it myself." Our house. We, us, our...such tiny words that meant so much.

He kissed Harley's forehead. "I will bring us muffins and bagels from the bakery in the morning." After they slept in. He didn't much care if they even saw morning.

"Mmm... Muffins." Harley sighed, going boneless. "Your favorite are the lemon ones, don't forget."

"Lemon poppyseed." He grinned. It had only been forty years, but it was kind of his sleepy boy to remind him anyway. Harley was easier. "You just like muffins."

"Uh-huh. All the muffins. And bagel sammiches. And waffles..."

"So...bakery food." He yawned again. "No more talking, petit. Sweet dreams."

His boy was heavy and quiet, and soon the soft inhalations and exhalations started, breath sliding over his skin.

Winter let himself drift, listening to Harley breathe, eyes closing and staying that way.

20

Harley woke up with his thigh throbbing, but it was tolerable, more an irritation than real agony. He was going to have to ponder how it was doing for Monday, but he'd cross that bridge tomorrow.

Today he wanted to be with Winter.

He'd woken up alone, but he didn't mind; he could hear soft classical music coming from the living room and there was light coming in under the bedroom door, and he knew there would be breakfast treats waiting for him and hot coffee.

He was a spoiled brat, but it felt so nice—to know Winter cared this much. He would totally return the favor. Totally.

The bedroom door opened slowly, and Winter poked his head in. "Petit? It's noon, love. Are you awake?"

His eyes went wide. He never slept 'til noon. "Noon? Oh, lover. I'm sorry. I crashed and burned. I didn't mean to waste the day."

"Waste? No, petit. Resting and healing are not a waste. I just wanted to be sure you weren't hurting too badly. I only got up a little over an hour ago myself. I like to sleep in sometimes; it's nice."

"Oh. That's not too bad. I don't want to miss a whole morning, but an hour is fair. Thanks for letting me rest." He sat up and swung his legs off the bed. Hopefully he hadn't bled on Winter's sheets.

"This looks a little better. Less angry. I'm sure it hurts still, though. Would you like more Tylenol? I'll get you some."

"Yes, I think that'll take the edge off. It feels more bruised today." More sore and less, fucking hell.

Winter went to the bathroom and came back with Tylenol and a cup of water. He got a grin that was slightly wicked. "I think you'll be pleased with my breakfast selections."

"Mmm... I love breakfast." He took the Tylenol, then chuckled at Winter. "You look like the cat that got the canary."

"I did not get a canary. But I did get cronuts." Winter winked and helped him out of bed. "You need pajamas, hm?"

"Unless you want my willy waggling all over..." he teased.

Winter laughed and handed him pajama pants. "Ordinarily I wouldn't object but...cronuts. I have berries and coffee too."

"You rock. Thank you." He bent his leg without thinking to put on the pants, and his breath caught as everything pulled. Whoa.

Winter caught him, hands steadying him. "Oh, my. Does it hurt that much?"

"Sorry. Sorry, it surprised me." And yeah, it hurt.

"Let me help, petit." Winter took his pants. "You can steady yourself on my shoulder. Will that work?"

"Thank you." He grabbed Winter's shoulders and carefully stepped in, feeling less shaky. "All I have to do is get through tomorrow, right? The third day is the worst."

"Is that right? Well, then we will take it easy. A quiet weekend. We can read and play cards." Winter pulled the pants up and carefully tied the drawstring at the top for him. "Shirt?"

"Please, yes. It's just a touch chilly. Breakfast sounds so good." He needed to make today better for Winter. Seriously.

Winter found him a t-shirt, helping him put it on even though he didn't need it, fingers roaming over his skin. "There are several choices. I waited for you. The coffee is hot."

"Thank you." He kissed Winter's cheek, loving the way Winter smelled. "You're good to me."

He liked the way Winter still blushed at his compliments too. "Come sit, lean on me. It's a beautiful day." Winter helped him into the living room where the sun was streaming in from the back garden through the French doors. The treats were set out on the little table and Winter sat him in a chair. "I'll get your coffee. And then—well. And then we'll talk. Hm?"

"Sure. I love talking with you." It was one of his favorite things, in fact.

"My good boy." Winter disappeared into the kitchen for a minute and came back with his mug of coffee and a couple of plates. "There are muffins, cronuts, a couple of slices of this amazing looking pumpkin loaf, biscotti..."

"Wow. It smells like heaven. What should we start with?"

He took one of the plates with a grin. "It's like an embarrassment of flaky riches!"

Winter chuckled happily. "There's a knife there. I was thinking about a bite of everything." But Winter reached in and took the lemon poppyseed muffin.

Oh, those were Winter's favorite. Excellent. "You can have that whole one. I know you like them."

"I can save you a bite. If you're a particularly good boy." Winter winked, then broke off a bit of muffin and ate it, humming as he chewed. "Mmm."

Harley nibbled on a bit of cranberry muffin and drank his coffee. Oh man, that was good. "I wanted to apologize for last night, love. I wasn't being the most logical man on earth."

"You've made better decisions." Winter reached over and took his hand. "I understand why. But next time you'll know better. We have time. If one night doesn't work out as planned, we have others."

"I hear you. I just... I got in my own head." He'd been unsure about Winter, if he was honest, and how he felt settled in his heart.

"You're used to being on your own. And trust is scary at first." Winter sipped his coffee, watching him. "But I'm going to need trust from you. You're going to need to rely on it sometimes. Do you think you can do that?"

"I do trust you. I sleep with you. That's the biggest trust ever."

"That's the most intimate trust for sure. But there are other kinds of trust. Trusting me to keep you safe. Trusting that if I ask you for something you don't understand, there is a reason. Trusting me to answer your questions honestly."

"I will do my best, totally. We're still learning each other, I think." But Harley thought he could do that.

"We are definitely still learning. Especially here at home, just the two of us. But I have a question for you, an important one, that I want you to think about. It's okay if you don't have an answer today." Winter smiled at him. "Have you had enough coffee for a complicated question?"

He chuckled, the question easing any tension the approaching conversation might have caused. "I am, yeah. Bring it on."

Winter relaxed back in his chair, eyes watching him carefully. "If I asked you to kneel for me sometimes, here, and at the club like the other boys, the subs...how would you feel about that?"

He tilted his head, pondering that. "It would be weird, I guess, and a little uncomfortable, but I wouldn't be the only one, so I wouldn't stick out like a sore thumb."

Winter nodded at him. "So, you'd do that for me, even if you don't know why right now?"

He nodded. "I think so. I mean, I really think so." He wasn't like a balky horse, and it wasn't like Winter was going to let anyone disrespect him. In fact, he thought it was pretty damn clear that disrespect was sort of a big deal in Winter's circles.

"You're a wonder, petit. And you really are mine." Winter lifted his hand and kissed his fingers before letting them go to sip his coffee. "I was very worried about asking you that question. I wasn't sure how you would take it. But it's...the club is both complicated and incredibly simple depending on how you approach it, and I've been a member for a very long time. Some of the rituals and customs there are important to me."

"Rules, yeah. Sam told me about that some." And he would try to figure them out.

"Thomas and Sam have found ways to make it work for

them, and we will do the same. I will make you a promise that I will not require you to do anything at the club that we haven't tried here first. I can't promise I won't ask for something new, but you may refuse. And I can't promise I won't ask you to do something you weren't fully comfortable with here, either. But if I do that it will be knowingly and understanding your reservations so I don't push you too far." Winter watched him while he took that in silently. "And you should remember, you always have your safe words. They can be used anytime, anywhere. It doesn't have to be a scene, your hands don't have to be restrained, those words are yours and carry weight always."

He didn't know what to think, but he was smart enough to understand when shit was important, to know when to nod and take it in and learn. "I'll do my best. This is all real new."

"I know. I know, petit. I appreciate that you're listening. That you're willing to try."

"I am. I just—who invented this? It seems so big, but it's not, like...anywhere hardly."

Winter chuckled. "Invented? Invented what, Harley? Kink?"

"I guess? I mean, I don't understand. Where did it come from?" It had to have come from somewhere, right? Everything had a start.

"I'm not sure. But humans want what they want, and they find a way to get it." Winter winked at him.

"Yeah. That's true, huh?" He was going to have to get on his computer and look.

"No kneeling any time soon, though. Not with your stitches." Winter stood. "Do you want some juice? I do."

"Please. Yes, please. I'm dry as a bone." He reached out, grabbed Winter's hand. "Thank you, Sir."

"Mm. I like that, petit. My boy." Winter left him, and he heard the fridge open and close and the clinking of glasses.

What an odd mood Winter was in. Unnerved and worried, but sure at the same time. Harley wasn't absolutely certain he got it, but he was here for it.

Winter handed him a big glass of orange juice and sat in his chair again. "I'm going to have a bite of something else. Maybe...this." Winter picked up the knife and peered at the treats on the table.

He chuckled softly, so in love it hurt. "You can't decide, love?"

"You're telling me this was easy for you?" Winter shook his head. "I'm going to try this chocolate thing. How do you feel about collars? Sub collars. Like the ones the boys wear at the club?"

"Well...you mean like the jewelry or the heavier ones? I can't do any jewelry at work, it's dangerous, but we could talk about it, sure." That seemed fair.

"We wouldn't break any work rules. No. I just wondered if there was something you'd seen that you liked...whether you preferred one kind over another. If I wanted to give you one."

"I like the chain ones—it seemed...natural. Is that right?"

"A chain would look very nice around your throat, petit. Very nice. Your eyes made up, a heavy but decorative chain around your neck, and something...a harness like Sam's or a corset like Oliver's...you would be beautiful."

His cheeks burned—less from embarrassment than pleasure, because he wanted Winter to watch him, think of him as beautiful.

"And that blush only makes the picture sweeter. Do you like that idea, petit? Dressing for me?"

"I like the idea of you looking at me. I like the idea of you wanting me."

"You like that I enjoy watching. Watching you. I like that you are mine after the watching is over." Winter sipped his juice and...watched him.

"I'm yours all the time, but I like how I turn you on." He'd never felt ugly, but Winter made him feel sexy and beautiful and necessary.

"You do. I'm waiting—patiently—for your thigh to heal enough that I can prove it to you. It's not a bad thing, having to wait."

"I was so mad it happened," he admitted. "I was looking forward to dressing up for you."

"I do like your fancy look. Dressy cowboy. Soon, petit. It will be delicious. We just have to be patient."

"Patience isn't my strong suit..."

"Nonsense. You just have to want it bad enough. Like when you wait all week for me, not touching yourself, even in the shower, saving all that need just for me." Winter set his empty juice glass down. "You can wait when you want to."

He swallowed hard, his body reminding him that Winter was absolutely right. "You have a point there..."

"Yes." Winter's smile was bright and happy. "You see? Wonderful boy."

"You make me ache some." And he didn't mind that at all.

"Well, if we're being truthful, you have a similar effect on me, petit." Winter winked at him. "I always want you."

"I like to hear that. I never felt hot before you. Never." Now he felt sexual, strong, desired.

"So many new things all at once. New feelings, new

desires, new lifestyles...but you're handling it all beautifully, petit. I'm so impressed. So proud."

"Thank you." It was mostly a lie, but he was beginning to understand that was being a grown-up—you faked it until you figured it.

The doorbell buzzed, making them both jump. "My goodness. Are you expecting anyone, petit?" Winter got up and went to the door.

Who was he going to expect? Raul from the work crew? Fuck.

"Is he okay? What was with all the blood?" Oliver sounded like he was high.

"Oliver? It's customary to call before you—"

"Is he okay?" Ollie pushed past Winter and into the apartment. "Harley? Are you okay? Where are you hurt?"

"Ollie? Are you high?" He sat up straight, frowning deep. "I got hurt at work. Nothing serious. A couple stitches on my thigh. Are you okay, man?"

Ollie rolled his eyes and sat with him. "No, I'm not—well, maybe a little but that's not—Raymond is at work. Don't tell on me. How is bleeding everywhere not serious?"

Winter stood a few feet away, arms crossed and silent.

What the actual fuck? Harley wasn't sure what was up, but he could be all comforting and shit. "I won't tell anybody anything. I bled on my jeans. Cuts bleed. What's wrong? Do you want a bite of pastry or something?"

"I just heard you were hurt, and you didn't come home... I mean I know you're with Winter now, but I—"

"Oliver. That's enough." Winter took Ollie by the shoulders and stood him right up. "Harley said he was all right."

Ollie's eyes were huge. "I was worried."

Winter raised an eyebrow.

"Sir. I was worried, Sir. I'm sorry, Sir."

Winter nodded. "You need some coffee and a shower."

"But—"

"Do not argue with me, boy."

Ollie dropped his eyes to the floor, nodding.

"I—" What did he need to say? He didn't even have clothes to offer Ollie, and honestly, he kind of wanted to hump Winter a little. "How can I help, y'all?"

There. Fall back on your manners. That's what Sam said.

"We're fine, petit. Oliver just needs to sober up and remember to be respectful." Winter was watching Ollie.

"Yes, Sir."

"You kneel right there next to the couch and don't bother Harley. I'm going to get you some coffee." Winter went into the kitchen, and Ollie did exactly as he was told. He knelt, eyes on the floor, and didn't say another word.

"I—Thank you for checking up on me, Ollie," he whispered. "You're a good friend."

Ollie glanced at him and nodded, then looked right back at the floor.

Winter crouched with Ollie and handed him a mug of coffee. "That's a good boy. Thank you for doing as I asked. Drink this. And then we'll see what's next."

Ollie nodded again. "Thank you, Sir."

Winter touched Ollie's shoulder and stood, then picked up his own coffee and sat. "I suppose word got around about your injury."

"It's just a simple cut. It's sweet, but there's no need to worry." Folks got hurt. It was a thing.

"Subs gossip. It probably started out as you having a cut to you losing your leg." Winter chuckled.

"Actually, he still had a leg; he was hemorrhaging blood

though. Bleeding everywhere." Ollie looked up long enough for Winter to stare him down again.

"A little bleeding, but Winter helped. I may have popped a few stitches."

"Popped! Harley! Are you insane?"

"Boy." Winter barked. He actually barked. Harley hadn't ever heard Winter raise his voice, let alone be so commanding.

"Sorry, Sir. Sorry. Sorry, Sir." Ollie stared into his coffee and went quiet.

He stared at Winter. Where the hell had that come from? His gentle lover was...intense.

Whatever that was, it disappeared as quickly as it had come on. "Do you need a warm-up on your coffee, petit?"

"Do I—Oh. I...please, lover? Thank you." He felt like his head was spinning.

"Me too. I'll be right back." Winter gave him a gentle smile, before going to the kitchen again.

"It—it's good coffee." Ollie's voice was soft, tentative.

"It is. I'm moving in with him. I'm going to still pay rent like I promised, but I want to be with him." The words tumbled out of him, and he had no control.

Ollie looked up at him sharply. "What? You're moving out? Already?"

"I love him. I want to sleep with him at night, huh?" Already? Was it too soon?

"Oh. Well. I get that. It's just... I'll be...alone. I'll talk to Raymond."

"So much chatter from a boy who is supposed to be silently contemplating sobering up."

"Harley just told me he is moving out, Sir."

"I know. I heard."

"I'm sorry, Ollie, but this is—" What? Important? Saying

that just made Oliver seem less important, and that was shitty.

"Oliver. I asked Harley to move in. We need each other, it's that simple. I'm sure you can understand." Winter handed him his mug. The coffee was hot and smelled so good.

Oliver nodded. "He loves you, Sir."

"And I love him too. Finish your coffee."

"Yes, Sir." Ollie took a big sip.

"If you're ever scared or need me, I have my phone, Ollie. You can call." He wasn't deserting anyone.

"Any of us at the club will help if you need it, Oliver. Or you can call Raymond. Perhaps it's time to take a long, hard look at that relationship."

"I—I want to." Oliver sighed softly. "It's complicated."

Wasn't everything? Harley didn't understand how the world spun, not really, but he could handle it. Sort of.

This time instead of barking, Winter smoothed a hand over Ollie's head. "Breathe right now, Oliver. You're not losing Harley; he'll be around to spend time with. How about a hot shower?"

"Yes, Sir. Please. My head hurts so bad..."

"Oh, dude. That sucks so hard."

Winter took Ollie's empty coffee mug and set it down, then helped Ollie up. That was more the man he knew, nurturing and kind. "Come with me, boy."

Winter gave Harley a smile and a wink.

He smiled back, and snagged half of a cronut, leaning back and nibbling as he thought about what he'd learned this morning.

It wasn't long before Winter was back, going straight for his coffee. "He's going to take a nice long shower, and then we can send him home."

"Is he—Did he just get fucked up?" He'd been there. More than once.

"Oliver is complicated, from what I know of him. I think he was probably coming off something, and he knew better than to be alone. I don't think he would have come to me ordinarily, except that you are here, and he trusts you. His current Dom isn't a lover; he's solely Oliver's Dom, so there are boundaries. Raymond may have not been available."

He didn't understand. "How does that work? He doesn't love Oliver?"

"Well, he may, or he may not. He cares about Oliver's well-being. He takes care of...a portion of Oliver's submissive needs and gets some of his Dominant ones fulfilled in return. But that is as far as their arrangement goes, as I understand it. Unless something has changed, Oliver is free to date as he pleases."

"Oh." Yeah. No. He still didn't understand. It was okay. He didn't have to. He was cool with that, and he would ask Ollie if he needed to. Oliver could *talk*.

Winter sat with him. "Are you all right, petit?"

Honest. Be honest. "I'm a little confused, but this is all new. You were...different. It was intense—not bad. A little hot, but intense."

Winter's eyes went wide. "Oh. Oh, yes, I'm sorry. I imagine that was—I don't like to raise my voice, but Oliver was spinning out and needed a firm response. He needed to get out of his head. It's not my style, but like anyone at the club, we take care of one another."

"Fair enough. You were what he needed. That rocks." He reached out and took Winter's hand, kissed it.

"I tried, anyway. Between that and the coffee, he seemed to settle. I'll give Raymond a call in a bit and see what he thinks we should do."

He nodded, but he didn't see what the relationship was. It wasn't meanness. He just didn't get how someone did this outside of love. It sucked.

"I think you need a good, old-fashioned cuddle." Winter put an arm around his shoulders and tucked him closer. "Just remember that in this lifestyle, everyone has to figure out what works for them. There's a lot I don't understand, except that I know when people are happy. If they're happy, then I don't need to be concerned with how they get there."

"Totally. That's true in everything, right? Everyone has a different thing, different needs." That he understood, bone-deep. Every relationship was its own thing.

"That's right. Good boy." Winter kissed his temple. "The best relationships are when both parties get what they want, but also what they truly need."

"You know it. I'm into that philosophy, lover. All the way." That was something he totally understood.

"Me too, love. Ours has been surprising to me in the best way." Winter hummed softly.

"Yes. This has been the...the most fascinating and wonderful love." That wasn't too stupid to say, right?

Winter chuckled. "We sound ridiculous, don't we? So smitten. But I don't mind."

"We do, but no one can hear us." And they were gay guys. They were allowed to be ridiculous out loud, weren't they?

"Master Winter?"

"Ah. Let me see what Oliver needs." Winter was up again and a minute later, led Oliver back to the living room, wet-headed and wrapped in one of Winter's thick robes.

"Better?" He sat up straighter, making room beside him.

Oliver nodded and sat close, leaning on him a little. "Are you sure you're okay?"

"Yeah. I won't even miss work, I bet. Just a little tenderized." And bruised. Whoa bruised.

Winter sighed. "Don't listen to him, Oliver. He'll be staying home from work on Monday at least."

Ollie beamed at Winter. "Yes, Sir. Thank you."

Harley was so tempted to stick his tongue out at Winter. And Winter just looked at him with a raised eyebrow like he knew it, too. That look was just daring him to say something.

He was almost willing to do it, but he wasn't feeling it, and he wanted a little of the cuddling. He wasn't used to it, and it made him feel...amazing.

He got a nod and Winter sat again. "Eat something Oliver. I went overboard at the bakery this morning. I just couldn't decide. We've been cutting bites off of everything."

"Just a bite. I'm a little queasy, Sir."

"Can I have more cronut next?" Those were two of his favorite things, smooshed up into one.

"Of course. They are spectacular." Winter cut a bite and held it out for him. "Open up, baby bird."

His cheeks heated, but he did it, didn't he? God, he was learning all sorts of shit about himself.

Winter smiled at him, and he knew, without a doubt, that he made the man happy. Him. Just...being himself. "Give your friend a bit, petit. A little sugar might help him."

"Here. You love berries. Try a bite of this." He cut off a bite of blueberry muffin and offered it to Oliver.

"Oh, you're feeding me now, handsome? I'll take it." Oliver opened his mouth and took the offered nibble, then chewed like it was the best thing he'd ever tasted. Harley could tell he was trying to smile, trying to relax. "Mmm!"

He reached out and squeezed Ollie's hand. "You got a friend, you hear? I got your back, whatever it is."

Oliver shrugged. "Thank you, but I'm just fine, honey. Don't worry your handsome head about me."

"That's what friends do, man. We're here." And that was all he could do.

Oliver looked at his hands and nodded. "I should go home. Huh? I'm...in the way. And tired." Oliver stood carefully. "I'll get dressed."

He glanced at Winter, not sure about this plan. Something was wrong. He could tell. He didn't know what it was or how to help or anything, but he was smart enough to see a friend was hurting.

"Oliver. Go take a nap." Winter pointed to the bedroom.

"I can nap at home."

"Boy." Winter's head tilted, but that was all he said.

"Yes, Sir. On...the bed?"

"Of course."

Oliver nodded and slunk back into the bedroom.

"All right, petit. You wanted him to stay, he's staying." Winter switched to the couch with him and patted his good leg. "You're worried?"

"Aren't you? Doesn't he seem...off?" Was this just normal? He didn't think so. He'd been living with Ollie for months. This wasn't normal. He wasn't silly.

"Well, he needs his Dom. I didn't ask, but perhaps something happened there, or perhaps Raymond simply wasn't available. Oliver isn't very good at asking for help when he needs it—I'm not sure he understands himself that well yet. Not like you do. You seem to have a handle on what you need. We'll let him sleep for a bit, hm?"

"We will." Him? A handle on things? Go team him because he felt a little like a poser.

"This has been an eventful weekend so far, hm? Should we go to the club tonight for a drink, or stay in?"

"Can we decide in an hour or two? It has been...busy. Surprisingly busy." And he was thinking about a lot of shit.

"Of course. I didn't know if you were feeling one way or the other." Winter sat with him and sipped his coffee and seemed perfectly happy just to hold him and be still and quiet.

It worked for him, because his brain was spinning, and the outer ease helped, a lot.

Winter's music was still playing softly in the background, and that was all the sound there was until Winter suddenly asked him, "If you hadn't come to New York, where would you have gone?"

"I thought about New Orleans and San Francisco both, but Jackson was the one I called, and it was kismet. He needed someone to rent, I needed out, and out I came." He'd been so lost, so fucking sad, and he needed family. It didn't have to be his mom, but he needed folks.

"Funny how things happen." Winter nuzzled his ear.

"Isn't it? I came here to find you." He didn't doubt that at all.

Winter nodded. "I still can't believe you just walked right over to my table. You're so brave."

"I had to. You were too beautiful not to." Winter was still the finest man he'd ever seen.

Winter shook his head, but he saw the shy smile. His lover was pleased.

"Seriously. I thought it was worth a shot. And it was. You were." He was a dork, but he was willing to put himself out there.

"The makeup thing was a little bit of a test, you know. I decided I had nothing to lose. I'd feel bad about it, but it all went so well; the real joke was on me. You were shockingly beautiful. Are beautiful."

"I was... I felt so different. Like someone fancy." And sexual and fine.

"I'm so glad you like it. It's one of my favorite things. It's sexy and sensual, it has a fantasy feel, and that you enjoy it is a real turn on. You looked good in the full makeup, but the eyes are enough...more than enough, really."

"No one has ever thought my eyes were pretty before you." He had brown eyes. He wanted blue or green.

"They're endless. Deep. Rich, enticing pools I'd like to dive into." Winter's lips brushed his ear as he spoke.

"Oh." His lips parted and he sighed, because suddenly he was awake, alive. Right there with Winter.

"That's my boy. This is a nice space to relax in." Winter's fingers slid over his abs. "Things we have to look forward to."

"It's exciting, isn't it? All the things we get to do together? Even silly stuff." Was it like this for all lovers? This anticipation?

"I'm used to doing things alone, and so... I don't do much. I don't go out alone much. I don't take long walks. I don't meet men. So yes, everything we do is exciting to me. Even just this."

"Maybe especially this." Because this was private and special and sweet.

"Yes." Winter hummed agreement and pointed to the shallow mantle over the little fireplace. "That's the horse figurine I painted."

"Oh, too cool!" He loved that—that Winter had given that memory a place of honor.

"I took it with me because I was proud of it. It's never been about memories or anything sentimental like that. I was just...proud of the way it came out. I thought that was important to have with me."

"I get that. It's cool." He thought he was more caught by the webs from back home, but he knew he hadn't had so long to be used to thinking about what he missed.

"You, though. You miss home some, I think." Winter kissed his cheek.

"I miss knowing that I had one back there. It hurts some." Because your folks were supposed to love you, no matter what, and that was a lie.

"You have to change your thinking. You had to leave so you could come to me. You needed to find your real home. A home of your own, of your choosing. This is healthy, and that wasn't. You see? Shift the narrative in your mind."

"I did, and it wasn't. I don't even want to go back. I just wanted to be important." Now, here, he was, he thought.

"That is not in doubt, petit. You are important to me. And I say that without reservation because I know I am important to you. I didn't trust that at first. That's been…a revelation for me."

"You are. Like truly. You are amazing." And his lover. That was so fucking right.

Winter kissed him. "You want me to read to you, petit?"

"I'd love that. Please." Winter always understood if he dozed off. Always.

21

"So Harley is doing better?" Deacon looked adorable this evening, wearing little more than a leather harness and a smile.

"Much. He got back to work on Wednesday." Though it had been a struggle to keep him home that long, and even then he'd insisted that Harley take it easy. The boy worried about rent, worried about keeping his job...it was maddening. And worth it.

"Have you seen Oliver? He hasn't been around this week."

"Mm. Yes. He had a rough weekend, and Raymond took him home." Though not until late Sunday evening. He'd been away with his husband. "I imagine they've been working together."

"Oh, I'm sorry to hear that." Deacon set down his glass of wine.

"He'll be all right. He seems to land on his feet." Raymond would make sure of that.

"Yes, Sir. I'm sure he will. Can I get you anything else?"

"No, thank you. I'm going to sit here a bit and wait for my boy."

Harley had gone for a retirement drink for a man at work, so he would be joining Winter here instead of at home, and he'd already had a couple of texts, one from the bar, and one from the subway.

He loved how impatient his boy was to see him. It made him feel warm, loved. That's why he'd decided to wait here at the bar instead of heading right for his table. He was eager too.

He'd worried the entire three days Harley had worked that his boy would come home with more popped stitches, and he'd fussed about the state of Harley's bandages, but it had worked out, mostly. He'd been glad at least that Harley had finally moved in so he didn't have to wonder all week how everything was healing.

Moved in was a funny way to look at it. Harley barely owned anything. He'd cleaned out half of his closet and a small dresser in the bedroom so that Harley would feel like he had some space of his own, but the boy had hardly used any of it.

He checked his phone and didn't see a new text from Harley, so he sent one of his own.

I'm having wine at the bar. Should I be embarrassed that I am watching the door for you?

Nope. Say hi, lover. And then the door opened, his boy right there, looking handsome, if a touch tired.

He slid off his bar stool and met Harley partway, giving him the kind of greeting that was on his mind, which was perfectly acceptable in this club. He slid a hand around Harley's waist and kissed him as if they hadn't seen each other in days, pulling his boy right in close.

"Mmm..." Harley hummed and pushed right into the curve of his body.

He danced Harley in a little circle before ending the kiss. "Come have a drink, let's sit. I want to hear about your day."

"Absolutely. I better stick with beer since I had some already." Harley kissed his cheek.

"Was it a nice party?" He led Harley to the bar for his beer. The scent of shampoo filled his nostrils, his boy smelled squeaky clean.

"It was a bar with pizza and beer. He was happy to be retiring, I think?"

"Most people are. That's hard work you do."

Deacon hurried right over with a big smile. "Harley! Don't you look so handsome? Glad you made it. What can I get you?"

"I'd like a... I think I want a Coke, man. I've had two beers already."

"A Coke it is." Deacon pulled a glass down and filled it with ice.

Poor Harley sounded worn out. "You're tired, petit. I can tell. We won't make it a late night." Winter wanted to stay a little while though, long enough to dance with his boy at least. It was one of his favorite things.

"It's not bad, lover. I want to dance with you." Harley's lips brushed his ear as he whispered low. "Then we can go home and..."

His boy. Always so ready for him. It made him feel proud, and a little swoony, to be honest. "And yes. My fingers are itching to touch you, petit." He turned to Harley and caught his lips in another brief kiss.

"You make me dizzy," Harley whispered against his lips.

Goosebumps spread over his arms and a not-unpleasant heaviness settled into his balls. He wanted what he wanted, but he was enjoying the wait. "Grab your Coke, and let's go sit."

"Sounds like a plan, Sir." Harley was relaxed, dressed in his good jeans, flat belly obvious in the tight t-shirt.

"What do you think about cuffs? On your wrists? Nice leather ones that are soft inside?" He'd been thinking. Fantasizing again. It wasn't a bad thing, but sooner or later he was going to say something and hit Harley's limit. He had no idea where that line was, so all he could do was test. Push his boy a little and see what happened.

"Soft inside? That's probably okay. I'd give it a go."

As long as they were comfortable...he loved his boy. So willing. So easy going. He reached out and circled his fingers around one wrist. "I'm going to see what I can find you."

Harley smiled and lifted his arm, kissing his closed fingers. "You spoil me."

"And I will keep doing it every chance I get." He loved doing it. Not only was Harley worth spoiling, but it never went to the boy's head. He was always grateful, no matter what Winter did for him.

"Is that Raymond? Oh, yes. It absolutely is and look at Oliver. Oh my." Raymond was turning heads in his full leather regalia—vest, pants, heavy boots, even a hat. There was a bit of a crowd between the Dom and where he and Harley were sitting, but he could see that Raymond was leading Oliver on a leash that was attached to his heavily bound wrists. The boy's eyes were cast low, but it was hard to see much else.

Harley glanced over, a frown creasing his forehead. "Winter?"

"Hm?" He picked up his wine and took a sip. Harley was concerned. That was interesting. "I think that's Oliver, yes?"

"Yeah... I..." That frown deepened.

"What's the matter, petit?" Now that the room settled down a bit, he could see that Oliver was in a tight corset with chains attached that went to black alligator nipple clamps and little leather shorts that left nothing to the imagination. Raymond all but ignored him as he ordered something at the bar.

He knew Raymond. Whatever the Dom was ordering would be alcohol free. He played hard, but safely.

"That feels...mean, huh? Ugly?"

He knew what Harley was saying, but the boy didn't understand what he was seeing. "Why do you say that?"

"I don't—I don't know. It's not to you?" Harley, for the first time, seemed truly vulnerable, like the boy needed him, right now.

"No, it's not ugly. Not to me." He tangled his fingers with Harley. "Everything you see in this club is consensual. That means that both parties have an agreement, and the sub has safe words he can use to get out of any situation instantly, no questions asked. Oliver isn't using his words, is he?"

"No. No, but I know Ollie. It's just not... I don't know. I'll figure it, I guess."

"I know what I think is going on, but I can't say for sure. The only way to know for sure is to talk to Oliver. Though, perhaps not tonight. He seems rather deep in his subspace."

Harley nodded, but he didn't say anything else, or look at Oliver even. Those eyes were on his Coke.

"Petit." He needed Harley to understand something important. "Look at me, please."

Harley glanced up at him. "Don't be pissed. Please. I'm trying. This is...a lot."

He blinked at his boy, startled. "Why on earth would I be mad at you? I agree, that is a lot to understand."

"I just... I know it's not cool, to be wigged out. Everyone's supposed to get it, but—I'm glad you're not mad."

He set his wine down and pulled Harley into his lap for a hug. "Petit. I don't care about cool. You feel whatever you feel, and we'll talk about it. All I wanted to tell you was that I am never going to ask that of you. I don't need that, I don't think you need, or want that. That's not us."

"No. No, it's not. I'm not... I need... I mean, I don't..." Harley stopped, blew out a hard breath. "Can we talk about this later, please? At home where it's just us?"

"Yes. Of course." He slid his fingers through his boy's hair. Poor boy. He was right; it was a lot to take in, especially when it was a friend, and it didn't make sense. "Shall we dance, petit?" He could hold his boy for a bit, settle him, enjoy the music.

"Yes. Yes, please. I would love to."

It was a rush, how Harley responded to him, immediately, trusting in him without question.

He smiled and stood, lifting Harley to his feet. He didn't need to say much, so he just pulled his boy along by the hand and onto the dance floor, under a pool of purple light.

Harley cuddled right in, almost, but not quite, clinging.

The boy was truly rattled. He swayed to the music and kept his arms tight around Harley, breathing with him.

Harley relaxed, breath slowing, body responding to him, melting into him. "Love this, dancing with you."

"As do I." He nuzzled Harley's ear. "Holding my sweet, beautiful boy." Nothing could rush him off the dance floor with Harley; it was a place he felt like they came together more or less as equals and understood each other best.

"Yours. Thank you. This is heaven."

"Mhm." He danced them deeper into the crowd, where they could blend in and disappear a little. So, his boy did have limits, at least in his head. Winter was going to have to tread lightly when Harley was ready to talk.

Right now, though, Harley was focused on him, on the music, and there was a freedom and a joy that they found out here, moving together.

This is it, Winter. He realized with clarity that this boy was going to be the centerpiece of the rest of his life. He couldn't bear any other outcome. So whatever Harley needed from him, Harley would receive. It was that simple.

He stepped back and twirled Harley under his arm, watching the smile bloom on his boy's face.

"Fancy!" They laughed together, just happy.

"That's me. So fancy." He twirled Harley into him so Harley's back was to his chest and hugged him close. "You're so graceful."

"I love to dance. It's so much fun." Harley's ass was grinding against him, matching rhythm.

Oh, he liked that game. He dropped his hands to Harley's hips and moved with him. "I'm going to take you home in a minute."

"Promise?" Oh, sexy kitty.

"I promise. It's going to be a long night." A little fun, a little nap, a little more fun until the sun came up. They might be having breakfast at dinner time on Saturday.

"I love how you think." Harley leaned his head back, looking up at him with dazed eyes. "I love *you.*"

"I love you. I've waited a lifetime for you, petit, and I love you very much." He spun Harley again, deciding it was time to go. They could dance at home with less clothing between them. "Let's go."

"I'm right with you. Let's dance at home in private."

He gave Harley a nod and pulled him off the dance floor. He deliberately steered them away from the tables and toward the bar to avoid the possibility of running into Raymond and Oliver. "A car, please, Deacon?"

"Yes, Sir." Deacon picked up the phone.

Harley stayed close but slipped Deacon a twenty in the tip jar.

"I saw that." He winked at Harley. He couldn't argue, the boy had found a way around the rules that suited him.

"He's a good bartender. That's important."

He chuckled. "It is if you want good drinks."

"Your car is outside, Master Winter."

"Thank you, Deacon. Have a good evening." He took Harley outside into a lovely evening and headed for the car.

They had a full dance card.

Harley cuddled into him in the car, fingers twined with his, body warm and solid against him. "You have plans for the weekend?"

He chuckled. "You. You are my plans for the weekend." He thought Harley could use some extra attention after his long week. "You work so hard, and your leg is probably still sore. I'm sure you probably need some downtime."

"Stitches come out Monday." Harley winked at him, because he'd caught his boy starting to remove the stitches this morning, and he had fussed a bit.

"Good boy." Winter slid a hand between Harley's thighs, hoping the driver was minding his own business. "We'll try to not pop any more this evening, hm?"

"If they come out, they're meant to, right?" Harley's lips parted and he wiggled under Winter's touch.

"I suppose so." He didn't get too frisky, but he left his hand there, hot against the boy's thigh and pressing into his groin. "I'm ready to be home."

"Yes, Sir. I hear that." Harley kissed his ear, tongue tracing the shell.

That made him shiver, brought his need into even sharper focus and reminded him how long he'd been waiting and how much he wanted his boy. "Mmm. Soon, petit."

"Not soon enough, sexy lover." He loved this confidence, especially mixed with the earlier vulnerability.

But the car did eventually get them home. By that time, he was buzzing and warm. And he hustled Harley out of the car and into his building.

Their building—his boy lived here now.

"Mmm...open the door, lover, so I can pounce you."

"Oh-ho. So eager." He opened the door and held it for Harley. "Home sweet home."

"Yay!" Harley grabbed his butt and squeezed, playing madly.

He closed the door and threw the bolt, then turned slowly on his boy, backing him into the apartment. "Naughty."

"Never..." Harley's eyebrows waggled at him.

He snorted and reached for Harley, tugging on his shirt. "I want you to take all of this off. Start here."

"Naked? Me?" Harley laughed and stripped off his shirt, shaking his butt.

"Yes. Entirely. And hopefully not too long from now." He'd settle the boy down in a minute, but he couldn't help his grin, watching Harley play, seeing his boy so happy.

"Not too long. Just a little anticipation." Harley opened his belt and fly.

"Mmm. Because we like that." He backed Harley into the bedroom. "Waiting just another minute."

"Yeah. Just." Harley licked a line up his throat.

He arched his neck for Harley, tucked a hand around one jean-clad butt cheek and pulled his boy closer. His

Harley was hard as nails, belly tight, and Winter loved how the boy fit in his hands.

His need for his boy was making his heart beat hard. "I don't want to wait anymore." He gently pushed at Harley's jeans. "I want inside you, petit."

"Yeah. I'm all in for that, lover. I want your cock."

"Take off your boots." Winter lifted his own shirt off and watched his boy as he kicked off his own shoes.

"Why hasn't a cowboy's uniform got flip-flops?" Harley was chuckling as he leaned against the wall and worked his boots off.

He laughed and undressed. "I'm not complaining." Not one bit. He watched Harley move, so graceful even just tugging on his boots.

The stitches on Harley's thigh looked like spiders crossing the tight skin, and Winter was ready for them to be gone.

Every time he looked at them he worried about that job; they reminded him that it could be dangerous.

"That leg." He sighed. "I want to wrap you in bubble wrap to keep you safe from everything." He took a light kiss.

"Scars are sexy, remember?" Harley licked his bottom lip.

"Maybe. But stitches are scary." He focused on Harley's eyes. They'd be gone in a few days. Right now he needed to focus. They'd been waiting so long. He slid his hand over one smooth hip and across those gorgeous, hard abs.

"Mmhmm..." Harley arched and pushed into his fingers. "Want."

"Yes, petit. All night." He slid both hands up and around to Harley's nape, pulling his boy into a deep kiss. Their hips ground together, cocks pinned between them, making them both moan as they moved.

He wanted to eat Harley up, snap him up and turn him inside out, but he had to be gentle, easy with that poor thigh. It was bad enough, that thing with Oliver had shaken Harley up a bit, he would just go easy, make sure his boy was okay.

"Come to bed, love." Winter backed toward the bed, pulled Harley along with him.

"Mmm...coming..." Harley chuckled softly, rocking against him.

"Good boy. Careful, petit," he said as Harley climbed up on the bed.

"I'm good. I just need you." Harley wiggled that tight ass at him.

God, it was too much. Winter tugged open a drawer and tossed a rubber and the lube on the bed, climbing right up after his boy. "Pretty petit."

"And all yours, right? All of me. I promise."

Harley's words made it hard to breathe as emotion swelled in his gut, his chest, and brought tears to his eyes. Winter nodded, believing every word that his boy said. "Yes, petit." He pushed Harley onto his back and took a kiss, it was easier than explaining himself.

Harley wrapped around him, taking every single thing he offered and begging for more.

He rocked against Harley, his own need making his eyes cross. "Beautiful boy. I am yours. I promise you too."

"Good. Fuck me now. Show me." His boy had a wicked, dirty mouth.

"Naughty." But he didn't argue, he wanted that too. He rolled his condom on first, then popped open the lube. "Such a mouth. What if I make you wait even more?" He pushed one of his boy's knees up and back and found that sweet hole with two slippery fingers.

Harley groaned and nodded. "Anything. I want your fat cock."

He couldn't stop his grin. "Such talk. You shall have it, soon enough." He slipped his fingers right in, twisting and moving them to get Harley relaxed and ready for him.

Harley groaned and panted, writhing underneath him like a sylph. It was luscious. Delicious.

"I could watch you forever, petit." But he wouldn't. He was out of patience. He yanked his fingers away, replacing them with his hungry prick. "Oh god." He took a breath before he moved again, he needed to find some control.

"This is better than watching." Harley rolled up, pushing down on Winter's cock, body like a fist.

"Harley!" he shouted. God, he never shouted. He pushed in deeper, hips grinding into his boy, helpless to hold back as he felt he should.

Harley's head bobbed, gaze fastened on his, drinking him in. He stared back and caught his boy's cock in his fist, working it, fingers gliding base to tip.

"Oh..." Harley's belly rippled visibly, and Winter could feel the pressure all around his cock.

Fuck that was so pretty. He surged into Harley, letting go, giving in to what he wanted—what they wanted. All he knew was heat and need and he felt so...free.

Harley met him, over and over, teeth clenched together. "Fuck yeah."

He pushed his boy's knees back farther, groaning because the change in angle was just right. Just so fucking perfect. He was breathing hard and working harder. "Yes... you...so good."

Harley was like fire around him, and he wanted to scream with it. His hips slapped lightly against Harley's ass, the sound a sweet counterpoint to their moans.

He'd reel it in, but he was so close, and Harley was right with him; they were riding this wave together and it was beautiful. He tried to focus on Harley and work that pretty cock through his fingers just the way his boy liked it.

Harley moaned and arched, cock leaving wet kisses on his skin, but it was the way the sweet body worked him that told him how close Harley was. "Soon."

"With you." He ducked his head and dug deep for what Harley needed, adding strength to his thrusts and gasping at the way that tight ass responded. He stared into Harley's dark eyes. "My boy."

"Yours. All of me. Fuck, Winter... I'm fixin' to shoot."

He nodded. "Good boy. Yes." Jesus, yes. Harley would push him right off the cliff, and he longed for it.

"Good... Fuck!" Harley's hips snapped and his boy shot, heat spraying between them.

God, the heat and the scent would have been enough, but the way that Harley's body tightened around him, the way his boy's climax made all those muscles around him flutter made his eyes cross. He thrust needlessly against Harley a few times before everything uncoiled and let go; his orgasm rocked him and stole his breath, and his jaw dropped open in a silent shout.

Harley relaxed under him, panting hard, tongue flicking out to wet his lips.

Winter kissed them, while they were shiny and wet. Just a quick peck between ragged breaths. He traced the line of Harley's jaw with more kisses as he worked to focus again, to think, to tell Harley how wonderful he was.

"Uhn." Yes. Yes, exactly.

What he wanted now was an armful of his boy. He shifted, dropped the condom in the trash can by the bed and rolled onto his back, tugging Harley into his arms. "Petit."

"Love." Harley cuddled in, breathing hard for him.

"So much love," he agreed, sounding hoarse. "So worth the wait."

"I'm glad." Harley kissed his jaw.

"Are you okay? Was I too...rough? I...you are irresistible to me." He rubbed his hand over Harley's back.

"Rough? You were great. I shot hard." Harley was almost purring.

"Okay...if you're sure. It's just that you're hurt so I worry." He nuzzled his boy.

"Shh... I'm fine as frog hair."

He hushed, because Harley did seem fine. He was better than fine, himself. He was...inexplicably happy. Devastatingly in love. And pleasantly exhausted. He let himself close his eyes.

22

Harley grabbed his bag and thought about going home, but...

But.

That but was unnerving. That but worried him. That but was something he didn't understand.

But, what?

Harley didn't know.

And that was weird.

It wasn't something he could talk to Winter about. Winter worried. Winter got stressed. Winter started to doubt.

That wouldn't work.

His phone rang, shocking him, and he smiled as Oliver's name showed up. Okay. Okay, this was a sign. He answered with a smile. "Hey, man."

"Hey, Hardworking Harley. You haven't called me in *days*."

"I know. I miss you, man. Bad." He was hardworking and fucking tired. He was considering calling in sick for a month.

"You do? Can you come over? We'll order pizza. Please?" Ollie sounded so hopeful.

"Yeah. Yes. I'll call Winter and meet him at the club. He's got a late meeting-retirement deal at the library anyway." Oh, that sounded like an amazing idea, seriously. He could use some one-on-one buddy time.

"Oh, this is so great! Yay! Oh, god I have to clean up around here. Okay, gotta go. See you soon. Love you. Bye!"

The call ended right there.

He texted Winter, letting him know that he was seeing Oliver and would meet him later so they could dance.

Maybe Oliver could help him work out this whole 'but' shit.

"I got you." Ollie shouted into the intercom before buzzing him in. He trudged up the stairs to find Ollie waiting in the open doorway to the apartment. "Sweetheart!" Ollie threw his arms open wide. "Come to Ollie, honey."

"Oh, I've missed you." He grabbed Oliver up and held on tight. "It's been weeks, buddy."

"I know!" Ollie hugged him hard. "I mean, I saw you but... I haven't been able to say hi. Come in! I ordered our favorite pizzas, and I found the remote, and there's even beer in the fridge."

There it was again—that 'but'.

Weird.

"You want one?" He headed for the fridge.

"Sure." Ollie locked them in, then flounced through the kitchen in his flowy shirt and comfy, harem pants. He didn't seem high, and he definitely wasn't in a corset. "Tell me everything. Are you living in a Winter wonderland? Basking in domestic bliss?"

"He is wonderful. He is so sweet and dear." And kind.

Generous.

Sexy.

Smart.

Ollie nodded, but he got a squinty-eyed look. "He is a great guy...but?"

"I know! Why is there a but? How can there possibly be a but? I love him!" What was wrong with him?

Ollie shrugged. "Well, I don't know. When did the 'but' start?"

"I—maybe when I got hurt? Around then?" He thought so anyway. He wasn't sure exactly.

"Oh." Ollie frowned. "Well, that explains why you didn't come talk to me sooner. I was on a bit of a bender, huh? Sorry about all that."

Damn. That sounded intense. "Are you okay? I mean, you're feeling better?"

"I'm good. Raymond is...you know why Raymond and I work? Because I'm a mess and he's good at cleaning a mess up." Ollie waved his hand. "But we're talking about you, honey. So. What happened after you got hurt?"

"I just... I feel like he thinks I'm...breakable, maybe? Fragile?" And he wasn't.

"Breakable? He-Man Harley the furniture mover? You can lift three of me. How can he think that?"

"I think it scared him—the stitches, the blood. I'm used to it. And then..." He freaked out about Oliver and all the...bondage?

Ollie leaned forward. "What? Did you faint or something?"

"No!" He sighed softly. "No, but it was big for him, and then I sort of...well, I saw you all gussied up and sort of... psyched myself out, to be honest. I'm sorry."

"Me, all...? Oh..." Oliver's eyes went wide. "Oh, that was

that night. With the leash and the...ooh. You didn't like that, huh?"

What was he supposed to say about that? He didn't want to be an asshole.

"That's cool. It's not everybody's thing, you know? It's my thing, and it's Raymond's, thing so we work. Master Winter doesn't like leashes, I don't think."

"I just...it was shocking. I didn't say anything much to him. We never talked about it."

The intercom buzzed and Ollie let the delivery guy in. A few minutes later he had a slice of pepperoni in his hand.

Ollie took a bite of his weird pesto and something white pizza and leaned back in the couch. "Okay. So. You never talked about it at all?"

"No. No, it never came up." Was that weird? He figured if it was a thing, they would, but they hadn't. "And we're having a good time together. I'm not unhappy."

"You don't look unhappy. But...let's talk. I mean about the whole leash and leather thing. What's bothering you? You're not going to hurt my feelings, I promise."

"It just creeped me out, you know? It felt..." Seriously, was he going to admit it was scary? No way. "I just didn't understand."

"What are your needs, Harley? That's what it's about. I need to give up control sometimes you know? And if it's not getting high, it's Raymond. Raymond is better for me for sure. What do you need? Have you told Master Winter? Does he know?"

He didn't know how to answer that; he didn't think. He just didn't want to have to be...treated with kid gloves.

"He doesn't know." Ollie frowned. "Well, you know what they say; the Doms may be all toppy and macho, but the subs are the ones with the real power. So, do you know what he wants?"

"For me not to hurt him, not to leave him, and I'm not interested in doing that at all. I love him." Harley rubbed the back of his neck. "I just want him to look at me like I'm the hottest thing ever. Like—he wants me so bad he stops thinking about the guys that did leave him."

Ollie's frown shifted slowly into a wicked grin. "He already thinks you're the hottest thing ever; everyone sees it. But if you want to eclipse a long line of broken hearts? Maybe...maybe you should dress the part."

"Dress the part? I got my good jeans on, man." But Winter liked makeup. "Will you help me do my eyes up?"

"Your eyes, yes. Your good jeans, your boots, and a little surprise under your dress shirt, I think." Ollie stood up. "Come in my room."

"Okay. You get it, huh?" He sort of felt like he needed that. Someone who was in his shoes a little bit.

Ollie turned and gave him another hug. "I get it, sweetheart. My kinks aren't your thing, yours aren't Jesse's thing...that fine. That's good! We just want our friends to be happy. You've hauled Master Winter out of a long funk, you know? He loves you, right? He just needs a little shock to leave it behind."

"Yeah. Yeah, I just want to be...so much he can't bear it." He wanted to be Winter's fantasy.

"We've got this. Eyes first. You just sit there and imagine yourself as the sexiest man on earth. This is going to be great."

Ollie looked positively gleeful as he went to work, the eyeliner going on cool and thick. "Here, so you can look if you want to." Ollie handed him a hand mirror.

"It's always so weird." It was like becoming someone else. Fun, exciting, but weird too.

"Good, weird? I mean if you don't like it..."

"Wonderful weird. It's like... I don't know, being special." Being a little magical.

"Yes, honey. That's it. A little boost isn't a bad thing, right? To help you feel like you but...more. More you. Better you."

"Sexy me." He took a deep breath and let himself relax and just be with Ollie, be in the moment.

"Okay. Eyes are done, have a look." Ollie tapped the mirror in his fingers. "I put on just a little smoky shadow too. I hope it's not too much. If it is, I can fix it."

He looked like a movie star, like someone that was mysterious. "It's perfect."

"Yeah? Cool!" Ollie put all the makeup away and disappeared out his bedroom door. "You trust me? Take your shirt off," Ollie called back.

"Okay." He stripped down, setting his shirt aside. His nipples were hard, his belly pulled in.

"I found the perfect thing." Ollie came back with something leather in his hands and opened it up. It was one of the corsets he'd seen in Jackson's closet. Black leather, dark red accents, lots of chains. "What do you think? It's even got a sort of western vibe, right?"

"Do you think I can pull this off?" Was he that sexy? He wasn't sure.

"I do, but let's get it on you and see how you feel. If you don't like it, we can take it off. Okay?" Ollie worked the fabric open. This one's easy, it zips up the front and then I can lace the back."

"It's fancy, huh?" He zipped the front up, the boning surprisingly strong, pressing at his belly a bit.

"Yep." Ollie settled it on his shoulders. "Take a deep breath, and push it all the way out, you know? Suck your stomach in."

He followed Ollie's instructions and as soon as he sucked in his tummy Ollie tugged on the laces and tightened the corset around his middle.

"Whoa." His body felt...different. Everything felt electric.

Ollie laughed. "Too tight? Can you still breathe? Mostly?"

"I can. I can breathe. Does my butt stick out?" He felt like his ass was pushing out.

"Your ass looks fabulous. Your hips too. You have broader shoulders than Jackson, this is going to look amazing on you. Wait until you see." He rocked on his toes, trying to keep his balance as Ollie tugged and tightened the laces. "Almost done. Have you thought about having your nipples pierced?"

"What? No!"

"No? You should. I have some magnetic ones, if you really want to drive him nuts."

"Magnetic? Really?" That could be hot...

"Yeah, they even have chains dangling from them. They hold nice and tight." Ollie walked around him and tugged on the corset here and there, then obviously checked out his nipples. "Yeah, I bet they'd look great."

"Let's try them. I mean, if you don't mind." He might as well be hung for a sheep as well as a lamb.

"God no. Black, I think. They'll look great. Should I get you some ice?"

"Ice?"

"Honey, you have to make them hard..." Ollie rolled his eyes. "Don't gape at me. I'm getting ice. You...here." Ollie opened up a closet door and there was a full-length mirror, then headed for the kitchen. "Look at your amazing self."

He couldn't believe how different he looked, how lean and different and sexual.

His butt did stick out though, like 'o fuck me now'.

"Mm. Yummy right? Look at that ass. You're hot as fuck, honey. Breathe." Ollie attacked one nipple with an ice cube.

He made a strangled noise, his eyes flying wide open. "Fuck! Cold!"

"Yes, honey. It's *ice*." Ollie held it there until he was sure he was numb and then fastened one magnetic clamp in place. "One down, one to go."

He stared down, and he'd be damned. It looked like there was a barbell with a little loop of chain dangling down. Whoa.

The other one seemed to go on easier, and then it was done. Ollie stood behind him as they looked in the mirror. "Look at you. You're a knockout. Master Winter is going to lose his mind. How do you feel?"

"Nervous, hot, excited." He felt ready to see Winter. To make an impression. To get fucked hard.

"Then it's time to go meet your man. Let's get you a car. I'll finish your pizza; you can't eat in this thing anyway." Ollie giggled and pulled out his phone.

"You're not coming?" How could he travel like this? He looked like a...horndog.

"No, honey. I've got plans with Raymond. Or...he has plans for me. Anyway, I'm busy." Ollie reached for his shirt. "Pull this on, and button up."

"Yeah. Yeah, okay." He grabbed Ollie's hand. "You're happy, though, right? You're okay?"

"I'm okay. I promise. I had a bad week, but Raymond is

the best. He cares about me." Ollie kissed his cheek. "You are going to have an amazing night."

"I care about you too. A lot." He hugged Oliver tight. "No matter what."

"Sweetheart, you're my best friend." Ollie wasn't shy about hugging him back hard. "I know, you're new here, but you are. I love you. I'm glad you're happy."

"I love you too. Can we have supper on Monday? Winter works 'til eight that night."

"Yes." Ollie gave him a bright smile. "Here, out, whatever we want. It's a date. Maybe we could make it a regular date if he always works late."

"I'd love that. Wish me luck?" He buttoned up his shirt.

"Nope. You don't need luck. You just need some confidence. Walk in there like you own the place." Ollie followed him to the door. "A little advice though. When those clamps start to ache, you ask Master Winter to take them off, okay? Especially since it's your first time."

"Okay. I'll ask. You think he'll like them?"

"Honey, he's going to love this. We'll talk Monday. Go. Your car is here."

Right. Going.

Please, God. Let Winter like this.

23

Winter was aggravated when he arrived at the club. He'd meant to get there earlier but so many people left his colleague's little goodbye party at once that he'd had trouble getting a ride. He'd texted Harley so he knew his boy wasn't waiting for him at least, but he liked things to go to plan.

He was here now, in any case, and he had just gotten to his table with his wine. He wanted to know how Harley's day was and how his leg was feeling now that the stitches had been out a few days. He took a sip of his wine and a deep breath. Harley was fine. And he'd be here. Soon.

There was a little commotion up near the bar, and Winter glanced up, less interested than irritated, and—

His heart stopped.

He wasn't sure he was even breathing anymore, and he didn't care.

He knew a piece of that boy—the piece with the eyes rimmed in eyeliner so dark and fancy and staring right at him. But the boy in the corset and—was that hardware? That piece of his boy he didn't know at all.

But his mouth went dry with wanting. Wanting to know everything.

He picked up his wine and took a sip, then set it down carefully. He heard someone say his name, but he didn't answer, because he only had one thing on his mind now.

Harley.

He couldn't move, so he held out a hand, beckoning, inviting his boy to join him.

Harley walked to him, laced up with hint of a waist making his boy's shape purely sexual, the sweet ass begging for attention. His nipples were decorated, red and pouty, chains swinging as they moved. Best of all, those dark eyes were painted and fastened on him.

"Petit." He slid his hands over the corset, the warm leather and boning exciting his fingers, and gently nudged the clamps with his thumbs. "You're...stunning." Stunning didn't seem to touch it, but it was the biggest word he could find. His boy took up the whole room. Every bit of oxygen.

"Hey." Harley licked his lips, making them gleam. "I was hoping I could buy you a drink."

"A drink?" He wanted a taste too. He pulled Harley closer and took a kiss, gliding his tongue along Harley's.

"A drink. A dance." Harley nuzzled his jaw, then bit his earlobe. "A hard fuck like I deserve."

"Is that what you want, petit?" He pulled his boy toward the dance floor, hands roaming and landing on that perfect ass, not caring who saw them. "Is that what you're doing? Seducing me?"

"Am I?" Harley's eyes flashed. "Do you want me?"

He tugged his boy close, so Harley could feel the answer to that question against those hard abs even through the leather and boning. "More than ever."

"Good." Harley cuddled in with a soft, hungry hum.

Winter whispered in Harley's ear. "Tell me about what it is you deserve, boy."

"I want every inch of your cock. I want to feel you next week. I want—no, lover, I need you to fill me to the brim."

"Every inch. Because you're mine." He heard the rumble in his own chest and swallowed hard. He could be a Dom. Get a key. It had been such a long time.

"Yes. I did this for you. So you could see how bad I need you."

"I need you. I love you, petit. You're so beautiful right now. Do you know how gorgeous you are?" He was dancing them back off the floor. He'd get a key at the bar. He didn't want anything but Harley.

"I don't. Show me." Harley held him tight, arousal pouring off his boy.

He wanted nothing more. "Go to the bar, ask for a key." He gave Harley a gentle push, following so he could watch that perfect ass move across the room.

Harley sashayed to the bar, and Winter was hard as nails as he followed, waiting to see what Harley would do. Everyone was going to be hard as nails looking at his boy.

"I need a key, please."

Deacon's eyes got huge, but his surprise settled quickly into a knowing grin. "A key? For Master Winter? His favorite room is open." Deacon went to a cabinet behind the bar where rows of fancy keys hung on little hooks and took one from a familiar spot. "Here you go. Room four."

"Thank you."

"You look amazing, Harley. Go you!" Deacon's grin was huge and knowing.

"I knew you had it in you, Harley." Jesse grinned at his boy as they walked by.

Everyone was watching them, and all he felt was pride. Well, pride, and a burning hunger for his boy.

Harley stopped at room four. "I'll take the key, please, petit."

"Yes, Sir." Harley stepped right up, pressed against him, dangling the key.

He loved this room. So plush and comfortable. Heavy curtains, which hid toys he wouldn't be using, a high-backed fainting couch, and a solid lock, which made a loud clunk when he locked the door behind them. "My own..."

"Yours." Harley moved away, hands sliding down his sides. "You like it?"

"Oh, petit. You have to know what I'm feeling is far beyond like." It was on another plane entirely. He wanted Harley with his whole self. He loved his boy beyond measure. He reached for his belt and loosened it, popped his trousers open and released his aching cock, stroking himself as he watched his boy. "I love that you did this for me. I love you. I'm going to take that sweet, tight ass of yours and show you, give you everything you need from me."

Harley's lips parted, the look on his boy's face pure hunger. "I'm all yours."

The first thing he did was pull Harley into a deep kiss, one meant to muss his boy up a bit, smudge that perfect makeup just a little. He slid his fingers over a nipple and gave the chain a gentle tug.

Harley groaned, the sound deep in his chest, eyes rolling. "Ollie—Ollie said to tell you something about the magnets..."

"Right. We need to take these off if they get sore okay? As soon as you're really feeling them." But for now, he'd take another one of those beautiful moans. He put light pressure on the other side of the chain. "Remember those words? Yellow...red..."

"Uh-huh... I remember. I remember." Harley was caught in a sensual haze.

He slipped his fingers low and went to work on Harley's jeans. He didn't care if the boots came off, or the corset, he wasn't going to wait that long. Neatly laid out on the tall table next to the couch was everything he needed now. He tugged the jeans open and slid his hand inside, getting a good grip on the warm, round globes of his boy's ass. One good squeeze and then he shoved the jeans down over Harley's thighs.

Harley turned and braced himself, offering that pale, taut, muscled ass, the corseted waist, the broad shoulders.

He didn't know why Harley had done this, but he was all in. He snatched up the lube. "Pretty petit. Is that for me?" He bent to take a nibble of one perfect cheek before getting Harley ready for him, slick fingers doing just enough.

"All. All of me." Harley glanced over his shoulder. "Like what you see?"

"Love it. Want what I see." He tore open a rubber, watching Harley ride his fingers. "All of it." He took his boy by the hips and didn't waste another second, burying himself to the hilt in Harley's tight heat.

There was nothing—nothing—like wrapping his hands around Harley's waist in that corset. His balls drew up and he squeezed tighter as Harley moaned.

He shoved aside a second's hesitation—the boy had safe words; he had to trust Harley would use them—and gave them what they both were craving. What Harley had asked for—

A hard fuck, like I deserve.

He took his boy deep, reveling in the soft creaking of the

boning and the leather as it protested against Harley's deep breaths.

Harley was stunning like this, and he couldn't stop staring. His need built in him, a growing pressure that wasn't going to stay contained long. "Petit," he whispered. "So beautiful."

"All yours." Harley stretched out tall and went up on his tiptoes.

"Yes." He found Harley's nipple and tugged on the chain again, pounding into his boy hard. "Soon, petit."

That sweet body gripped him like a fist, a flush covering the broad shoulders.

He found Harley's hard prick, pleased to feel it leaking and hungry. "I've got you, petit." He ducked his head and didn't wait, using his boy, chasing down his climax.

Harley barked out sharp, wild sounds, noises that made him dizzy.

"Boy!" He shivered and his hips snapped and stuttered as his orgasm overtook him, so intense, blood roaring in his ears and making his thighs tremble.

Harley was limp and quiet under him, sweet and sweaty.

"Petit." He kissed Harley's nape. A million little aftercare thoughts nagged at him, but this was their moment, Harley's moment and he wanted to stay in it a little longer.

"Yes. Oh, lover. Thank you." Harley sighed and stretched.

He shifted and disposed of the condom, then went after the laces in Harley's corset to loosen them a bit while he caught his breath. Every so often he dropped a hand down to fondle Harley's smooth, pale ass. "This was quite a surprise, love. A very welcome, wonderful surprise."

"I wanted to...get your attention. In the best way."

He helped Harley to his feet and let his boy wiggle his

jeans back up. "You have it. You always have it. But you were after...different attention, I think."

"I wanted to make you wild. I wanted to make you need me."

He nodded. It was never too late to learn something new about someone, was it? Even the love you'd been looking for forever. "Do you like it? Are you comfortable? Is it...fun?"

"Yeah. It's fun. Hot. I feel sexy and well-fucked."

"You do know how to make me smile. And...other things." He pulled Harley in for a kiss. "I can't wait to go shop with you."

"Mmm...shop?" Harley was heavy-lidded and did, indeed, look well-fucked.

"Mmm. Yes. For something custom fitted and even more perfect." He sat on the little couch and pulled his boy into his lap. "But first we'll rest here a minute."

"Sounds perfect." Harley dragged soft, damp lips over his jaw. "This is pretty damn perfect."

EPILOGUE

Harley headed up, entire body slick with sweat, muscles trembling from a day of good, hard work.

He didn't stop for anything, just stripped off his filthy clothes, shoved them in the washing machine, and got in a cool shower, letting the water sluice over him.

He knew Winter had come home when he heard the bathroom door open and close. "Hello, petit." Winter drew back the shower curtain, leaned in and kissed his wet shoulder. "Did you have a good day?"

"Hot. It was killer hot today." It was the teeth of July and they worked in a lot of un-temperature-controlled situations. "Looking forward to being with you tonight. Going out. Showing off."

Winter's smile was wide, and Harley saw his cheeks pink before the shower curtain fell closed again. "You'll be hotter than the day was. We'll make a lovely little scene when we enter, won't we?"

"Mmhmm...you going to dress me up and make me pretty?" He beamed as a bottle of icy cold water appeared. "Oh, thank you."

"I am. I have a fancy new bronzer to try. I wanted an excuse to use that lovely angled brush you gave me," Winter said over the hum of his electric razor.

"Mmhmm." He swallowed the water down, and that took care of the last of the heat. He was beginning to love the reactions his lover gave with each new fancy brush, each little bit of jewelry or decoration.

"And I can't wait to lace you into your new corset." Winter had a towel for him as soon as he shut the water off. "Dance you around until you're breathless."

"Mmm... It's beautiful." The longline corset held him tight, kept him right where Winter wanted him, and framed his ass like a dream.

Winter slid a hand under his towel. "Very nice. Still waiting for me. I'm going to keep you waiting all evening. No sneaking off to a plush back room tonight."

He pouted, but they both knew it was a game, an exciting addition to their Friday night. "Not even a little orgasm? To get the edge off?"

Winter laughed and pulled his hand away. "You like the edge. The edge is exciting. Did you shave?"

"Of course I did. You need a good, clean canvas."

"Good boy. Come on then." Winter led him back into the bedroom where his corset was already laid out for him on the bed with his good jeans. Next to that were Winter's leather pants and a white button down.

He turned, snuggling right into Winter's side, teasing them both, luxuriating in a bit of naughtiness. "You smell good, lover."

Winter hummed, lips pressing to his temple. "Old books. It's my favorite scent next to you fresh out of the shower. I'm glad you want to be close; you're going to dress me when I'm done with you. Naughty boy."

"Mmm... There's not one thing wrong with that." Nothing about helping his Winter slide the leather on was bad in the least.

"I'm going to recommend you for club membership tonight." Winter moved them to the dressing table with its enormous mirror. "So the club will be our place, not just mine. You're not a guest anymore. You're mine. You belong."

He couldn't stop his smile, and it was so big it stretched his cheeks. "Really? Our place. Our club."

That sounded amazing in his ears.

"Our place." Winter pulled him in for a kiss. "Are you ready?"

He stared into those beloved eyes, his entire soul alive and awake. "God yes. I'm all yours. Let's get ready to go to our place."

End.

The Cowboy and the Dom Series
By Jodi Payne and BA Tortuga

Sin Deep is set in the Cowboy and the Dom universe. Thomas, Sam, Clint, and others from the club are featured in that series. It's a romance with suspense elements, and you can start that journey with book one—First Rodeo.

First Rodeo

When a killer strikes, Texan and former rodeo cowboy, Sam O'Reilly, loses his older brother. Unbeknownst to Sam, James was also the lover and sub of a sophisticated New York City Dom named Thomas Ward. Sam comes to the city determined to stay until he can bring the murderer to his own brand of justice, while Thomas' more ordered mind is hoping for a legal solution.

Neither man expects their connection to the other, but having each lost someone irreplaceable, their hearts are crying out for comfort almost as loudly as their bodies are screaming for each other. Some yearnings refuse to be ignored, but transcending their differences to explore the fragile connection between them will prove to be a steep a hill to climb--the first of many.

As Sam and Thomas take the first tentative steps on the rocky path that might lead to a relationship, the killer steps out of the shadows...And this time, his sights are set on Sam.

Note to our readers: Each of the three books in The Cowboy and the Dom Series has a fully realized, romantic happy ending

(HEA). However, the overarching suspense element will leave readers on a cliffhanger after books one and two, to be fully resolved in book three.

Buy it now or read in KU!

Hey, y'all!

We want to thank you for giving Sin Deep a try and we hope you enjoyed the story. If you can spare a few minutes to post a review at the eBook website where you made your purchase, we'd very much appreciate it!

Don't forget to "like" our Facebook pages and groups to keep up with all the news--new releases, sales announcements, giveaways, sneak peeks-- and of course the rodeo pictures, coffee memes and just general fun. We'd love to have all y'all!

Yeehaw and thanks for reading!

BA & Jodi

Interested in learning more about BA's cowboys and Jodi's gentlemen? Want free fiction and news? Join our newsletters!

What's Up with Jodi
http://bit.ly/whatsupjodi

Spurs and Shifters
https://lp.constantcontact.com/su/A9CRUzp/baandjulia

ABOUT JODI

JODI takes herself way too seriously and has been known to randomly break out in song. Her men are imperfect but genuine, stubborn but likable, often kinky, and frequently their own worst enemies. They are characters you can't help but fall in love with while they stumble along the path to their happily ever after. For those looking to get on her good side, Jodi's addictions include nonfat lattes, Malbec and tequila any way you pour it.

Website: jodipayne.net

Newsletter: http://bit.ly/whatsupjodi

All Jodi's Social Links: linktr.ee/jodipayne

ABOUT BA

Texan to the bone and an unrepentant Daddy's Girl, BA Tortuga spends her days with her basset hounds, getting tattooed, texting her grandbabies, and eating Mexican food. When she's not doing that, she's writing. She spends her days off watching rodeo, knitting and surfing Pinterest in the name of research. BA's personal saviors include her wife, Julia Talbot, her best friends, and coffee. Lots of coffee. Really good coffee.

Having written everything from fist-fighting rednecks to hard-core cowboys to werewolves, BA does her damnedest to tell the stories of her heart, which was raised in Northeast Texas, but has heard the call of the high desert and lives in the Sandias. With books ranging from hard-hitting GLBT romance, to fiery ménages, to the most traditional of love stories, BA refuses to be pigeon-holed by anyone but the voices in her head.

BA loves to talk to her readers and can be found at http://batortuga.com/ and her newsletter signup link is http://bit.ly/BAJulianews

AVAILABLE FROM JODI & BA

The Cowboy and the Dom Trilogy

First Rodeo, Book One

Razor's Edge, Book Two

No Ghosts, Book Three

The Soldier and the Angel, a Cowboy and Dom Novel

Sin Deep, a Cowboy and Dom Novel

East Meets Westerns

(single titles)

Wrecked

Window Dressing

Flying Blind

Special Delivery, A Wrecked Holiday Novel

Temptation Ranch

The Higher Elevation Series

Heart of a Cowboy

Land of Enchantment

Keeping Promises

Bigger Than Us

The Triskelion Series

Breaking the Rules

Making a Mark

Making the Rules, coming soon!

Les's Bar Series

Just Dex

Hide Bound

The Lone Star Series

Tending Tyler

Roped In

The Collaborations Series

<u>Refraction</u>

<u>Syncopation</u>

Puzzles Series

Cryptic